THE
CURE

JEN KINGSFORD

The Cure

First published in Australia by Jen Kingsford 2025

Copyright © Jen Kingsford 2025

*A catalogue record for this book is available
from the National Library of Australia*

ISBN: 978-0-6486042-6-6 (pbk)
ISBN: 978-0-6486042-7-3 (ebk)

Cover photography: Depositphotos
Cover design: miblart

Typesetting and design: miblart

10 9 8 7 6 5 4 3 2 1

For Brooke

SYMPTOMS OF HYSTERIA

The patient becomes restless and excited, or melancholy and retiring; listless and indifferent to the social influences of domestic life ... She will always be ailing, and complaining of different affections ... Often a great disposition for novelties is exhibited, the patient desiring to escape from home, fond of becoming a nurse in hospital ... or other pursuits of the like nature, according to station and opportunities.

To these symptoms in the single female will be added, in the married, distaste for marital intercourse, and very frequently either sterility or a tendency to abort in the early months of pregnancy.

These physical evidences of derangement, if left unchecked, gradually lead to more serious consequences.

Dr Baker Brown (1866)

PROLOGUE

London Surgical Home for Women

Case XIII – Age 32, married. Admitted August 5, 1862.
Extreme Hysteria, verging on insanity. 5 years illness.

August 7, 1862. Operation.

The woman could not move a limb or flutter her eyelids open. Her flesh was bare against a table and covered with a sheet, but the chill seeped in. The sweet scent of chloroform clogged her nose.

She heard the rumble of male voices coming closer.

'I am pleased that you have come around to my way of thinking, Dr Butcher. I think we both agree with Dr Copland that the increased reflex excitability of the nerves of the female generative organs is one principal causative condition of hysterical affections.'

Her wooden legs remained immobile as the sheet was removed.

'See here, how there is evidence of peripheral excitement of the pudic nerve. I've often noticed this in those who have epilepsy.'

There was a murmur in response.

'Given there are no conscious women in the room, I will speak plainly. So, by examining the clitoris, you can determine that this woman masturbates frequently?'

The woman's heart clenched. Surely, Dr Baker Brown, to whom she had spoken only days before, was not discussing her in such a manner.

'Yes, and of course that overstimulates the woman, which makes her prone to fits. For some, like the other woman I have examined, it can lead to melancholia. I hope that by observing me today, you will be able to perform this procedure on the other poor souls that require it. Let's begin. First, we use these forceps – see how the hook grips the clitoris.'

Her brain fired, and she willed her limbs to move, but they remained leaden.

'The cautery iron needs to be red hot. Take the thin edge of the iron around the base until you sever it ... like this.'

A burnt-flesh smell filled the room. Her stomach roiled.

'Is that it, then?' Dr Butcher asked. His voice sounded reedy rather than mellow, like Dr Baker Brown's.

'Oh no. We pass the iron over each side of the nymphae, using a sawing or cutting motion ... oops, I accidentally tore them, but there, they are gone now.

'Now we complete the procedure by taking the back of the iron, and sawing off the labia and other parts of the vulva – rubbing backwards and forwards, like so. This can also be done with scissors, of course, which I often prefer. There, now I have destroyed the parts and cured the woman.'

Cured? By destroying her most delicate feminine parts? It was beyond her comprehension. Numbness filled her from deep within. How could Dr Baker Brown savage her like this?

All over her fits of anger with her husband. No, she didn't like it when he ordered her about as if she were only a servant. Nor did she like him to take her in the bedroom, as if she were one of the women who frequented the pleasure gardens. Her numbness became molten.

Did *he* know what Dr Baker Brown had planned for her?

'Now, we plug the wound with compresses of lint and a pad, well secured by a T bandage. Place a grain of opium in her rectum, and she is ready to be moved to the infirmary. The nurses need to be mindful of haemorrhage and keep still her and quiet. Keep her on an unstimulating diet: milk, fish and chicken should be fine, but no alcohol. In a month, all will be well. There has been some debate about the most effective mode of destroying the nerve and irritation, but I find this most effective. Where will you begin your practice of this operation, Dr Butcher?'

'I plan to cure the poor souls at Bloomfield House.'

'Most admirable. I am sure the asylum inmates will be grateful.'

What! They were planning to inflict this on lunatics? Part of her willed herself to remember everything, so that this would not happen. Another part wanted to suck in the chloroform and forget it all.

'Mr Levy, you must continue to hold the inhaler over the nose for the whole time, or the patient may wake up – and that would never do.'

She heard the screams that couldn't be expelled echoing in her head.

CHAPTER

ONE

'Ouch!' I bit back a curse word as my husband raised his eyebrow. I sucked my bleeding finger and set aside my needlework with a sigh. 'I don't know why I can't seem to manage a simple sampler when I can stitch a woman after birth so easily.'

'Ruined another one?' Spencer asked as he turned his attention back to the journal he was reading. *The Lancet,* I noticed, a medical journal.

I examined the blood-stained material. 'Most likely. Did you come across the lecture on uraemic excretory puerperal fever? I am not so sure I agree with Dr Barnes inferring that insanity springs from disturbed renal excretion.'

The ambience of the parlour seemed to chill. The mantel clock ticked along with my breath, and my heart dropped with the curl of Spencer's lip. While courting, he had seemed to find my thoughts on medicine interesting; now I kept forgetting it was not my place to have intellectual discussion with my husband. I missed those days.

'Now, now, dear Adeline. You must not waste precious energy worrying about childbed fever or causes of insanity. Thankfully, your days of midwifery are over, and you can rest.' He flicked the pages, the discussion over.

A flicker of resentment rose within me. It was eighteen sixty-five. Was it not possible for him to respect a woman with a medical mind?

I gave my burgeoning stomach a rub. It was odd to be on the other side. To feel the roll of a babe within.

As I looked around the attractive parlour, I admired my latest creation. While my papa considered redecorating a waste of funds and had therefore barely touched his Georgian townhouse, I had taken pains to furnish our parlour with lovely wallpaper patterned with a blend of pomegranate fruit, flowers and leaves. I had ensured the damask curtains matched the colour of the pomegranates and the tassels were a rich gold. My cream button-backed chairs and chaise longue provided a beautiful contrast to the mahogany side tables and display cabinets.

I should have been well satisfied I had made the London townhouse a respectable, if not welcoming, doctor's house, but I felt it lacked the conviviality of my father's. Now that I had completed the refurbishment, how was I to fill my time? Restless and uncomfortable, I tapped the arm of the chair.

Spencer frowned, and my fingers stilled. He blew air through his nose and set his journal on a side table. 'I'm going to check on Mrs Whitmore, then I'm going to Red's. Don't wait up.'

I bit my lip. I had irritated him again, sending him to his gentleman doctor's club, but I too experienced prickles of irritation. How was it possible for a man's charm and humour to fade so much? I was obviously far from worthy of his attention these days. Yet how might he expect me to be pleasant company, confined all day as I was with few diversions?

I sighed with relief at the sight of Charity being led through the door by Mrs Smith, the head housemaid. My closest friend and fellow midwife would most certainly welcome a lively discussion about childbed fever.

Charity set aside her bag. 'Oh, my goodness. Did you read about it, that childbed fever comes from the decomposition of the urea poisoning a woman? What rot.'

I nodded my agreement.

'Oooh, the letter that Dr Sims wrote, defending his so-called simple, safe, and efficient operation. Who would cut an incision in a cervix for painful menstruation?' Charity's cheeks heightened in colour, becoming almost as deep as her auburn locks. 'So smug in his defence.'

My spirits soared as my brain fired. 'Yes, I agree with his adversary Dr Gream. I wonder what his reaction was to reading that a possible cause of the miscarriage was his exploration of the cavity, rather than the excessive cervical cut. I would be livid.'

Charity snorted. 'I am sure Dr Gream will respond. We must keep an eye out. Is Spencer still discouraging you from reading his journals?'

I sighed. 'Yes. He believes they're unsuitable for a lady's eyes. A faint trace of horror struck me when I read of them cutting into women. It seems much more civilised to offer motherwort, an infusion of yarrow, or a ginger tea for such pain.'

She nodded. 'I agree. Now we should get on and see how things are progressing.'

'All is well,' Charity said when she had completed her inspection and I was tugging my skirts back down. She was flicking her fingernails, and I frowned. She did this when she was anxious, but Charity would never lie to me about the state of my baby's health.

'What is it? Is it Papa?' I slid from the examination table in Spencer's surgery and stood next to her as she packed up her kit. When she refused to look at me, I touched her arm. 'Tell me.'

'Let us sit in the parlour.' Her eyes glinted in the lamplight. I could not interpret her expression, but her subdued manner quickened my pulse.

Once seated, I watched her draw breath, and I feared for my papa.

'Oh, Addie. I apologise for unintentionally causing you concern. I saw him this morning when I gave him the lemon balm, and I suspect cholera—'

A gasp escaped from my lips. 'I told him to avoid—'

She shook her head. 'You're one to talk.' Noting the stubborn set of my chin, she tutted and moved on. 'He is quite ill. He has a robust constitution, though. It is what I came upon as I walked up the stairs that troubles me more.'

A log cracked and rolled in the fireplace, sending sputters of sparks onto the hearth. I flicked a burning ember with my slipper, no doubt smudging the satin tip. As Charity poked the log back into place, I wanted to poke her.

'Tell me,' I begged.

'I overheard an argument between your papa and husband. By all accounts, it appears Spencer has been borrowing vast amounts of money to pay off his gambling debts, but once he has paid off one, he accrues yet another. Your papa warned him he was reaching the end of his funds and could not offer more support. Spencer dismissed his warning and confidently claimed that everything would be fine once your papa passed away! He said that he would then discover the full extent of your true inheritance. I was so shocked I dropped my packages. Such a clamour was clearly audible to them, and Spencer stopped speaking and stormed past me. Your papa did not mention a word of it.'

I released a slow breath. 'Thank you for telling me. Concerning inheritance, I am clueless. Papa has never discussed his family with me at all, only that he had a terrible argument with them many years ago and he has seen none of them since. When Mama was alive, she would not betray his trust and tell me what it was about, either. I wondered if their match was approved. I must see him.'

Charity took my arm, trying to guide me back to sit. 'I should have said nothing. You are in no—'

I shrugged her hand away. 'Don't tell me what a delicate condition I am in. We both know how sturdy a pregnant woman can be, and I'm fine.'

It was apparent to both of us I was not fine, but that had little to do with being with child. She put her hands up in surrender. 'At least let me walk with you, then I'll return tomorrow.'

As we stepped into the dank fog of the London afternoon, I shivered. If Spencer was gambling at such a rate, would my child be born on the street?

TWO

'You shouldn't be here.'

I ignored my papa's grumbling and willed my hand not to rise to my mouth. His face twisted into a grimace. His sunken eyes and the bedroom's odour made everything clear. I touched his cold, damp forehead. 'And you shouldn't have gone to Poplar. What were you thinking?'

He shrugged. 'They needed me.'

I held my tongue. There was no persuading Papa not to attend to the wretched of the East End. His heart rode roughshod over his intellect, but I admired his dedication to all patients, those who could pay and those who could not. I added some fuel to the dwindling fire. My father, like many doctors who advocated for hygiene, kept his bedchamber sparsely furnished with a bed, wardrobe, washstand, and chair. There would be no vermin or germs breeding among such simplicity.

'Do not touch the pot,' he said. 'Cook will be back any minute. I am sure she would have barred your entry if she had been here.' I took in his look of mortification at me for finding him in such a state. 'She has gone to the apothecary for some more willow bark for my aches.'

'I don't understand. You claimed cholera stemmed from contaminated water, rejecting the miasma theory. If you were aware, *how*?' Maybe this wasn't the moment to rebuke him.

'Oh, Adeline. I am uncertain. I did not drink any of the water while I was there. 'Tis no matter whether I believe the work of Mr Snow now. I have contracted the dreaded thing, and I am having the devil of a time keeping anything down.' He seemed to sink even further down into his pillow. 'Don't you worry; Cook will take care of me. You'd better be getting back to your husband. I doubt Spencer would want you here.'

I bit my lip; now wasn't the time to inquire about Spencer's gambling. Papa sighed and closed his eyes, every wrinkle bunching together in his hollowed cheeks. I stroked the jutting bone of his cheek, then dropped my hand to my stomach. A draught blew from the top and bottom of the sash window and clutched at my neck with icy fingers.

He opened his eyes. 'You're still here. You've been a wonderful daughter. I should have listened to you. I'm not sure if I did right in introducing Dr Parker to you.'

I frowned. 'What do you mean?'

'I realise you're unhappy,' he mumbled. 'I wanted you looked after, but I didn't suspect he would prevent your work as a midwife or be so ... he is far more flawed than I understood.'

'What flaws?' I asked. My heart began banging in my chest, but his eyes stared into space. 'Papa, tell me.'

It was of no use to ask any further or shake his frigid hand. He had drifted off again.

'I'm back, Dr Ward,' Agnes Cook said. 'They didn't have any willow bark, but I got some,'— she saw me perched on a stool next to Papa—'Miss Ade...Mrs Parker, you shouldn't have come.'

I ignored the housekeeper's frown. 'That's what Papa said. I was unaware his condition was so serious.'

Mrs Cook softened. 'It happened so quickly. Oh,'—she wrinkled her nose—'it smells like he's brought the East End home with him. Let me clean things up. Would you tell Kitty to boil the kettle for his tea?'

As I made my way down the stairs, I realised I had left quite a mess in my haste to see my papa. Muddy footprints marred the gleam of the polished wood on the stairs and in the hall. Mrs Cook had picked up the rain-soaked cloak I'd dropped off myself when I'd charged through the entry door; I had come to my father as soon as I had farewelled Charity.

I entered the warmth of the kitchen where the young maid, Kitty, was stirring a large pot of soup on an open range.

The maid clutched her cap. 'Oh, Miss Adeline.'

'Do not fear so; my papa has a robust constitution.'

Her enormous brown eyes teared up at my words. 'I'm done for when Mrs Cook comes back down. She'll be ever so mad with me. I'm forever about to burst into tears when I see the state of Dr Ward.' Kitty was worrying the soup. 'Oh, now I've gone and burnt it.'

She was right. The scent of the soup had changed.

I smiled. 'Do not fear.' With her cherubic face, it was impossible for me to be angry with Kitty. 'Let's focus on getting my papa back to health.' I wiped the sweat forming on my upper lip. The heat of the kitchen was stifling.

She burst into tears, grabbing her apron to mop them.

I patted her arm, biting back my own tears. 'Come now, Kitty.'

Her sobs faltered to a hiccup and sniff. 'It's my fault he went to Poplar. He learned Ma was unwell, and with the two little ones. I'm so sorry.'

A bubble of anger fizzed and popped. 'It's no use getting worked up about that now,' I assured her. 'I need the kettle on.'

Kitty wiped her face and nodded. 'Right away, Miss.'

I took a cup of tea up to Papa, relieved to see Mrs Cook had cleaned both him and the dreadful stench of the room up.

'Don't be too long now,' Mrs Cook said. 'He needs more rest.'

I nodded as she bustled past me.

I waited until Papa had sipped his tea and then blurted out the fears in my heart.

His thin lips hung wordlessly open like a Billingsgate fish. 'How did you figure that out?'

'It doesn't matter. Is it true? Is my husband, whom you so generously helped to set up his own practice, harassing you for further funds to pay off his gambling debts?'

As his pale face grew waxier, I regretted asking.

'Yes. I have told him that this well is almost tapped dry. His promises were false. He said that if I would settle his final debt, he would gamble no more. With the babe coming, he would stop ... but it seems he is fast held by his vice. I will do what I can to ensure that you—,'

Unable to bear the deepening of his wrinkles and sag of his mouth as he spoke of Spencer, I lifted my hand. 'Do not give him another farthing. We will be fine. I want you to focus on regaining your health.'

He nodded and sank back into the pillow, and a gentle snore soon wheezed into the room.

I left Papa's townhouse on Harley Street and returned in the dark to my own in Devonshire Place. It was a mere couple of streets away, but it felt as if I was trudging all the way to Ireland.

I tiptoed in stockinged feet along the hallway. To remove my street clothes swiftly was necessary, but my head was throbbing with fatigue. I should have a thorough wash with my rose-scented soap; despite trusting Papa's assertion that cholera was spread through contaminated water, I understood I should cleanse myself thoroughly, even though I was tired. That meant asking Mrs Smith to organise a hip bath, and that would no doubt mean a scrubbing of another kind. She'd made it very clear who ran the household once I'd dared cross the threshold as a newlywed. She was made of far sterner stuff than even Agnes Cook was.

'What might you call this, sneaking in at all hours as a thief might to steal the silverware? You need to stay rested in your room.'

I froze mid-step and made a slow turn. Mrs Gwen Smith stood there in her nightdress, cap, and gown, with her candle sputtering in its holder.

'I did not wish to disturb anyone.' Her raised eyebrow and cynical expression annoyed me, so that I broke off an apologetic explanation. 'Regardless, I do not need to answer to you. I'd like a bath drawn.'

Her eyes widened. 'What? Now?'

I gave a firm nod. 'Yes, now.'

'You may not have to answer to Mrs Smith, but I am sure you must answer to me,' Spencer said. 'What led you out in the dead of night? Did you not think about how perilous that might be?'

I noticed he too was still in his street clothes. Was he only just coming home now?

I tried to steady my quivering chin. 'Why did you not inform me of Papa's serious illness? I needed to see him. I would like a bath and a cup of tea.'

'You understand, then, that he suffers from cholera?' Spencer's usually appealing face seemed gruesome in the shifting light and shadow. 'I'm sorry. I was concerned for the baby. Go on, Mrs Smith; Mrs Parker requires a bath.'

As I washed, I worried about Papa. I felt fortunate to have had such a father. One who ignored society's rules of withholding affection and regarding the female species as feeble. Yet, since marrying, I'd never been so feeble. I was accomplishing little of true importance.

Ignoring the emptiness echoing within, I bathed and then found comfort in my four-poster bed. I had been distracting myself with my frantic decorating. I had been trying to create a warmth and welcome in our house that was not there in my marriage. Things were only going to get worse once I confronted Spencer with my knowledge of his gambling. The gloom of the room's corners seemed to swallow the timid candlelight. The darkness engulfed me.

THREE

I waited all the next day and night, pacing for so long I imagined I would wear a hole in the parlour's Turkish rug. Eventually, my eyes and body drooped, and I accepted there would be no confronting Spencer that night. I went to bed and fell into a restless sleep, only settling when I dreamt of happier times. My mind wandered back to when I first made Spencer's acquaintance. What an impression he had made.

The clop of horses' hooves sounded much more muffled in Regent's Park than on the streets of London. I almost enjoyed the rhythmic clip-clop as Charity and I strolled in the crisp autumn air.

'We are becoming far too soft, needing a morning walk,' Charity said. 'Much like these young ladies getting in their exercises with their governesses. Perhaps I need to stop having the women stay with us so much and get myself back into traipsing all over London.' Charity gave her trim belly a pat.

'You look fine, Charity. There is not an extra ounce of fat on you.'

Charity stooped to pick up a crimson maple leaf. 'This will look beautiful in my collection.' She tucked it into her skirt pocket. As she withdrew her hand, a puff of wind picked up a paper from her pocket, and it fluttered to the ground. We laughed as we chased it before it could end up in the boating lake.

I caught it and handed it back. 'I hope it was important.'

She snatched it and hid it away, then grabbed my arm, intending to continue our walk.

I refused to move. 'Charity?'

She blushed. 'Just a note from—'

I crossed my arms. 'Mr Appleby?'

'He's not that bad.'

I watched the breeze ripple the maples, sending a sprinkle of leaves over the lake. 'You are aware of his terrible gambling addiction?'

Charity sighed. 'It's not like we're courting with any serious intent.'

'Even though he is wealthy, there is not polish enough to remove the tarnish to his reputation.'

'I can assure you; he will not marry a mere midwife.' She kicked a pebble. 'It's clear that you and I both favour assessing a man by his character rather than his possessions. And he kisses rather well.'

I softened and laughed with her.

Charity turned to face me, her eyes twinkling. 'You are my dearest friend and understand I don't care for the shackles of marriage. I appreciate a handsome man taking me to dinner and a show now and then, though.'

I spoke to Charity slowly, as if to a young child. 'As long as he does not expect you to show *too* much appreciation for his efforts.'

She snorted like a horse at me. 'You are being ridiculous.'

I sighed. 'Maybe, but you don't want others to suppose you are a coquette.'

'Oh, I may flirt a little, but I am long way from being a fallen woman.'

My eyes widened – that she would say such a thing in public! The closest governess clapped her gloved hands over her young charge's ears and led her away.

We watched them all but bolt to their waiting carriage and take off at a speed far too fast for the park. A chuckle escaped my lips, and we were soon bent with laughter, which only sent more young ladies scuttling.

After wiping our tears and readjusting our bonnets, we continued on our walk.

We slowed as we came across a man kneeling by the lake. Dried and decayed bunches of flowers lay at his boots.

'Oh, he looks terribly sad,' Charity whispered. 'Do you suppose he may have lost someone? Didn't a few children drown there last winter?'

I shrugged. 'The idea of skating on the lake sends shivers down my spine. What if you fell through a thin patch of ice? It's an accident waiting to happen. A horrid way to die, to be sure.'

The man stood and seemed to search his pockets as he sniffed.

Charity nudged my elbow. 'Oh, I say, he's rather handsome. Such a shame I don't have time to stop and minister to him. Go; he needs a handkerchief.'

I did as she bid and stepped forward with a handkerchief. 'Excuse me, sir. I do not mean to intrude.'

I handed him the hanky, and he wiped his bloodshot eyes. They glowed the blue of a clear summer sky. 'Thank you. I am making quite the display.' He gave a rueful grin that touched my heart.

Charity was right: with a finely chiselled face set off by a neatly trimmed black beard, he was quite pleasing to the eye.

'I must attend to Mrs Bates,' Charity said. With an apologetic nod to the gentleman and a wink at me, she scurried away.

'We are midwives,' I explained.

'Ah, how wonderful. I am a doctor. You've caught me in a moment of failure, I'm afraid. I did little to save a poor drowned lad pulled from the water right in front of me last winter. I come here to remind myself that I may fail when I become too sure I cannot.' He gave the water a pensive look.

'We are but human,' I agreed. 'It does dull the heart to lose a patient.'

So began my romance with Spencer. A man I deemed both dashing and compassionate. Papa had believed so too.

The stench of whiskey filled my nostrils; it was clear Spencer had returned from Red's, undoubtedly intoxicated. He fumbled about. A thud here and there, then a heavy plop on the bed. He flopped down, and I remained motionless. An arm lay heavy on mine.

Before long, the arm turned into wandering hands. I batted his insistent fingers from my breast.

'Come on, Adeline. The baby won't mind.'

Throwing his arm off me, I sat up. 'How might you even contemplate such a thing? I am in no mood for that.'

'Most men do not find the female form in such a state as you are now very attractive. You are fortunate I have let you rest.'

Heat shot through my body – a heat not born of any physical desire save the one to punch him hard.

'Yes, you are most kind. Letting me rest while you are out gallivanting at the club, gambling away money we no longer have.'

With this, he shoved the covers aside and stood. 'I am your husband, and the money is mine to do with as I see fit.'

I heaved myself off the bed and stood across from him. 'That might be correct, but a good husband would not make his family destitute.'

He charged at me, grabbed my hair, and wrenched my head back. He shoved me, and I sprawled onto the floor, my knees taking the brunt of my weight. 'How dare you challenge me in this manner?' He clawed at my nightdress and shoved a hand over my mouth, muffling my screams.

After he took me, he held laudanum to my mouth and ordered me to drink. 'There will be no more behaving like an alley cat in this house.'

I was not sorry I had scratched his face and back. When he left the room, I curled into a ball, hugging my belly, and sobbed into my pillow until the shroud of laudanum sleep cocooned me once again.

My limbs were heavy and my brain cloudy, but I experienced a deep twinge of pain within. My babe ...

CHAPTER

FOUR

My mind was empty. I was only a rolling ache and twist of pain. An animal, groaning, losing all hope of survival. Until a firm touch and the scent of lavender pierced the veil.

'Not long now, Adeline.' Charity stroked my cheek, then returned to her midwifery duties.

My throat closed as another roll of thunderous pain engulfed me. A different tug took over, and I sensed something moving back and forth within me.

At my request, Charity was the only woman with me as I birthed in the confines of my bedchamber, so there was no chatter, nor extra hands to offer support. The velvet softness slipped between my thighs. There was only silence.

'I'm so sorry, Addy,' Charity murmured.

I glimpsed a blue bundle, but Charity whisked it away and spun back to me to encourage me to finish. When it was over, she deftly placed the afterbirth into butcher's paper. The ache of emptiness in my stomach was overwhelming.

As we had both worked as midwives before my marriage, we were familiar with many a birth that had ended with a still, blue-marbled baby. We had both shared a soothing cup of tea with the mother and wished her well for the next baby. We had not lacked compassion, but I had not understood. I was grateful for the tears in Charity's vivid blue eyes, a mirror to my own.

'It was my fault. I went to visit my father ... who knows what I exposed—' I began.

Charity held up a slender hand. 'No, do not do that to yourself. If that was the cause, then I would also be to blame. But the cholera is not the reason that you've lost the little one. Now lie back and let me check you.'

I threw a limp plait behind my head and slumped into the pillow. I wanted to close my legs rather than open them, now all too aware that the pain was gone.

Charity rested a hand on my knee and waited. 'There, now. We've got to be sure you are not losing too much blood.'

I murmured and let her get on. 'How am I going to tell Spencer?' I experienced the burn of shame of having angered Spencer and provoking his subsequent push. I would not tell Charity that my wildness had cost me this babe. A seed of anger niggled beneath the shame. How dared Spencer lose his temper and treat me so?

'It's not a straightforward path for some. I'm sure he'll understand. Everything looks fine. Let's get some raspberry leaf tea to help things along. *I'll* speak to Dr Parker.' Charity finished tidying up the room, removed the bloody rags, and changed her apron. I didn't watch her leave the room with my baby.

'She wants to be left alone.'

'We can't leave her in that darkened hole any longer.'

'Dr Carter says that the shock of losing her baby has been too much. The laudanum is helping her sleep, and with time she'll recover. Dr Parker agrees.'

'No, she'll sleep forever on that concoction. She needs to be among friends. Let me in.'

I stirred as I listened to the exchange between Mrs Smith and Charity beyond my door. I shook the fuzzy heaviness away and cleared my croaky throat.

'Please come in, Charity,' I called.

Charity burst through the door, pushing Mrs Smith aside. Her face paled. 'Oh, Adeline. What are you doing? Please bring a bath up.'

Mrs Smith wrinkled her nose and nodded.

'You stink worse than the Thames at low tide,' Charity said.

Before a protest could escape my lips, she'd flung back the curtains, opened the window, and pulled out some fresh house clothes. Like a child, I let her bath me, wash my tangled blonde hair and dress me. She gathered up the collection of glass bottles on my dresser and dumped them in her nurse's bag.

'Now, to eat. I've bought your favourite damson drops.' I looked at Charity's stern nurse expression and understood it was unwise to challenge her. Once I'd eaten one of the proffered sweets, she smiled. 'Now, let's get you out of here so they can change the linen.' Charity placed a bouquet of pink peonies into the vase on the chiffonier.

She took my arm and led me down to the parlour. Once I was settled next to the fire in my favourite Queen-Anne style chair, we drank tea and she chattered away.

As my smile drooped, Charity took my hand. 'Even though he is a doctor, Dr Parker is at his wits' end with what to do with you.

The ladies at church ask about your wellbeing, and he is unsure what to say. I assisted that awful Clara Hughes with her third, and she told me he was considering an asylum.'

My eyes widened. 'What! He believes I've become a lunatic?' My hand went to my aching heart.

Charity sighed, then sipped her tea. 'Given that he is forever out, it surprised me he would even notice your melancholy.'

'Our discussion of his gambling did not go as planned.' I would not tell her how badly.

Her compassionate gaze showed me she was privy to far more than I'd disclosed regarding my marriage.

To add to his vice and appalling behaviour when I had confronted him, I had a growing consternation that Spencer did not doctor as Papa did. He lacked a generous heart, often demanding large fees from his mostly wealthy patients, many of whom were elderly widows. He seemed most uninclined to share his expertise with those who needed it most. I had hoped having a child would improve my marriage and give me another focus, but it was not to be. Regardless, I needed to rise above this fug that was soupier than a London fog.

Just having Charity sit across from me slowed my breath. My mind flicked back to a time when we chatted, giggled, and huddled over failed romances, ecstatic birth experiences, and dreams of our future.

'I had better get on and prove to him I have come to my senses.'

I swallowed my fear at this pressure, but I would tuck my grief into a box and behave like a model wife.

CHAPTER

FIVE

Now that I was clear of the haze left by ingesting laudanum far too often, the needles of grief continued to spike me as my needle did the sampler. Often, I found myself with my embroidery or sewing lying in my lap as I stared into the distance, only to be jolted back into movement when Mrs Smith came into the parlour to bustle around me.

It was clear she regularly informed my husband of my daily activities, or lack thereof. Tired of her scrutiny, I decided to go out to the dressmakers. Much of my clothing was ill-fitting now and, as I still lacked any appetite, I was sure I would remain a skinny wretch for a while yet.

Not wanting any companionship, I slunk from the house like a naughty street urchin that had stolen from a street cart. I closed the door behind me, and the bustling life of London assaulted me.

The miasma of horse dung, damp wool and lavender soap was familiar yet strange, as if I had left London for a long time and had only now returned. I took a deep breath before I entered the swish of crinoline exuberance. The colour of these lampshade dresses seemed to have brightened in my absence. I must have seemed quite subdued in my more practical grey poplin promenade dress against the magenta, emerald and lazuline of summer fashion dotted around me, but I had not wanted to fuss with a train or worry that lace or tassels were being soiled.

As I walked along the street, I wanted to shield my ears from the rumble and scrape of omnibus and cartwheels and the clop of horses' hooves. It was getting too much. To add to my distress, I was becoming breathless – enough to wonder if my corset had been tied too tight or I was just no longer fit to leave my townhouse. Perhaps Spencer was right. Maybe grief was addling my brain, and I was in a downward spiral towards lunacy. I set my chin but was relieved to make it to the dressmakers at last. As I stopped, I bumped into someone, knocking a brown paper parcel from her arm.

My cheeks burned as I retrieved the parcel. 'I am so sorry.'

I recognised those eyes. 'Kitty!'

'Oh, Miss Adeline. I mean, Mrs Parker. How do you do?' Kitty and I moved to the side of the doorway. 'Given your papa's grave illness, I was hoping we would see you.'

I frowned. 'I was not aware. I have been rather ill myself and was told he had recovered and was back to his duties.'

Kitty's cheeks coloured. 'Oh, I was probably not to bother you if you were sufferin'.'

'I'm on the mend now.' A hot spike of rage ran through me.

Kitty's eyes dropped.

'What is it? Speak plain.' The heat running through me ran to ice.

'Dr Parker has been visiting, sayin' he is doctoring.' She looked among the flat caps and bowler hats, as if expecting Spencer to leap upon us at any moment. 'I know your papa would be heartbroken, as he thinks the world of you, and it seems ...'

I wanted to shake the poor girl, but I set my face in as kind an expression as possible. 'Seems what?'

We waited while a lady fussed at her skirt in the doorway until she had narrowed it down enough to enter the shop. We waited for her to pass, and then Kitty whispered, her eyes wide and solemn, 'It seems Dr Parker has been a right regular gambler, and I heard that he's racked up an enormous debt. I heard Dr Parker and Dr Ward arguing. Dr Parker promised him he'd stop and get the debt paid.'

'Oh, you are brave to tell me.' That's all I could say.

Kitty's drawn face was etched with worry. 'The thing is, Dr Ward was cuttin' costs here and there, but he told me last night, he was awful sorry, but I might have to go. He'd get me a suitable position with one of his friends ... but I enjoy working there.'

The good, solid foundation of wealth that Papa had worked so hard to build and had hoped would offer us a cushion to fall in should we need it was more than likely gone, or soon would be. Of course, I had heard of men frittering away family fortunes their fathers had built, leaving the next generation in ruin – but before we married, I had never heard even a whisper of *Spencer* having this affliction of character. 'Thank you for telling me. I will look into it.'

'I am awfully sorry, but even though Mrs Cook says I'm always sticking my too-big nose where it doesn't belong, you've always been kind to me.' She shifted the package under her other arm. 'I'd best be getting back.'

I nodded and watched her scurry away. How could Spencer's gambling have led to Papa casting his faithful servants out? I did not know what I could do to set things right.

'You have been asking what I have been doing with my time?' Spencer asked as he paced.

I sucked in a breath. Was he angry? I wasn't certain, yet his clipped words and set mouth indicated he was.

I rose from the parlour lounge. 'Yes. I am aware you haven't been giving free medical advice or treatments at the ragged school. Nor have you been earning any money at the—' I stopped as he whipped around, his hand up. I glared at him until it fell by his side. 'Regardless. Papa will not be giving you any more funds, and if any further debts accrue, I will be forced to discuss the matter with—'

'You will not ruin my career or my reputation by talking to anybody else. I am grateful for your father's generosity and discreetness. There is no need to trouble his colleagues from whom he has borrowed.'

I sagged back down into the lounge. My father had *borrowed* to pay my husband's debts? This was worse than they had led me to believe. I took shallow breaths to avoid choking on the cloying smell of the Spanish Leather cologne that Spencer usually insisted on dousing his clothes in. I had always found the scent of carnations unappealing, but when blended with patchouli and musk, it could be overpowering. If only he used a mere dab on a handkerchief, it might save me from a headache. He insisted it was a fine scent for a gentleman and reminded him of his grandfather. He was not behaving much like a gentleman at present.

But this time when I drew breath, I noted that the scent of jasmine rose above the usual smell his cologne. I had smelt that when he'd come home another time.

Spencer's pinch of my cheek stopped any scent-laden memory from surfacing. 'I mean it, Adeline. Keep your mouth shut. I always do well at Ascot. I will repay them in time.' He released my cheek, and I resisted rubbing it. He returned to his chair.

I picked up the *Englishwoman's Domestic Magazine*, feigning fascination with its pages of fashionable clothing for those on a tight budget; however, the magazine offered little guidance on coping with a husband's poor behaviour. After a while, I returned it to the side table, then held up a few of his issues of *Sporting Life* and a new magazine I was unfamiliar with, *The Sporting Times*.

More persistent than a dog with a butcher's bone, I could not let go. I disregarded the flare of his nostrils and the crack of his knuckles as he settled in to his chair, nursing his empty whiskey glass.

'Having a little flutter on the horses is one thing, but playing card games like Faro is quite another.'

My body tensed as he stood and snatched the magazines from me. I watched his eyes harden to granite ... then become glassy with unshed tears as I instinctively moved my hands to my barren stomach.

'Oh, Adeline. My intention was to repay my debts and remove any temptation without causing you sorrow. I only wanted the best for our unborn child. I deeply regret the trouble I have caused for both you and your papa. What can I do to make amends?'

Focusing on his glistening eyes and down-turned mouth, I was sure his regret was real, as was his hope that I would forgive him. I softened. 'If you spend more time doctoring, then things should be set right soon enough.'

He smiled. 'Of course.'

When he gave me a draught of laudanum to ensure I slept well after he had caused so much consternation, I took it as an apology. He was right. Exhausted after so many sleepless nights spent worrying about confronting him, I welcomed the heavy slumber.

CHAPTER

SIX

It had not been a dream. Dulled by laudanum, I had sensed something was wrong, yet was not alert enough to figure out what it was. The sway of movement overcame me, and I surrendered to velvet nothingness. I did not know where I was. I sat up and took in my strange surroundings.

My bed was one of eight lined against the whitewashed walls. The bed frames were wooden rather than metal, and the floor made of seasoned oak. There was an acidic scent of carbolic soap and vinegar in the air. I pushed aside the linen sheet, ignoring the chill, and made my way to the window. Verdant hills studded with woodlands and broken by a river greeted me.

Good God! What had Spencer done? Drugged me and then transported me here during the night?

'Quick, get back into bed,' a voice whispered.

My nerves clanged as I looked down at the woman lying in the bed closest to the window. She looked about my age and had beautiful features: large green eyes, a glossy dark plait emerging from her nightcap, and a ready smile. She nodded towards the end of the room, and I gave a slight gasp as I noticed the observation window looking into our room. A woman attired in a blue dress, white cap, and apron was behind the window at a desk, writing, with her head down.

'That's Matron Wright. You don't want to start here by getting into her bad books on day one. Olivia Hall,' she offered in introduction.

I bobbed lower. Taken aback by her informality, I answered in kind. 'I'm Adeline Parker. Where am I?'

Olivia kept her eye on the matron. 'This is the most illustrious recent addition to the lunatic asylums of Britain. The latest and greatest, Bloomfield House.'

My knees gave way, and I tumbled onto the floor. Olivia leapt from her bed to help me up.

'Miss Hall, leave that woman alone! Look at the commotion you are already creating for Mrs Parker.'

Meaty fingers gripped my arm where Olivia had held me. Other heads were now popping up from the surrounding beds.

'Stop your gawking and get up, the lot of you, while I see to Mrs Parker.' The matron guided me to sit on my bed. 'Let me introduce myself. I am Matron Wright. You have not gone through the usual admission process, but Dr Griffiths will attend to you after breakfast. Welcome to Bloomfield House. Your clothes are in the locker there. You will find drawers, socks, stockings, and a blouse. As it is summer, you'll find petticoats and a dress. There is a straw hat and boots to wear on your walks outside. There is also a tartan shawl, should you feel the cold.'

I followed the other women to an adjoining washroom and watched with astonishment their lack of concern for modesty as they completed their morning wash at a lavatory stand with four bowls, soap, and towels, not bothering with the privacy screens. The screens, I realised, were providing a partition for a commode chair. I wrinkled my nose.

'Don't worry,' Matron Wright said, hands on her ample hips. 'In other dormitories there are water closets and privacy screens for your ablutions. Now, let's get you dressed. Are you able to tend to yourself?'

'Yes.' I scuttled off to do so, not wanting any strange hands upon my body. An older lady watched me with softness in her eyes as she noticed my hesitation at using the sharp-smelling soap. It reminded me of childhood. Spencer had spoiled me with scented soaps for too long; I was no longer used to those based on animal fat and caustic soda. I gratefully accepted the woman's offer of rosewater.

With a rub and a rinse, I was soon layered into my asylum clothes. Being made to fit a much larger woman, as most of the dresses seemed to be, the cream-and-rosebud print swallowed my bones. I tugged on the slippers, then put up my hair.

Matron Wright gave each woman a quick inspection with cool grey eyes and nodded to let us know that we were presentable for breakfast. Olivia gave a more reassuring nod as we filed from the room.

We went down a set of stairs and along a covered walkway to a cavernous dining hall. Here, as in the rest of the asylum that I had seen so far, the walls were whitewashed, and the floor made of oak. Some women, already seated at the tables and benches that were dotted around the room, were being served from a wagon. My spirits lifted as I breathed in the scent of coffee. Normally a tea drinker, I sometimes succumbed to coffee when I felt lethargic. I would need coffee today.

I ate the simple fare of black rye bread coated with butter and sipped my coffee as I tried to take in the reality of what Spencer had done. How was he able to confine me to an asylum? There had to be a way to put this right.

'Ladies, this is Mrs Adeline Parker,' Olivia said. 'Adeline, may I introduce Miss Sophia Miller, Mrs Leonora Thompson, and Miss

Edna Green.' She pointed out each woman and my brain scrambled to find an anchor, so I'd remember who was who. They were Sophia (freckles on an upturned nose), Leonora (sad puppy-dog brown eyes) and Edna (withered-apple skin but twinkling eyes, also the generous soul who had offered me the rosewater). I found it odd that Olivia gave me their Christian names and that using them was the preference. Most unusual.

There was a mix of blankness and curiosity from the women. I wondered how it was they were here and what affliction cursed them.

'Dr Griffiths is lovely,' Olivia said. 'Although he means well, I doubt he comprehends what goes on in a woman's mind. He will be influenced by whoever has put you in here, so it is best to refrain from making any accusations of falsehood for now. He won't listen to those when you are first admitted. It would be wise to put paid to any thoughts of a quick release, too. The medical officers agree at least six months of treatment are needed before release, as that offers the best hope against a relapse.'

My stomach dropped at Olivia's words. 'But they have sent here me under false pretence! My husband wants me out of the way so he can continue to indulge a terrible gambling habit. He is all but a bird of prey, waiting for my papa to die so he can fritter away my inheritance.'

Her beautiful face was grave. 'That is what I mean. For now, be the good, compliant woman who needs a restorative vacation in the country, and you will find your release that much closer.' She studied me and smiled. 'It is also a bad idea to consider trying to escape. You don't want to end up in the refractory ward; they are rather violent in there.'

'She's right, love,' Edna said. 'It is not such a tough time to be insane right now, and this is a lovely asylum. I've been in far worse.

There'll be none of that filth and squalor, chains, or beatings as to be had in so many others. It's no Bedlam here.' Edna chewed her crust slowly. 'This bread is getting beyond me. I must ask for oatmeal tomorrow.'

I combed my fingers through my hair. My hopes of securing my release by showing I was a rational woman evaporated. Was I supposed to be grateful to Spencer because he hadn't dumped me in an old public asylum? Maybe I was going insane, because right then I wanted to gouge his eyes out.

CHAPTER

SEVEN

I followed Matron Wright along the corridor of offices for the medical men. When we reached the receiving room, she directed me to take a seat. The walls of the receiving room were lined with glass cabinets full of bottles and boxes with various labels, shelves of books, and a machine combining scales and height measurement. I sat in one of the comfortably padded leather chairs in front of the table.

'Ah, Mrs Parker. Welcome. I am Dr Griffiths.' He gave me a beaming smile and sat at the chair behind the desk while Matron Wright sat next to me. 'As you can see, we are a progressive and caring institution here, and we will hold private meetings to discuss your needs and treatment with utmost confidentiality.'

He stroked his beard as he read a paper. He was a solid man of average height, but even though he had oiled his hair back, a shock of dark curls framed his handsome, craggy features. His expression was one of kindness and curiosity, and it put me right at ease. Perhaps Olivia was mistaken, and he would listen to me. I held myself steady, though, wanting to hear his thoughts.

'Matron Wright tells me you've settled well already. That is welcome news, as I understand it must have been quite a shock to wake in an asylum. Your husband was extremely concerned, or he would not have brought you here. He tells me you have been dreadfully melancholy after losing your baby. He said he had ensured you rested with the aid of laudanum and that once you had rested enough, all was well – until you had a recent outburst and attacked him.'

While I desperately wanted to defend myself, I saw some steel in his eyes.

'I was indeed very sad after losing my baby,' I agreed carefully.

He nodded with satisfaction. 'Now, I know laudanum is seen as the panacea for all human woes. But we have some other therapies that we use here to soothe and revive. We have a modern approach to medicine here, so there will be little call for the old-fashioned approach of bleeding and purging. Much can be done with good, simple nutrition, fresh air, exercise, and productive contribution. Once we observe you for a week, we will have a better idea of what regime of treatment will be suitable.'

With that, I was dismissed and taken to the dayroom. As with the rest of the building, the dayroom had very tall ceilings, giving the room an airy feel. A wooden beadboard painted bright blue ran around the room. Above it, the wall was whitewashed; below was a warm, stone colour. A large oak-framed sash window was open, and I took a breath of the clean country air. An unlit stove surrounded by an oak mantelpiece with a framed mirror was the centrepiece for the pretty room.

Some women were seated around a table in padded smoking chairs, playing cards. Others were reading on birch settees or on the benches set into bay windows, which looked out onto an airing court. The trilling of a tangerine canary entranced me as the bird darted about in a cage next to the window. Surrounded by potted plants and the hum of conversation, I might have been in a drawing room anywhere in London.

'There is a letterbox near the attendants' office, if you'd like to write to anyone,' Matron Wright told me. 'Dinner will be at 12.30 pm. There is plenty to occupy you for now. If you'd like to play draughts, dominos or bagatelle, just ask an attendant to get you a set.'

She gave a quick nod to another blue-dressed nurse and left me to it. Of all the horrors I had imagined of an asylum, this scene was not what I had pictured.

I had no idea what to do about Spencer's deceit. Maybe I'd write to Charity. My closest friend surely would intervene. I found a small writing desk, which was equipped with paper and an inkwell, but no pen. Before I could ask for one, Olivia sidled up to me.

'Oh, I didn't notice you were in here,' I said, pleased to see her.

'If you are hoping to write to someone to tell them what has befallen you and to beg that they intercede on your behalf, I wouldn't bother,' she said, pulling up a chair next to me.

I frowned. It was as if she knew what I was thinking. 'Why not? I am sure my friend Charity will vouch for me.'

Olivia gave me a sad smile. 'I'm certain she would. The problem is that the super, Mr Bugwell, reads all these outgoing letters and decides which ones will get passed on. If you are going to create any doubt about your need to be here, he will decide you are delusional, and you may end up in the back wards. There is the refractory ward for the aggressive patients. I've heard there are other wards for other things. You will find the women in our ward most civilised and agreeable company.'

My skin chilled. 'The back wards?'

'Yes. In order not to disturb our delicate sensibilities, they hide away the real lunatics. There are other methods for controlling those who cannot be controlled. Of course, they regard the methods used as a necessary evil, but you don't want them to become necessary,' she said with a dark expression. 'Perhaps write your letter, although it is doubtful they will pass it on until you have been here a few months to settle in.'

What were these mysterious methods used in these back wards? I did not know, but I heeded Olivia's warning and set the paper aside.

'How about a game of Euchre instead? Or perhaps dominos, if you are a little preoccupied.'

More like *defeated*. I sighed. 'That sounds lovely.'

As we sat and played, my mind wandered. 'How long have you been here?'

'Oh, two years now.'

I closed my eyes. 'Two years. My impression was that this was the convalescent ward.'

She laughed, a beautiful, genuine sound. 'Don't look so distraught. It hasn't been that awful. Yes, for some in this ward, convalescence means they go home within weeks. You know, it *is* nice to see a new face. If I had to keep jollying up Leonora for too much longer, I might despair. I know you are curious, so I will answer the question. They have diagnosed me with epilepsy; apparently my fits are quite alarming. Definitely not suited to genteel London society.'

'I'm not sure I understand why you are here, though. My papa is a doctor. He has been most impressed with the work being done at The National Hospital for the Paralysed and Epileptic. Apparently, bromides are doing wonders,' I said as I placed a tile down. I bit my lip at the thought of my dear papa. How was I supposed to know the state of his health while they had me trapped here? I swallowed hard.

'Really? I hadn't heard. My mother is sure I am possessed by some form of devil, and they assured her I would be cured here.

Between the church services and warm towel wraps, and of course plenty of useful work, it would only be a matter of time before I became better.' She flicked a ringlet from her eye and set down her own tile. 'It's fine with me. The London Season is quite tiresome, in my opinion. I care little for fashion, neat needlework, or charity. I'd rather be painting my landscapes or writing any day. Thankfully, I don't experience regular fits; otherwise, they would sedate me and deprive me of any real life.'

That she would consider an asylum a fitting refuge from the dullness and disdain of London society was a peculiar thought. 'I expected to find meaning in charity work, homemaking, and family, but reality differed from my expectations,' I told her. 'I longed for my more independent life as a midwife.'

'Yes, I agree. I found sitting idle all day rather tiresome. Being treated as a delicate doll left me quite feeble-minded, but every time I read a broadsheet and offered an opinion, I was told not to trouble myself and return to my needlework. I've actually enjoyed the challenge of doing housework here, even the dreaded laundry. How fascinating – a midwife! You must tell me more.'

I basked in her attention. It had been months, if not years, since anyone bar Charity had offered any sense of friendship. I had not realised how deeply lonely I had been in my marriage.

CHAPTER

EIGHT

Even though I was fretful for many reasons, my appetite returned, though it was difficult to make my way through a dinner of roast pork, boiled potatoes, and beans without a fork (apparently considered a weapon). Even plum pudding made its way into my bloated stomach. To prove Spencer had made an error in committing me, I needed to remain strong and healthy.

Olivia remained by my side, chatting away, and it was only as I finished the last of my milk that I realised she had stopped talking. I followed her gaze, which had rested on a woman a few tables down.

The woman was sylph-like, with a crown of glossy blonde curls. Her doll-face glowed with health, and her china-blue eyes crinkled with warmth as she dazzled Nurse Talbot with a smile. Despite dressing in the same style as the other asylum inmates, she stood out because of the higher-quality and well-cut material of her attire. The dress actually fit her.

'What is it?' Edna asked as she turned in her chair to look. 'Oh, I saw her come into admissions. I thought it was the older woman with her who was to be admitted.'

Edna often floated around doing her duties near areas other inmates were not permitted to be in. She leaned forward. 'I heard them say that she wanted to come here for the rest cure. Her parents seemed very wealthy, by the looks of them. That lot usually keep their delicate flowers at home for such things. This one seemed determined to come here of her own choosing.'

'Her own volition? How odd,' I commented.

Olivia sighed and continued stirring her mashed potato with a spoon. 'Imagine having a choice about it. I'd say that Mr Bugwell was more than happy to take their money.'

'It seems she is to come and go as she pleases,' Edna said. 'It's a poor reflection on society if an asylum is the only place a young lady finding the Season too bothersome can get some rest. Miss Shaw was her name – Prudence Shaw.'

Over the next week, I adapted to the asylum routine. After breakfast, there was voluntary attendance in the chapel for morning prayers. They had assigned me to a small working group where I tore strips of old newspaper to make stuffing for the bedding of those who might wet or soil themselves, or I combed horsehair for pillows or rags for fuel for the boiler. It was simple and repetitive.

I hoped it would show that I was an agreeable patient who was well enough to secure release. Did it matter if I squirrelled away a sheet of newspaper now and then into my apron to read at my leisure? I noticed Edna doing the same with the obituary pages. She muttered something about having a large group of friends before they committed her to the asylum and desiring to check which ones had departed this earth. I hoped they would not trap me here for years, wondering what had happened to Charity and whether she was still alive.

'Are we permitted visitors?' I asked Olivia as we walked along a gravel path in the gardens.

Olivia adjusted the ribbon of her straw hat and shook her head. 'The medical officers have said that visitors disrupt treatment, so not until a person is almost ready to leave. Those of us regarded as actively insane used to receive a monthly visit – until Gladys couldn't bear for her husband to see her in such a state and somehow found her way to the roof and tossed herself from it.'

I cringed at the mental picture she had casually handed me.

My hope to contact Charity and have her visit was dashed.

'Now visits for anyone are few. I miss my brother, Sam. He is not a diligent correspondent, so his visits were much to look forward to.' Olivia stooped to pluck a daisy that had dared rear its head among the irises and handed it to me. 'Don't fret. I'm sure your husband will reconsider and come to collect you.'

I twirled the daisy in my fingers as we strolled. 'He is no doubt squandering the last of my money as we speak. There were nights I could have sworn he was wearing the scent of jasmine – not his usual cologne, but the extravagant sort of scent worn by the likes of Miss Brown. She loved to fawn over my husband. I am sure my so-called insanity is very convenient for him.'

'I know I told you to expect to stay for at least six months, but sometimes, for whatever reason, the authorities keep many of us here for years. I don't mind, but I can see the idea bothers you enormously. You don't want to fight it too hard, Adeline, or it will actually draw you into true madness.'

I looked behind at Leonora, plodding along with Nurse Talbot, who closely monitored us. A tall, solid woman possessing an air of authority comparable to the matron's. Despite such scrutiny from these women and a few other attendants, I must admit that, having become used to Spencer's cool examination, I did not find being watched too bothersome.

Olivia waved me over to admire the double cream flower of a Jeanne d'Arc rose I recognised as the flower my mother had adored. I bent over and sniffed the sweet scent. As a cloud of nostalgia descended, I blinked rapidly.

Olivia noticed. 'Don't despair so; one day all of this will be a dim memory for you.'

I raised my head and touched the velvet petal. 'I'll be fine.'

Olivia took my arm as we continued walking, our boots crunching along the gravel. 'You must do all that you can to show you are earnest in regaining your good health. It would be terrible to end up lost in the back wards with those that cannot be cured.'

I tried to ignore the swish of fear swirling in my stomach. 'They really keep some women in here forever?'

What causes some to stay insane was unknown to me, but I had once heard of a woman being held in a padded cell, no less, wrapped in a jacket and unable to utter a sentence of any sense.

Olivia let me walk in silence. I did not want to succumb to any madness lurking within me.

I stopped and turned my face to the warmth of the sun and the clearest of blue skies. Birds twittered in the nearby trees, and a couple of butterflies danced among the flowerbeds.

'Be careful or you'll get freckles.' Sophia's caution reached my ears.

'I like *your* freckles,' I said as she joined us.

Sophia wrinkled her button nose. 'I'd much rather have skin like yours and Olivia's. Just like the finest porcelain. Mind, you are both so pretty that even with beautiful skin I would not fare as well as you in London's Season.'

'There are far better things to aspire to than catching a gentleman's eye. That can be the undoing of you,' I said, bitterness in my tone.

Sophia raised an eyebrow. 'So, noted. But I wish for a bonnie babe in my arms one day and, of course, that would require a gentleman.'

'Unfortunately, yes,' Olivia and I said in unison. We all chuckled.

'Oh, such sour old biddies you are,' Sophia said. 'I had a sweetheart once, but his family declared I was beneath him. My belief was that we'd elope, but he wed someone else. He was reluctant to forgo the family title and manor for the love of a common girl. I took it hard and made such a scene at their wedding celebration that they dispatched me here, and here I remain. The hysterical jilted lover. Then I started having fits ... and here I stay.' Sophia sounded so forlorn, my heart ached for her. How many sad tales would I hear in this asylum? She sighed. 'Time for us to head in and get back to work.'

Matron Wright nodded at Olivia as we re-entered the building. 'Time to see Dr Griffiths.'

Olivia smiled and almost skipped off with the attendant. Stopping to retie the laces on my boots, I saw Nurse Talbot lean in to Matron Wright's ear and heard her murmur, 'Her brother Sam was at the front door again this morning. He does not understand why she is still here. I did not know what to tell him, as I wonder too.' Nurse Talbot stood straight and smoothed her apron. I waited for Matron Wright to take her to task for questioning the doctor's length of treatment.

Instead of being angry, the matron looked pensive. 'She is a pretty thing.'

They exchanged a look, and I ducked my head and finished my knots.

I did not miss the curl in Nurse Talbot's lip as we walked back inside. What could have disgusted her so?

'Mrs Parker. Time for your first treatment,' Matron Wright said, interrupting my cleaning. I gave the stair banister one last wipe with my lemon oil-soaked rag, handed it to Olivia, and wiped my hands on my apron.

'I intended to speak to Dr Griffiths before starting any treatment,' I said as I followed her down a corridor to the treatment rooms.

'Oh, this is fairly standard. Nothing to worry about at all. Dr Griffiths knows best.' Her clipped manner left my questions on my lips.

She ordered me to strip down to my undergarments and then swathed me in layer after layer of cold wet sheets until I was entirely swaddled. I squawked in protest at the cold, but it was to no avail, and it was my impotent rage that eventually warmed the sodden linen.

'There now, Mrs Parker. We regard this to be a very soothing therapy for nerves that are overexcited. It is also beneficial for stimulating the circulation of an unwell person and helping the body to purge any ills.'

I was far from soothed. 'I thought purging was no longer used as a treatment for the ill here.'

Matron shook her head. 'It can still be vital when treating certain illnesses. Following this will be a cold sitz bath, which will help draw down any humours from the head. Very useful for women's complaints in general.'

After sitting in the hip bath filled with a few inches of near-freezing water, my feet hanging over the edge, with buckets of icy water being poured over me, I did not feel relaxed or expunged of ill humours. My spirits dropped even further when I was told that this would be my treatment of the week. To be carried out every day for at least six days.

'I would like to speak with Dr Griffiths, please,' I asked as I wrapped my shawl around my quaking body.

'He will see you at your allotted appointment time next week,' Matron said, taking the towel from me.

'This isn't a suitable approach for my situation,' I argued. A familiar tightness grew in my chest. Whenever Papa or Spencer overlooked my concerns and continued their work as planned, and I could not object, my chest ached. I took a breath, knowing that pleading or stomping my feet would only worsen the situation.

'You are here because you cannot judge what is best for your health. Leave that to us, and you'll be fine in no time. Let's get you to the dining hall for supper. A cup of tea will finish this off nicely.'

I gritted my teeth. Obviously, my opinion about my treatment was going to be ignored. I shuddered to think what else the good doctor had at his disposal.

As we walked along the hall, Nurse Talbot grabbed my arm. 'No, not that direction. It's quite the maze.' Another nurse carrying a meal tray, coming from the direction I had turned, nearly collided with us.

With an apology, the nurse stopped to tell Nurse Talbot of a new admission.

I peered down the long corridor to the left and saw a door that was bolted at the end. A muffled scream came from beyond.

The nurses stopped talking, and Nurse Talbot bustled me along. 'Who was screaming?' I dared to ask.

'Screaming?'

I ignored her blank look. 'Yes, I heard screaming coming from beyond the locked door.'

She shook her head. 'It was probably the wind.'

From her expression, I understood I would receive no more information.

What might happen beyond to make a woman scream?

Olivia took one look at my damp locks and shook her head. 'I hope that means that Matron will excuse you from our weekly bath tonight, although at least *that* one is warm.'

With my metal cup of tea in my hand, I sighed as its warmth filtered through me. 'I witnessed many an argument between my parents about treatments for the ill when Mama was alive. God bless her. Mama came from an extensive line of midwives and wise women and believed in the power of her herbs, rest, and laughter among friends as the cure for many an ailment – while Papa supported some of the newer discoveries, though he was not interested in some of the heroic treatments of surgeons. I doubt either of them would have regarded a wet pack comforting.'

Olivia, sitting across from me, laughed. 'Oh, yes, the sitz bath is most refreshing. Brings all the senses alive.'

Leonora's gaunt face also transformed with a smile. 'Now, I much prefer the Tickleator.'

The table burst into laughter. What was it they found so amusing? I doubted any treatment would raise a laugh from me.

Leonora raised her tin cup to me. 'I hope that husband told the good doctor that you were reluctant in the bedroom. Mind, even though you are beautiful, if you *did* show some fire in the bedroom I expect he would have been just as concerned.'

I blushed, and she grinned. 'Ah ha. This part of melancholy can totally befuddle a man. If a woman came out of that sad condition only to be asked to attend to her wifely duties, she might feel some anger at the man. A woman might refuse, yell, or strike such a man – and be deemed to have moved on to hysteria. Of course, there are many things that lead to hysteria. Our wandering wombs and all.'

Leonora's doe-brown eyes twinkled.

Sophia nodded solemnly. 'Oh yes, all of our madness can be linked to that wandering womb.'

Tea sputtered from my mouth. 'Our wandering *what*? Surely, after all this time, and since doctors have been cutting into poor dead women, they know the womb stays right where it is.' I wiped my chin.

Leonora scanned the room, then leaned in and continued, 'Maybe the Tickleator would be daunting for some, given it's attaching a machine to our most intimate parts. Those that we are told are not to be touched – and certainly not by our own fingers, and not for pleasure.'

'Good grief. They use a machine … what on earth for?' I had once overheard Papa discussing rumours of such a device with a colleague, but they had agreed that to submit a woman to manual or mechanical stimulation of delicate parts would cause such a scandal that it would be regarded as a totally inappropriate treatment. Especially as much of their medical focus was on *avoiding* overstimulation.

Olivia no doubt noticed colour in my cheeks as heat ran through my body. I was used to having personal conversations with women around the time of childbirth and its recovery … but to talk of some machine applied to those delicate parts! It seemed quite scandalous.

She flicked hair from her eyes and suppressed a smile. 'The good Dr Griffith assures us that some women who have become melancholy or suffer from hysteria may need some stimulation or relaxation to soothe them. It is quite a frightful-looking machine – takes up half a treatment room – and is rather noisy, but ooooh, yes, the stimulation is most delightful.'

I straightened, trying to appear blasé about it all. 'My mama was confused when times changed. When she was a girl, she learned as an apprentice midwife it was important for women to be pleasured to have a good conception – and, of course, the only way to do this was by rubbing the clitoris.'

Olivia's eyes widened, and she started giggling.

I frowned. 'Oh, don't be silly. That's what the female pleasure part is called. It does nothing but give us enjoyment, but it seems over time that pleasure has become no longer considered our due, and the clitoris has been forgotten, so I am surprised it is now a focus for treatment.'

'Oh, yes. They have some of these machines in pharmacies, I have heard, in London. Were you unaware? Very popular with the bored aristocrat, who may pop in for a lovely time and then be on her way.'

Now we were both giggling. After we had made a few snorting noises, Matron Wright warned we would be separated if we were to continue behaving like disobedient children.

Once my mirth had subsided, I dismissed the idea. 'I'm certain that's not the case. I have heard of no such machine at a pharmacy. It is true some doctors have thrown ideas around in their circles, but I am sure they would have decided that, given we are such delicate and refined creatures, we would not abide such an inappropriate treatment; nor would they link it to a woman's mental state.'

I did not understand how hysteria or melancholy might benefit from a woman's being stimulated to orgasm, unless, perhaps, men complained their wives were not 'in the mood' while in melancholic states. It confounded me, and I had no wish to submit myself to such a humiliating experience. Was such stimulation not something for the bedroom, rather than the treatment room? Not that Spencer knew his way around a clitoris.

Perhaps that was the problem ... such exploration was only deemed suitable for mistresses or worse. Either way, I resented that a doctor might presume I was in need of any such stimulation or that he would be in control of its application.

'Stop looking so horrified. It is far better than the wet pack, let me assure you,' Olivia said. 'Do you suppose your husband would have called you reluctant?'

I shuddered as images of Spencer clawing at me flashed through my mind.

When my eyes regained focus, Olivia's eyes had darkened to an emerald colour. She touched my hand. 'Many of us have been ill-treated or ravished. I am sure that has caused some of the insanity in here.'

'I heard a woman scream from behind a locked door. Have any of you heard screaming?' I asked.

All of them denied any knowledge, although something in Edna's expression suggested I should ask again in private.

'That's enough idle chatter. Time for a bath.' Matron Wright's lip curled as I groaned.

As we lined up, Prudence stared at me as she ambled past, even turning her head to look back.

'As beautiful as she is, she gives me the shivers.' Olivia's pale face was almost grey. 'It seems she has taken an interest in you, Adeline.'

I took her arm. 'Pay her no mind; she isn't bothering me.' My stomach clenched in denial.

I was glad to have been forewarned of the Tickleator, as the women called it. As soon as Dr Griffiths mentioned the need for a little stimulation to check all was well down there (as my awful husband had indeed told him we had quarrelled about the act and hadn't engaged in it since I had lost my baby), I held up a hand in protest.

'I assure you that, as a midwife, I am confident I am in good working order. Our quarrel had far more to do with my discovery of his gambling habit than me being unresponsive to his needs.' I ignored the burn in my cheeks and jutted my chin forward. That should put paid to it.

'Either way, we need to be sure. Most women find the pelvic massage from the Manipulator very restorative.' He gave a smile that seemed almost a leer. 'It induces a hysterical paroxysm that restores the circulation. A steam engine in the room next door runs it.'

I stood. 'Oh, I really don't believe this is necessary. My melancholia has responded very well to the serenity of the asylum already. On what evidence are you basing the theory that a woman's mental state is connected to her need for a paroxysm?'

The doctor's eyes narrowed, and he left his chair. He opened his door, calling out, 'Matron Wright, would you mind offering some assistance?'

Before I could shut my hanging mouth, Matron Wright forcibly escorted me into the treatment room. A platform as large as a dining-room table stood in the middle of the room. At the centre of the platform, a metal sphere rose from a hole cut into it. Matron stripped me down to my undergarments and had me lie on the table with my legs and arms strapped down, putting me into position so that I felt the cold sphere at my crotch.

'Stop with all this wriggling. I understand you questioned the doctor's expertise. That is very unwise. You are to do as the doctor orders,' she said. I prickled under her scrutiny. 'All seems to be well here; I'll start it. The ball will vibrate against you.'

I shivered; a tear traced a path, its wetness dripping into my ear. 'As a midwife who knows much about the female anatomy, I can assure this is not—'

Matron rechecked the straps on my wrists. 'There's no need to be upset. This will set you right. We use this for backache and other aches too.'

I was unable to meet her eyes and instead looked up to the pendant light in the centre of the ceiling. How awful, to be stripped and strapped with my legs apart for all to see, with a machine ... I couldn't bear it.

'I'll leave you for a few minutes, usually all that's needed.'

I nodded, grateful at least that I would be left with a shred of privacy.

The sphere whirred into life, and I jolted, fearful of pain, but I experienced only the mildest of tingles.

My stomach rolled and clenched as the tingles intensified. I frowned as my whole body warmed and tingled. This was the strangest sensation. My eyes closed, bursting with stars, as I rode wave after wave of bliss.

So much better than a wet pack.

CHAPTER

TEN

I assisted Edna in scrubbing the floors of the consulting rooms. It was backbreaking and smelly work, as the floor had to be scrubbed with sand and then rubbed with a stiff brush and lye. The floor would then be moistened with a diluted solution of hydrochloric acid, and a thin paste of bleaching powder would be applied. It was all washed off in the morning after it had been left overnight.

'You've been in various asylums. Why haven't they released you in all this time?' I asked. Edna seemed perfectly sane to me. She enjoyed mopping the floors, shredding the rags for the furnace, chatting as she did her needlework or played cards. She must have been subjected to some terrible treatment in the days before the insane were treated with more humanity. How she preserved her cheerful demeanour was a mystery to me.

'Oh, I am too honest. I told them I doubted I should ever be cured of my affliction, so it would be best I stayed on. My great nephew writes regularly now that my sister has passed on. He enquires of my health, writes to the doctors. They confer and agree to me staying on.' Edna stopped scrubbing and crossed her arms over her shawl.

When I met her eye, her rigid posture softened.

'As much as I might make some fun and mischief here, I like we can share the burden of anything that troubles us. That others may understand, and care and true friendships might be made.' Edna's voice trembled with emotion. 'I see how lonely you are. I am aware you have Olivia, but I want you to understand I'm also available for support. The fact is, even she is unaware of my affliction, and if it becomes known, it will impede every friendship I ever forge here.'

What was this affliction that was so awful it could not be shared? I frowned, but took her wrinkled hand. 'Edna, it sounds as if you are carrying the heaviest of burdens. If you choose to free your heart of it, I promise to keep your confidence. It will make no difference to me, as I would appreciate having another dear friend in this place.'

Edna closed her eyes and squeezed my hand. 'Oh, I've been told I am most wicked and have no place in civilised society. My mother abandoned me to an asylum when I was sixteen. That was fifty years ago. How I have lived to this grand old age in such places, I do not know. I should have perished in the gloom of York Asylum.'

As her face fell with the pain of grim memories, I remained silent. With a sniff, she shook off her mood, as if removing her shawl.

'We can thank the Quakers for how asylums are today. If one of their own had not suffered at that asylum in York, we would still be regarded as little more than animals. Those reformers, such as Mrs Fry, saw the horror of asylums and conditions of the gaols and raised their voices for change. They set up York Retreat, and if I have understood the Friends' approach correctly, it became the blueprint for asylums such as this. You know: the gardens, exercise, and work ethic, the gentle listening and family-like connections. Maybe not some of our treatments, though.'

'No wet towels or Ticklelator?' I asked.

Edna grinned. 'If word got out, I believe it would be regarded as quite the scandal. I don't think the treatments for those in the convalescent ward are too concerning. Yet, behind the grand façade here, I wonder. When someone has power over another, there will always be trouble.' She got back to work as I pondered her words. She took in my frozen posture. 'There's always more shadow than light in asylums.'

My pulse raced. 'Really?'

'Some doctors here think they need to do more than what the Friends offered as therapy. I have heard and seen things here that might curl your hair. Not that I want to scare you. I might not be as educated as some, but these doctors ... it makes little sense to me, what they do. They call themselves alienists, saying the self has become alienated from itself; they think that removing body parts or spinning us in a chair can cure us.'

'Body parts? What parts?' I tried to keep my voice from escalating into a scream.

Edna bit her lip. 'It depends on the doctor.'

'For my "hysteria" ... how would removing any body part cure that?' I shook my head. 'And what would they need to do to cure *you*?'

Edna nodded. 'Who knows what an alienist would chop off? So far, I've been left to it.' She paused and gave me a wary look. 'My mother placed me in an asylum because she found me in a compromising position with my lover.'

'Someone she did not approve of, then?' I asked.

'No. She never took to Lily.' She watched my slight intake of breath.

'I wonder what your mother would have thought about the asylum treating you with a Ticklealator, then?'

Edna burst out laughing. As tears streamed down her cheeks, I ended up chuckling too. It was expected of me to view Edna's behaviour as shocking and unnatural, but I judged abandoning a daughter to an asylum to be far more reprehensible.

Edna opened the tin of caustic soda, and I wrinkled my nose. 'You'd best get some work gloves and a scarf for your face, to cover your nose from the stench,' she said. 'I have some spare ones upstairs for this work.'

I made my way to the dormitory and found what I needed in Edna's cupboard. As I tied the scarf around my face before I started downstairs, the ties were yanked back by invisible hands. The scarf moulded itself to my face, and I struggled to breathe. Who was trying to suffocate me?

A voice whispered in my ear. 'I wouldn't go walking around here by myself any longer if I were you.'

As my vision darkened, a bony hand shoved my back, and I cartwheeled into the air. Thud, thud, thud, down the stairs.

CHAPTER

ELEVEN

I was fortunate that Nurse Talbot had been heading up the stairs as I tumbled down. Even more fortunately, she was a strong woman; she caught me and, apart from a few bruises, I was none the worse from the fall. In body, that is. In spirit, I was rattled.

I had been expecting too much from women in an asylum. They had all been so friendly and accommodating that I had been tricked into regarding this betrayal of Spencer's as just a retreat from society. A woman's sojourn to Bath for the healing waters, not a sane woman's committal against her will. I should not have been shocked that there were indeed some insane women within the walls of Bloomfield House.

For a few days I flinched at every branch tapping against a window and every flutter of a shadow in a corner, and was very mindful around the staircase, but with no further incident, I decided that beyond keeping an eye out as a woman would for a pickpocket in Coventry Market; I had little to gain from becoming a Nervous Nellie. Olivia had been keeping a watchful eye on me since I told her I had been pushed down the stairs.

Long after we settled in for the night, I was sure I heard a strange blend of a groan and a scream. But no other nightcap popped up from a pillow. Was it my imagination?

'Olivia,' I whispered to the bed next to me.

With a rustle of linen, she turned towards me. 'What is it?' She was far from alert.

'Did you hear that scream?' My eyes flicked around the dark ward.

After a pause, she answered, 'No, not even a moan from the wind. It must have been a nightmare. Go back to sleep before the night nurse catches us.'

With a rustle, then a soft snore, she returned to slumber. I sighed. No matter how hard I tried, my heart would not settle. As happened on many a night, I was troubled by images of my ill papa, of Spencer's contorted face, as he shoved me down, and of my still babe. The clouds must have parted, for moonlight flooded in, allowing me to feel safe enough to drift off.

I awoke with a start, my skin tingling. A silhouette hovered above me, and then breath touched my cheek. My throat closed over, and my limbs froze. In my head, I screamed for Olivia. As my eyes adjusted, I saw a flash of golden hair, then the glint of silver in the moonlight. The silver hovered above my chest. I made the slightest gasp, enough to pause the movement towards me.

A lamp bobbed behind, and Prudence was revealed.

'Miss Shaw, what are you doing out of bed?' a night nurse asked.

'I thought poor Mrs Parker was crying. It seems she must have been dreaming.'

I sat up. 'My cheeks are dry. I was not crying.'

The nurse moved the lantern from Prudence's face to mine. 'All is well. Back to bed.'

Prudence gave my leg a pat as she left, yet I felt something hard in her palm. I gulped as I realised the silver glint had been a knife in her hand.

Were these women far more insane than they appeared?

A sound night's sleep became a luxury I could no longer indulge in.

CHAPTER

TWELVE

Olivia and I looked up from our cards as Dr Griffiths led two gentlemen into the dayroom. My inward groan was echoed by Edna's outward one. She stabbed the needle into her sewing with extra vigour.

The tours of the Visiting Committee had their purposes. Some were to educate, some to ensure women were being cared for appropriately, and others to check how allocated funds had been spent, and so on. We had all been instructed many times how we must behave as they passed through (more often than not with nothing more than a nervous glance our way), while Dr Griffiths spouted the wonders of the asylum. It was the only time I experienced the burn of shame that came with the label of lunatic. I did not want wealthy gentleman to look upon me with fear, judgement, or even sympathy.

One man was elderly, stooped in posture, and seemed to compensate for a loss of hair on his scalp by growing an extra-long beard. The other held my enquiring gaze with his own. His sculpted features were easily as handsome as Dr Griffiths's, but his air was more serene, almost languorous. He asked Edna what she was sewing and took great interest when she explained it was part of a costume for an upcoming performance. Although he must have been aware of intense scrutiny from all quarters and of the old man's grumbling, he persisted in his chat. This was the first time I had seen a committee member stop to talk to patients.

Olivia tapped my leg, and I returned to the card game, trying to ignore Dr Griffiths and his guests as they drew near.

Dr Griffiths began the usual the spiel about how progressive and wonderful this institution was. 'Here at Bloomfield House, we believe in following the moral regime to restore health. Women here respond well to compassion, industry, and various tailored treatments. This asylum takes its role as a refuge from the evils of society seriously.'

I looked up as I finished mouthing the last of these words along with Dr Griffiths and noticed the visitor's eyes twinkle as he bit into his lip to stifle his grin.

'Well, that sounds like a very admirable venture indeed.'

'It is, Mr Ashton, I assure you. It is wonderful that you have taken such an interest. Your father may have given generous donations, but he did not step foot inside the asylum. Now, if you'd like to continue ...' Dr Griffiths showed him the side door, but Mr Ashton was watching Olivia and me play.

'I've heard that I can have a word with the patients here. I wonder if these fine ladies would mind answering some of my questions. You can continue the tour with Mr Grinstead and collect me afterwards,' he suggested.

Dr Griffiths flushed. 'I'm sorry, we can't leave you unsupervised.'

'I'm sure Matron Wright can keep an eye on things. She seems like a very capable woman.'

'Right you are.' Being left with little choice, Dr Griffiths and Mr Grinstead left the dayroom.

Mr Ashton gave a charming smile and asked if he might sit with us, which, of course we readily agreed to.

'If you don't mind me asking—' he began.

'I have epilepsy and Adeline melancholy, although they have admitted her as hysterical,' Olivia jumped in.

'Olivia. Mr Ashton may not have been asking such forward questions,' I said, noting his blush.

'I must admit, I was curious, but did not want to pry. Pleased to meet you, Adeline and Olivia. Since we are being informal, may I introduce myself as Morgan.' We gave a nod of acknowledgement.

'So, what brings you to be on our fine committee?' Olivia asked.

I enjoyed watching him squirm as we abandoned the rules of social protocol that usually kept all in their place.

'Oh, my father has recently passed, and as he has always made such large donations to the asylum, I felt it appropriate to educate myself and continue his good work.' Morgan's blue eyes became more vibrant as they slightly teared. 'I hope they are treating you well.'

Unprepared for such candour, Olivia and I sat in silence for a moment. Neither of us could meet his eye.

'I am sorry for your loss,' I whispered.

He looked upon me with such intensity that my cheeks blazed. 'I get the sense that while all is in *order* here, all is not *well*.'

I wanted to spill all my woes there and then. 'My husband imprisoned me here when I became addled with grief over the loss of my unborn child.'

Morgan's face softened with compassion, and my heart ached. He looked about the room.

'May I ask what troubles *you*?' I asked, and immediately regretted my outburst.

He gave me a soft smile, but I saw his distress. 'I was a tad nervous about visiting you all.'

I laughed. 'Are we not the lunatics you were expecting? Don't concern yourself; I too, was surprised at how lucid everyone is. It makes one wonder about what constitutes madness. This is only one ward of the less serious cases, though.'

'Mr Ashton, forgive me for interrupting, but it is time for dinner,' Matron Wright said as she stepped between us.

'Oh. I'd best find Dr Griffiths. Thank you for your company, ladies.' Morgan stood and smoothed down his waistcoat. 'I'll see you another time.'

Olivia waited until Morgan had ambled from the room and Matron Wright's sharp eyes were targeted at someone else.

'He's a smitten kitten,' she teased as we packed our cards away.

'He was being polite,' I said, yet my happiness at her words was evident. 'Even if he was even the slightest bit interested, he is far above my station. I'm married and a lunatic.'

Olivia laughed. 'That's what makes this so entertaining.'

Long into the night, it was Morgan's eyes and gentle smile that haunted me. My head must have been tainted from reading one of Olivia's romance novels. That was the only place for dreams of a handsome man whisking a lonely woman away from her sad lot in life.

THIRTEEN

I will admit that my heart gave an extra beat when I saw Morgan enter the dayroom a few days later. I was definitely distracted from my novel.

He sat in a chair beside Edna and seemed most absorbed in her wig- and beard-making. Edna continued to make intricate point knots of hair, attaching it carefully onto the flesh-coloured silk net.

'The secret is to use real human hair, not goat or horsehair,' Edna explained as she set her knotting hook down. 'I don't like to take advantage of the poor girls, so my nephew pays them well for their locks.'

As Morgan stroked one of the sorted piles of hair ready to be woven, Edna gave a slow smile, and I sensed she was up to mischief. 'Oh, of course I boil them good, to get rid of the lice.'

As if licked by a flame, his hand shot back, and Edna cackled.

With some hesitation, Morgan picked up a piece she had set on the table. 'Is this a beard?'

Edna nodded and held the wiry grey-and-black mass to her face. Morgan gamely touched it.

'That looks so real.' He stared at it in wonder. 'How do you put it on?'

'Oh, it's much like the wig. It has been made to measure for Adeline. You loop it over your ears like so, and the netting moulds to the face. Now, the moustache is more complicated. Don't tell Adeline, but it's sewn into a pig's bladder to make it sturdy so it can handle the dabs of a concoction I made to stick it to the skin. I've made another to remove it.'

I tried not to grimace; I was certain Edna understood I was eavesdropping. She paused as the canary took this moment to trill. Oh dear, wearing a poor London waif's shorn hair and a pig's bladder. Until now, I had given little thought to the effort Edna was putting into her costuming.

'It is a messy business, to be sure. This is made from a man's actual beard. That's why it's nice and wiry. It's important to blend in assorted colours so it looks more natural.' She puffed with pride as he admired her work. 'My mother was a fine wigmaker. When they fell out of fashion somewhat, she made them for the theatre folk, and I helped her.'

'You are a marvel. I will leave you to your work.'

I pretended to gaze out of the window as Morgan made his way to where I was seated.

'Miss Adeline, how are you this fine morning?' he asked.

I laughed, as the view from the window was obscured by the rain beating against the pane. 'Perhaps sunnier than the weather, although it is only a summer shower.'

'Good to hear. May I?' He took the chair across from me, and I shot Olivia a pointed stare as she puckered her lips and sat, giggling, with Edna.

Even though I appreciated Morgan's fine looks, it was his warm manner that held my attention. He had a way of making me feel I was the only person who mattered to him in the world. The conversation flowed as easily as the raindrops trickling down the window and was just as mesmerising to me. I didn't realise that a man could be as engaging to talk to as a close woman friend. Still, I would not be fooled again by a charismatic man, as I had by my husband. His words had been false, like linsey masquerading as silk.

'I heard you were given the leading role in the Dickens play,' Morgan said.

While it had been flattering to be chosen for the lead role, it bothered me that the play was to be performed at Christmas, months away. It did not give me hope for a quick release.

'Oh, yes. I blame my father for encouraging my dramatic flair. We would often imitate those we had encountered in the day for our own amusement. The women here were quite taken with my imitation of various staff members. Obviously not something I partake in when they might hear. I would not want to offend,' I said.

Before long, I had an opportunity to demonstrate my acting skills to Morgan. I waited until Matron Wright and Dr Griffiths left the room, and only Nurse Talbot was in attendance. When she was sufficiently occupied with helping Edna gather up her completed costumes, I launched into character, swapping from Matron Wright to Dr Griffiths.

Morgan laughed so hard he almost choked. I stopped to pat him on the back, waving Nurse Talbot away. I noticed the tug of a smile on her lips, which I had seen before when I had entertained our ward in such a way one evening. She had not tattled on me then, and I hoped I had not overstepped the mark now. She gave a warning cough as Matron Wright returned.

'That was genius,' Morgan said. 'You have mastered the voice of each, and that little snort Dr Griffiths does when he's trying to impress. How can such a delicate woman sound so much like a man?' Morgan wiped the tears from his cheeks.

I was thrilled to have entertained him. 'I am uncertain that I can manage performing for a longer time, but I have been given little choice. It is a wonderful idea to base a performance on Mr Dickens's novel. I once saw him do a public reading, and he has far more talent in devising different voices and styles than I'll ever have.'

'Oh, I'm not so sure about that, but I too have had the honour of seeing one of his performances. I hear he will read in Dublin, and even all the way to New York City, in the coming years. A most talented man.'

I agreed with him. 'I hope I will do him some credit. Although, I can say he has not enhanced a nurse's reputation with his character Mrs Gamp. As a midwife, my mama was already vying with the male midwives, the accoucheurs, who were trying to oust her out of business.'

Our talk meandered to many topics.

Though unsure of my ability to judge the man, I told Morgan my concerns about what Spencer might do while I was being held here.

His brow furrowed deeply. He leaned against the window as we sat in the alcove, pointedly ignoring Matron Wright's hovering and tut-tutting. 'I do not understand the appeal of gambling myself,' he said. 'My father would have been horrified if I'd wasted the family fortune on such folly.'

What a relief that he didn't gamble. 'Were you close to your father?'

He sighed. 'He gave me the correct amount of attention and the tuition he felt necessary, more so than some fathers, because of my unfortunate lack of siblings, but much of his time was spent at a gentlemen's club or out riding. Thankfully, I was an imaginative child and rather than lament my loneliness I used to invent stories and play with woodland animals or annoy my nursemaid. Our head gardener had a son my age, and we had many an adventure together. Rather than separate us, my father generously gave Isaac a wonderful education – we even attended Eton together. He is still a loyal friend.'

'I, too, have a loyal friend from childhood rather than a house full of siblings. Charity would do everything in her power to release me from here. I am sure she is ignorant of my fate. I spent most of my childhood tagging along to births with my mother or in my father's study, asking him question after question about medical matters. Perhaps he would have preferred had a son to follow in his footsteps, but it was not to be. He is against so much of the quackery that abounds in London and, unlike many, values the apothecary and wise women.' I felt my lip tremble and bit down. 'He was very ill when I last saw him.'

He touched my hand. 'You must be concerned about him.'

I nodded. 'Terribly. My mother died when I turned sixteen, and I felt certain I could not bear it. Then my baby. I cannot imagine a life without Papa's wise counsel and humour. I'm afraid I grieve with my whole heart and soul. Very unladylike of me. Mind, I am of the middling class, so I lack the finesse of a lady and the stoic nature of the poor.'

'Ah, I would rather be grieved fully than have life carry on as if I had never trod upon the cobblestones of this world at all.'

My fingers tingled at his touch, and my head became light. 'I am sure someone would grieve much at the loss of you.'

I am sure we were both blushing at this stage.

'Isn't this a pretty picture? I don't think I've had the pleasure.' Prudence smirked as Morgan withdrew his hand and rose to greet her.

He murmured an introduction, but his eyes did not light up at her attention. Prudence prattled on and tittered at Mr Ashton's replies as if they were most amusing, but he seemed impervious to her lilting smile and lily-white complexion. In fact, the more she tried to engage him, the more distant he appeared. He was polite as Prudence leaned in far too close to him, but left her side as soon as possible. He gave me a warm smile as he moved toward the door.

The air became dense, Prudence's eyes narrowing as Morgan waved his farewells at us. 'I was unaware that committee members took such an avid interest in patient welfare. You must learn to share, *Mrs* Parker.' Prudence puffed out her ample bosom, which looked out of proportion with her tiny frame, and I almost laughed at her display, but my skin prickled. 'What a shame you are married. He'd be quite the catch.'

As she glided past me, she stopped to whisper in my ear. 'Seems you landed on your feet here ... like an alley cat ... but there are many ways to skin a cat.'

My blood chilled. Spencer had called me an alley cat. That rasping whisper. I gulped. It was Prudence who had pushed me down the stairs.

I barely noticed Matron Wright until her coffee breath was upon me. 'This is not your drawing room or parlour where you entertain gentleman callers. I am not to be considered your chaperone. This must stop.' Matron Wright huffed off, leaving the women in the room initially silent – until they erupted into giggles.

'Oh, yes, Mrs Parker. That will never do. A married woman consorting with such an eligible man. Not that he has an eye for any other woman here.' Olivia fanned herself.

I recovered myself. 'Stop casting aspersions upon my fine character. We are merely engaging in conversation that will assist Mr Ashton with his work on the Visiting Committee. He is ensuring that Leonora will be released, as she is meant to be in a few weeks.' If only it were me.

Edna and Olivia rolled their eyes.

'Thank goodness not all the committee members want to socialise. I imagine Mr Grinstead would be poor company. Did you hear him fart down the hallway?'

Olivia gasped at Edna's words. 'You're hardly one to talk.'

'Let us all pray that there is no cabbage soup again today,' Edna muttered as she folded up her sewing.

I laughed with Olivia, but my mirth was forced. While I had enjoyed Morgan's conversation and attention, I had lost all sense of ease. For whatever reason, Prudence meant me harm. Arsenic posing as toffee.

FOURTEEN

I was under no illusion that it was to round out my character that I stood before a washing-tub in the asylum laundry. Matron Wright was punishing me for Mr Ashton's gentlemanly attention. My fingers reddened and chafed above the steaming hot water, and my back ached under the load of the heavy linen. What Matron Wright did not realise was that I was finding the release of pounding and stirring the cloth with the washing bat quite wonderful. With each strike, I pictured Spencer's nose bursting. Now, that was more therapeutic than cold towels.

As I scooped the last sheet of the day out and passed it to a hefty woman operating the mangle, I had to admit I was done in. At least Matron hadn't put me on ironing duty. Once everything was arranged and our departure for dinner was possible, I was near collapse. I hobbled along with the other women, trying to ignore the soggy clothes chilling my skin, the scent of sweat, and the rat-tail hair drooping in my eyes. A hot cup of sugared tea was all I cared about.

'Mrs Parker?'

No. Please. That was impossible; Mr Morgan Ashton was not calling my name when I was in such an appalling state.

'Mrs Parker, it's me. Morgan.'

I turned and offered a smile. 'Oh, good evening, Mr Ashton. Isn't it rather late for you to be visiting?' As he seemed to care little about my bedraggled appearance, I straightened up. The other women, obviously curious, glanced at him, then walked past me into the dining hall. The attendant frowned, but then, on seeing a gentleman, dipped her head. She stayed near the entrance, keeping me in view.

'Yes, indeed it is late,' Morgan agreed. Before he continued, another gentleman pushing a contraption along the hall came up behind him.

'Mrs Parker, allow me to introduce to you my friend, Mr Walsh.'

I pushed back my lank hair and gave a genuine smile to his friend. 'Mr Walsh.'

Mr Walsh was dressed as well as Morgan was, with a fashionable single-breasted and semi-fitted coat, simply embroidered waistcoat, and cravat tied as a scarf. Somehow, he wore it in such a way as to make him look as dishevelled as I no doubt appeared. I wanted to tidy the cork-screw curl that fell upon his forehead. His unusually clean-shaven face added to his boyishness.

'Ah, Mrs Parker. Would you be so kind as to try out my newest invention? Mr Bugwell has approved a trial.'

I could not resist his enthusiasm and found myself seated in some kind of wheelchair.

Mr Walsh stepped in front of the chair. 'This new wheelchair design has yet to secure a patent, so I am very keen for it to be tested. As you will note, it has large wheels at the back and small castors on the front so it can be self-propelled.' I looked at all the wheels and nodded.

He beamed at me, and Morgan raised his hands behind him in surrender. There was obviously no stopping his friend. 'If we can attract investors, we might even experiment with rubber wheels.' No doubt noting my blank but expectant look, he allowed me to give the enormous wheels a push.

I watched his eyes gleam as I rolled forward. 'How clever. What inspired you to make this? Are you a medical man?'

Mr Walsh nodded. 'I was indeed. Although, this was for my ma. Pa was in the Charge of the Light Brigade and lost his leg when a shell burst in front of him. Mind, he was more upset at the loss of his horse. When he got home, he did not want to be wheeled around and gave my mother such grief ... so now, he can get himself around.'

Morgan gave Mr Walsh a clap on the back. 'It seems he is far too clever to be wasted on medicine. He was a fine physician, now an astounding inventor.'

'I'd better give this a run, then.' I rolled the chair down the full length of the hallway. 'What a wonderful invention,' I said.

A smatter of applause and other women asking for a ride filled the hallway. Apparently, there had been an audience to the experiment. I laughed as Edna shoved her way through and plopped into the chair that I had barely vacated. I wheeled it around, and she was off. Prudence's squeal echoed as Edna rode over her foot.

'What is this ruckus, ladies?'

We each donned the face of a naughty child, complete with a hung head (even Morgan and Mr Walsh) as Matron Wright stalked up the hallway, indicating for Edna to stand.

'Please return to the dining room, ladies,' Matron Wright directed.

I gave the men a wave in farewell.

'Not you, Mrs Parker. You are a sight. Attend to yourself first.' Matron Wright held on to the wheelchair. 'We have no need for a self-propelled chair at Bloomfield.'

Mr Walsh narrowed his eyes and took the chair from her grip. 'Mr Bugwell seems to think it is a wonderful idea. The committee also approves.'

I admired his light manner as he addressed her. He ignored her puff of impatience as she returned to the dining hall.

'Until next time, fair Adeline,' Morgan said as they left.

I warmed at his words. I had to admit I felt a tingly lightness with the promise of 'next time'.

FIFTEEN

I roamed Bloomfield's corridors while most were at the chapel, except the most devout, who were forbidden (it appeared excessive Holy Spirit was possible) and those, such as myself, who chose not to go. I had been more than patient. I had done my best to show I was a sane and well-behaved woman, yet it had made little difference to the medical men here. I had still not been given any indication of when or if I might ever be released.

I wandered into the art studio and studied the works in progress, wishing I had an iota of talent myself. While some depicted scenes of nature I recognised from the grounds around the asylum, others were more imaginative, with fairies and the like. A beautiful one that was very much like Millais's Ophelia stirred both awe and sorrow within me.

My mother had taken me to see Mr Windus's collection at Tottenham years ago. While I had admired Turner's paintings, it was the depiction of the tragic demise of Ophelia that had caught my heart. Perhaps I had always been slightly melancholy. I sighed, then drew in a deep breath, enjoying the scent of linseed oil and even the turpentine.

'It's not just about the accomplishment of a fine painting, dear Adeline,' said Edna as she worked on an etching in the corner. 'There is much to be enjoyed in the process. It can be soothing.'

I nodded and moved away from the easel to stand next to her as she continued with her sketch, her fingers dancing over the malleable wax ground.

'That's all well and good to say when you are clearly talented. The intricacy of the pattern on her dress is beautiful.' I watched her deft hands add more detail, amazed that a woman of her advanced age had the dexterity to produce such a beautiful etching of a woman dressed in a ball gown without even a model.

As she kept drawing, I noticed another etching, already printed on thick paper. It too was a remarkable etching of a scene in London.

'How beautiful. I feel as if I am there, looking across the Thames at St Paul's.' I peered closer. A similar pattern to the one on the dress was etched onto the jacket of a gentleman in the foreground. 'Is this your work, too?'

'No, I am one for portraits, rather than landscapes.'

She didn't offer any further explanation. I kept studying the two etchings, then noticed a bemused smile on Edna's lips.

'There's obviously more to this. Please tell me.' I put the etching back on the side table and sat on a stool next to her. The light-flooded room revealed every crinkle and wrinkle in her face as she weighed up whether to tell me her secret.

She held up the London scene. 'Yes, you are right, you clever girl. My nephew, who sent me this, is not a talented artist. Lily, however, is.'

From the bittersweet expression and the tenderness with which she gazed at the etching, I knew who she meant.

'You have been in contact all these years?'

She nodded. 'Yes. We have a code that we incorporate into all the drawings. My sister was far more sympathetic to my plight than my mother and passed them on every month. She ensured her son would continue to do so after her death, although he is unaware of my love for Lily.'

Edna sighed. 'Apart from personal news, Lily keeps me abreast of news of our mutual friends. The rest, I gather from ripping the newspapers here. She has mentioned a concern for Mrs and Miss Whitmore. Are you acquainted with either of them?'

I nodded. 'I met them both when I was invited to an archery meet at Powderham Castle in Devon, of all things.' One of my very wealthy women had been so grateful after a safe birth that she had insisted I would enjoy such a spectacle.

My mind trailed back in time. I was gawping at the brilliant hues of colour the lady archers were wearing, when Miss Whitmore noticed I was a complete novice in such a setting. We stood in the shade of an oak tree, one of many dotting the extensive grounds of the deer park.

'It is a wonderful sport for fashion,' she said. 'The wraparound style of the bodice means we can move our shoulders easily, while still looking fashionable. I quite like the feathers in our hats.' Miss Whitmore touched her pheasant's feather with a plump finger. She was dressed rather plainly in cream, with a matching lavender ribbon tied around her waist and black hat.

'They are rather elegant,' I agreed as a woman in a scarlet skirt and green-trimmed jacket sauntered past. She had a large white ostrich feather attached by a knot of green ribbon to her white hat.

'Are you—'

I laughed. 'No, I am here to spectate today. I do not own a lady's set.'

Miss Whitmore picked up her bow, which she had laid on the ground next to her. 'I would be happy for you to use mine. I may not be adept at calisthenics or croquet, but I am rather good at archery. I can show you how.'

A regal-looking woman, as sharp in features as Miss Whitmore was rounded, came toward us. 'Shouldn't you be getting ready to shoot, Matilda?'

'Mother. May I introduce Mrs Parker?' Miss Whitmore fiddled with her bow, while Mrs Whitmore's eyes narrowed then softened.

'Ah, the newlywed. Where is your delightful husband?' We scanned the crowds. 'Oh, there he is. With Lady Elizabeth Telford, I believe. Doesn't she cut a strikingly slender figure in her green dress?'

I was unsure if it was a barb at her rotund daughter or a dig at me. Spencer was looking rather too comfortable with the sweetly laughing Lady Telford. I had heard rumours he had been turned away by her father, the earl, as being too below her station to be considered as a match. But I'd heard other rumours, too, about the earl: whispers of depravity, of an immoral taste for young boys. No doubt it was all just cruel gossip; I would not entertain the thought. As Mrs Whitmore studied my face, I sensed she was aware of Spencer's former attachment to Lady Elizabeth and wondered if I was too. I swallowed the niggle of doubt and gave her my best effort at a smile.

I nodded in agreement. 'Yes, she looks lovely. I never realised exercise could be so graceful.'

Mrs Whitmore pursed her sour-lemon lips. 'He is such a kind and attentive doctor. I had hoped he would have a heart for Matilda. You are a very fortunate woman, Mrs Parker.'

'You must come closer and cheer me on, Mother.' Miss Whitmore offered an apologetic glance back at me as she steered her mother away.

I rubbed my arms, suddenly feeling chilly in the shade. How many women here were aware of Spencer's failed pursuit of Lady Telford's hand? Was I a poor second prize?

'Are you listening, Adeline?'

Edna's question jolted me back to the present. She continued speaking when she was sure she had my attention. 'Miss Whitmore – Matilda – has been a wonderful support to Lily. Her widowed and wealthy mother has gone to the trouble of making a will and plans to bequeath a substantial portion of her estate to the doctor who has been attending to her – thus reducing her daughter's share. Matilda is not a greedy or selfish woman and deserves to be taken care of. I do not believe that same can be said for the doctor in question. Mrs Whitmore is not the only wealthy widow to have offered this same doctor the same promise or already given him funds.' She watched me expectantly.

My brow furrowed and my head ached. 'Spencer was once her doctor. Does she mention the name of the doctor in question?'

Edna waited. The ache deepened, and I rubbed my temples. Oh!

'It is Spencer?' More of a statement than a question. How could he?

My mind raced as I recalled the extravagant jewellery and gifts that Spencer had given me as we courted, the expensive items for his curiosity cabinet, or the fine painting that adorned our drawing room. He had told me that wealthy clients liked to show their appreciation, and later I had assumed some of these prizes had resulted from a lucky flutter. I held my stomach as nausea threatened to evacuate my breakfast.

Edna set down her etching. 'You had no idea.'

'None at all.'

'It seems your husband has few redeeming qualities.'

I gritted my teeth. 'I cannot call to mind a single one. He is beyond redemption. I did not believe his greed would extend so far. I do not understand his obsession with wealth at all.'

She gave a slight nod to a blank canvas set up in front of one of the floor-to-ceiling windows. 'You might want to capture the beauty of the rose garden beyond. You might find it equally wonderful to let your brush express what cannot be said.'

Much might be expressed, but it would go unheeded. Following Edna's encouragement, however, I took up the brush. I dabbed a range of oil colours from the tin paint tubes onto a palette. While I was quite taken with the cadmium yellow and cerulean blue, my emotions were far too dark for them.

Edna dug around her own paintbox. 'You might like this one. Egyptian Brown.'

'Yes, I am feeling quite murky. Brown would be wonderful.' Her eyes danced with mischief as I took the tube. 'What is so special about this one?'

She cackled. 'It's actually made from ground-up Egyptian mummies.'

I gasped. 'Surely that's not true.'

She gave me a dark look and handed me another tube. 'You'll like this one too, then. Indian Yellow. Made from the urine of cattle fed on mango leaves.'

I dropped the tube, and she laughed even harder. 'I'll leave you to it.'

She took back the tube of yellow and gathered the rest of her things. Her chuckle followed her as she walked along the hall.

I loaded the thickest paintbrush and slapped it onto the canvas. I kept going. Slashes of red, brown, and black covered the canvas. It looked a fright when I was done.

'Now, that's got to be a sign of hysteria.'

I did not turn to the doorway to acknowledge Prudence. I continued my painting and added a very thick splash of red.

She came and stood behind me, close enough for me to feel the whisper of her breath on my ear. I held the brush tight, lest she notice the tremble in my fingers.

'One might conclude your recovery is non-existent. You are getting too comfortable ... enjoying the company and the ambience such a fine institution offers.' She flicked a stray curl from my neck, laughing when I flinched. 'There are other parts of the asylum to explore that are far less pleasant.'

'Leave me be.' I whirled to face her, my brush smearing a vivid red line across her linen dress. It had looked as if I had taken a sharp knife to her, leaving a blobby line of congealed blood.

'You'll pay for that,' she growled.

CHAPTER

SIXTEEN

Dearest Charity,

I am writing to you in a state of desperation. I can only hope that the gentleman, Mr Ashton, agrees and succeeds in passing this letter along to you. He is one of the Visiting Committee members and has been most kind to me. I understand this is a terrible imposition on him, so hope through his generous and courageous heart that it makes its way into your hands.

First, Spencer has locked me away in an asylum. I suspect he has no intention of reclaiming me, though I pray for release much as a child dropped on the stairs of an orphanage might. This leaves me in the hands of the doctors here, who are in no hurry to release any woman here, whether or not they be sane.

I am fortunate that many of the women around me are lovely, though I am in mortal fear of one. The treatments are quite odd. I wonder whether the medical men are more concerned with attracting more funds through so-called 'progressive' treatments that will attract accolades – or if they truly believe these treatments might cure the maladies of women. I have no faith in anything on offer here and worry there are even more severe treatment options being tested out of a civilised person's view. It may seem my imagination is running wild, but I can feel in my bones that something deeply sinister is happening.

Speaking of which, I am very concerned about Spencer's more wealthy patients (in particular Mrs Whitmore). I suspect he is manipulating them into making him a beneficiary of their wills. Please warn your friends not to take any treatment he offers. I realise I sound quite deluded now. I promise I have my wits still.

Please give word on the state of my dear papa's health. I worry about him.

I beg of you to aid me in obtaining a release.

Yours with affection,

Adeline.

I held the letter in my apron pocket, having snuck into the dayroom early to scribble it out. I hoped Charity could decipher my scrawl, complete with tear smudges and blots of ink. I hoped Morgan would come again today.

I all but leapt up and hugged the man when he sauntered in a couple of hours later. Olivia was cross that I wasn't able to settle and play cards with her, and from the wink she gave me when Morgan came in, she thought that my attachment to him was the reason.

I swallowed my nerves, aware of the crackle of paper in my lap when I moved, and returned Morgan's smile.

He looked extra pleased with himself. 'Good morning to you, Miss Adeline. I am pleased to find you in here rather than slaving over a laundry tub,' Morgan said in a rather loud voice.

'Good morning to you too, Mr Ashton. I agree, the dayroom and its activities are far more to my liking. Though I am never one to hide from hard work.' I gestured to the empty seat near me, which Olivia had thoughtfully vacated. I pondered how I should ask him to take my letter and pass it to him.

He sat and gestured to the small collection of books on a shelf near me. 'I have guessed you are an avid reader, and that is quite a measly collection. I hope you do not mind; I would like to give you this.' He handed me a small book with a pretty cinnamon-coloured cloth binding and gilt wreath on the front. *A Christmas Carol.* It had a red and green title page, and even beautiful illustrations throughout.

I gasped. 'This is far too extravagant a gift,' I said, although I did not offer it back.

His smile widened at my pleasure. 'Aren't the illustrations by John Leech wonderful?'

I looked at a colour engraving of Mr Fezziwig's ball next to the title page and laughed at the plump man in a bright blue coat dancing with a woman in yellow. 'Very captivating.' I flicked to another of Marley's ghost. 'Ooh, I feel almost sorry for Mr Scrooge there. Can you imagine a ghost coming toward you while you are sitting in front of your fire?'

'I would think meeting a ghost would be quite terrifying,' he agreed.

My neck prickled, and I turned to see Prudence staring at me. 'Sometimes people are more terrifying than any phantom.'

Following the direction of my eyes, Morgan noticed Prudence, too. Her sourness became sugar as she smiled at him.

He coughed and looked away. 'Forgive me ... I dislike speaking ill of others. Miss Shaw ...' he tapped his fingers on his legs.

'Yes, quite,' I said. 'The only woman I have encountered here who fits the mould of a lunatic.'

His eyes popped. 'I was going to suggest that her scrutiny was rather intense. I will defer to your judgement, as it sits well with me. Is there anything I can do to help?'

I reached into my pocket and removed my letter.

Matron Wright lumbered toward us, and I tucked it away. 'Why, Mr Ashton, Mr Griffiths told me you were visiting again. Nurse Talbot should have sent an attendant for me. It is lovely of you to take such an interest in our asylum. You must accompany me to see the new hot-water heater for the shower bath. Mr Maughan is generously allowing us to test it out. How wonderful to have a warm shower. What an exciting invention. He calls it the Geyser. Heaven knows why.'

With a shrug of apology, Morgan stood to follow an insistent Matron Wright from the dayroom. I mouthed my thanks for his gift and clung to it as he left. The letter would have to wait. My knees bounced.

Prudence slid into his seat. She grabbed at the novel as I held on to it.

'I'm sure that was meant to be shared with everyone in need of entertainment,' Prudence said, all but snarling.

'It's clearly a gift for someone Mr Ashton finds especially entertaining,' I snapped.

The temperature seemed to drop.

Even though I hid the precious novel later, I was horrified to find the page with Marley's ghost on it sitting on my pillow that night. On another piece of paper, words were written in neat copperplate: *You will wear the chain you forged in life, and I will place it link by link and yard by yard around your slender neck and pull. There will be no light part of your penance.*

I did not care for Prudence's version of *A Christmas Carol*. I showed Nurse Talbot the note, but because identification of its author proved impossible, she was powerless. If only I could have given Morgan my letter.

CHAPTER

SEVENTEEN

As I swept the hallway floor, melancholy notes washed over me. I put the broom against the wall and stood in the doorway of a small music room. Leonora was bent over the pianoforte, playing with passion. I closed my eyes and let the music envelop me and the tears I'd suppressed fall. The last note faded away, and I wiped my eyes.

'I did not see you there,' Leonora said, as she stood.

'I did not mean to intrude. That was such a beautiful melody.'

She ran her slender fingers along the piano keys. 'This allows me to share what cannot be shared.'

I nodded. 'I hear the depth of your sadness.'

She sighed and sat back on the padded stool. 'Dr Griffiths believes I am ready to leave Bloomfield and return home.' She chewed on her lip. 'I know you would give anything to be in my shoes. As beautiful as Bloomfield is, as serene and inviting, we are not here by choice, and so it does not matter whether we have a golden cage or a pit. We are trapped. But in returning home, I would merely replace this golden cage for another.'

Leonora's shoulders drooped as I pulled another stool next to hers, cringing at the scrape on the oak floor. 'Surely you would prefer to be a lady of the house again, rather than being ordered about by Matron Wright.'

She gave a tight smile, almost a grimace. 'My mother-in-law makes her look like an angel of mercy. Now that she is widowed, she lives with us. I can do no right; her barbs of criticism dig daily. Her son can do no wrong, and I am not worthy of him. He seems oblivious of her treatment of me. I may have a beautiful townhouse, fine clothes, and many books ... I do not have the love and passion of my husband. I am but a shadow of who I once was or even could be.'

I frowned, her words striking my heart. 'I understand. I suspect it is a common experience among women.'

'I have no doubt many women experience a loveless marriage, though some cope with it better than others. There is far more danger in my head and heart than whatever Dr Griffiths may concoct in his attempts to heal me.'

I gave her slumped shoulders a gentle touch. I could find no words of comfort. What did she mean about danger in her head and heart?

'I understand you desire release,' Leonora said. 'But what would you be returning to?' She tapped a few soft notes out when I sat in silence. 'It's not for me to say, though I can not help but observe the affection between you and Mr Ashton. If there was a way, I would follow that path. It would be far richer than the one you'd leave behind.'

Now it was my turn to sigh. I gazed out of the large window to the blaze of autumn colour in the woods beyond. Sweet gum, golden larch, redwood, maidenhair, and maple trees reminded me of the beauty life held far beyond material wealth and told me it was natural for my heart to want to unfurl in the spring and discard what was no longer needed into the mulch below. Leonora was right. Even if Spencer took pity and arranged for my release, my marriage was in tatters. As dry and crusty as the brown, discarded leaves. Was there *any* way we could recapture the green of spring in our marriage? That Morgan would play any role in my future was in the realms of impossible romantic dreams.

I shrugged. 'You are right. Take heart, Leonora.'

Leonora moved over to a harp in the corner. I sat, mesmerised, as she played the same melody on its strings. I pictured myself in London's best parlour, being entertained before delicately eating a charity tea, not in a small asylum music room.

'What a talent you have, Mrs Thompson,' I said as I applauded.

Leonora blushed and gave me a small curtsey. 'You are too kind.' She tucked an escaped brown tendril under her cap. 'I guess it will be lovely to play my own instruments again. I even have a hurdy-gurdy that has been passed on by my grandfather.'

'That sounds fascinating.' I was relieved to see some spark return to her eyes and colour to her cheeks. 'I had better get back to the sweeping. It was a pleasure to listen to you.'

It was not a pleasure, though, to bump into Prudence in the hallway and have her accuse me of being a lazy slug.

As we settled down for dinner later that day, I noticed Edna and Leonora missing from their usual places. When Edna finally shuffled in, she could barely speak.

'What is it?' I asked.

'It's Leonora,' she whispered.

I leaned in. 'I just saw her, only an hour ago, and she was fine,' I said.

Edna's eyes clouded. 'She got into the medicine cabinet and took all she found. I found her all covered in vomit, and ... there was nothing to be done.'

My fingers gripped my cheeks as they covered my mouth. I had been a fool. I knew she was desperately sad about being released, and I had said and done nothing to ease her burden. I could not think of what I might have done; I only knew that just listening to her was not enough. I had failed to notice she had lost all hope.

Our last conversation haunted me as I twisted in bed. In a flash of clarity, I realised Leonora did not want me to suffer such a fate. I would no longer deny my heart, for that would lead to an empty life, devoid of love and hope.

A groan echoed down the corridor outside the dorm with such mournfulness my heart raced. I half-expected to see Leonora's ghost wafting toward me. Surely her choice had left her a tortured soul. Had I had any part in adding to her pain?

EIGHTEEN

'I have been informed by a reliable source that you have been stealing newspapers to read, making a parody of hard-working staff – in front of a Visiting Committee member, no less – and questioning our doctor's expertise in letters that, thankfully, were never sent beyond these walls,' Matron Wright said as she held the offending letters and scraps of newspaper I had buried in a hole in my mattress. 'Even worse, you were the last person seen talking with Mrs Thompson, and I am certain you must have disturbed her, considering the events that followed.'

The other women in my ward froze, then scurried to dress as the matron's beady eyes flicked over them. Her gaze came to rest upon Prudence, and a smug smile formed on Prudence's thin lips. What made Matron Wright believe I was connected to Leonora's death? No use defending myself. Reliable source indeed.

Nurse Talbot and another imposing nurse I was not acquainted with stepped into the room.

'You are to be escorted to another ward.' Matron Wright gave a nod, and the nurses stepped to either side of me. Olivia gasped.

My limbs fired up as I considered running. As if they sensed my intent, the nurses clamped strong fingers on each of my arms and tugged me along.

Before long, we had left the familiar part of the asylum, and I was lost in the labyrinth of progressively gloomier hallways.

'I want to go back to my ward,' I protested, but this only made their grip on me even tighter.

'Only women who follow the treatments recommended and behave with decorum should be on the convalescent ward. You are nowhere near ready for release,' Nurse Talbot said. These were not the words of reassurance I was seeking, and my legs grew heavier with every step. 'I do not understand how you could believe such a thing of me.'

Nurse Talbot faltered for a moment. 'Matron Wright told me you neighed like a horse when I left the room.'

I gasped. Nurse Talbot had a long, slightly horse-like face and large teeth. No wonder she was being cold towards me. 'I would never do such a cruel thing, Nurse Talbot.'

She continued prodding me along, ignoring my protests. 'Here we are. Now, behave or you will be taken to the seclusion cells.' She unlocked the door with a key and shoved me inside.

Most of the patients were bedridden, but one paced towards me.

'Mavis, leave her be and go check on Hattie.' The nurse guided the old woman to a chair beside one of the beds and placed her in it. Mavis grabbed another old lady's hand and began chatting to her.

I wrinkled my nose at the smell of mingled urine, faeces, and carbolic acid solution.

'Why isn't she medicated?' A nurse asked, tilting her head at me. She had a lumpish body with hunched shoulders and was wearing a thunderous expression on her sallow face.

Nurse Talbot took a step back. 'I'll leave you in Nurse Bell's capable hands.'

Nurse Bell rolled her eyes. She said to me, 'The other nurses don't like to spend much time in here. As you can tell, many of the woman here are older and have dementia. Some cannot control their bladders or bowels. I hope you are in control of yours.'

'Of course,' I stammered.

'Mmmm, you look fine to me. You can help strip the beds of linen once I've moved any patient needing a wash. Nurse Hodge will help me move the women into chairs by the windows, and then we'll make up fresh beds.'

Another nurse that I took to be Nurse Hodge was wiping a young woman's face with her bib. 'It takes so long to feed them; we're barely done with it before we start on the next meal.' Nurse Hodge had dark rings under her eyes. She was as stocky as Nurse Bell and made quick work of hoisting various patients into chairs.

I got on with replacing sheets, checking the mattress for moisture, replacing the newspaper strips if needed, and making up the beds. It reminded me of my midwifery work. Cleaning up the mess of humanity and restoring dignity. It was something a doctor or medical officer would regard as far beneath him, yet one of the most basic acts of generosity in assisting the vulnerable.

Once the flurry of activity was completed, the ward settled.

'If we're lucky, Mavis will have one of her good days and we can have a rest.' Nurse Bell watched Mavis pat Hattie's hand as they chatted. 'Looks like a good day.'

As we settled on some chairs, Nurse Bell groaned with pleasure. 'Ah. To have a sit.'

'So, what's Mavis like on a difficult day?' I asked. 'She seems very sweet.'

The nurses swapped a look. Nurse Bell's brown eyes clouded with tiredness. 'On a hard day she will pace all day. She'll go on and on about some crime she thinks she's committed and ask when she's due to be hanged. Other days she sits next to the door and waits until someone walks past. She'll try to grab their arm and bite them. It varies, as it does with many of them. On a wonderful day she'll tell you the most marvellous tales of all her travels. I'm not sure they're entirely true, but they *are* entertaining. The saddest times are when she feels I am her daughter, Abigail, and wonders why I deserted her here.'

Nurse Hodge nodded. 'It doesn't help that your name is Abigail. Most of the ladies here are not aware of much, so they're far more settled. I think it's unhelpful when they add other women with mania in here now and then.' She stopped short, realising that I was a patient too.

'That would be difficult,' I said, ignoring her hesitancy. 'My father once tried to treat a woman with such mania in a workhouse ward. She would talk strangely, gesture wildly, and rip her bedding constantly. Those around her were quite scared, but when she tried to burn the place down, they became even more concerned, and he secured a place in a better asylum.' I was babbling, desperate to have a professional conversation. I wanted to show I was a sensible woman who did not belong here.

'Yes, they are very difficult to treat. We do not favour using restraints, but in some cases, they are indeed a danger to themselves and others.' Nurse Hodge smiled and stood, stretching her back with a crack. 'Back to it, then.'

I had hoped that if I persuaded the nurses that I was quite sane and might even assist them, they would speak on my behalf and restore me to my ward, but my bubble of hope was soon popped. After I had eaten a bland meal of watery soup and stale bread, Dr Griffiths returned and ensured I took my medication. Before long I was another body in a bed, oblivious of all around me.

CHAPTER

NINETEEN

'You're very fortunate. One of the first to use the soothing chair,' Nurse Bell told me. 'Most in our ward are beyond it. I don't know if you saw Mr LeMott's demonstrations of his electric light above the Duke of York's column ... back in '48, I think it was.'

I had no idea what Nurse Bell was chattering about, but I was happy to be free from the ward and smelly dayroom.

She unlocked a small room and told me to sit on a couch. 'There's no need for us to wait for Dr Griffiths to get started. He said he would be along.'

I settled on the couch, looking at a strange box below a table of mechanical parts. Nurse Bell sat in a chair. 'See, this here is the magic of electricity. This device is like a Leyden jar, storing the electric charge.'

Although I usually tried to understand scientific matters, this was beyond my addled brain. The dementia ward had softened me. I took the metal handle that she gave me.

'Settle back and close your eyes. You'll sense a lovely buzzing within you and will be quite restored, I'm told.'

I did as she asked and felt an odd, though not painful, sensation beginning in my fingers and travelling up my arms.

I heard a soft groan from her. I opened my eyes and noticed her gripping her stomach. 'Are you poorly, Nurse Bell?'

As she blushed, I guessed the origin of her discomfort. 'Some willow bark might be of use?'

Her bloated face wore a glum expression. 'I don't like to leave you, but I need to go to the privy.'

I smiled. 'I'll be fine.'

'I'll be right back. The doctor will be along any minute now,' she said in warning as she closed the door.

I had intended to sit and tingle until she came back. Could I help it if the clomp and shuffle of footsteps to the room next door alerted my catlike curiosity?

I slid off the couch and padded to the slightly open door and risked a peek in, expecting it to be set up as mine was. But instead I saw a chair, rather than cushioned couch, with wires all over it. A woman I did not recognise, who was clearly in the throes of a deep melancholy, was being placed by two attendants onto the chair and strapped in.

'I hope this one goes better than the last. Singed hair and a fracture to boot,' a rail-thin nurse said to one of the attendants.

I jumped as Dr Griffiths came through a side door to the room. Thank goodness he had not entered through mine!

'Now, Mrs Melville. It's time we got some spark back into you.'

The nurse tutted. 'This is hardly the time for such humour, doctor.'

Suitably admonished, Dr Griffiths suppressed his smile and got to work.

He attached various wires to a contraption on her hands, then another to her head. 'I believe this will work if we apply it directly to the skull, sending a pulse through her brain, which will cause a fit. I doubt melancholy and epilepsy can occur together.'

What on earth was going on? Was this one of the things Edna had been talking about?

'Here we go.'

A tendril of smoke wafted up from the woman's head. Her body throbbed, then trembled. She groaned. I covered my mouth and stepped back. This asylum was a chamber of torture.

I scurried back to my couch, huffing, and gulping air. Nurse Bell soon followed.

'It must be working; you are glowing,' Nurse Bell said as she sat. I grabbed the metal handle before she could notice I was no longer holding it.

'Oh, yes. It's quite soothing,' I agreed.

She frowned as thuds and groans sounded from the next room. 'I wonder what that is all about. I'm sure it's nothing for you to concern yourself with.'

The noises stopped. There was only the hum of the machine next to me.

'Ah, Dr Griffiths. As you can see, Mrs Parker is doing very well.'

I did not open my eyes. I set my face in as tranquil an expression as I could manage.

'Ah, yes. Looking quite like a sleeping angel. I'm glad. I'd hate to use the wet towels again. She did not find that a healing experience at all. Plenty of other things to try for these poor women.' I heard the door close and his footsteps recede.

I had given life in an asylum very little thought prior to entering one. Those with mental maladies were hidden away, either in asylums or in homes. It was not for me to ponder. Now I was locked away in one. The layers were being peeled away. I did not want to be subjected to its dark centre. My assumption, at first, had been that Spencer intended to punish me and that, upon concluding his lesson, he would collect his newly docile and biddable wife. Now, I wasn't so sure.

But if he was not coming to release me, then I would have to help myself.

CHAPTER

TWENTY

'Abigail! Abigail! They are trying to poison me. You must help me!' Mavis slapped the medication from Nurse Hodge's hands and leapt from her bed. She grabbed Nurse Bell's skirts and gripped them tight, dropping to the floor and clinging like a child. I watched from my bed next to hers.

'Now, now, Mavis, all is well. Nobody is trying to poison you. This will help you sleep,' Nurse Hodge said as Nurse Bell tried to release Mavis's claw-like hands.

The poor woman shuffled on her bottom to hide behind Nurse Bell's skirt.

Nurse Hodge sighed and handed the sleeping draught to Nurse Bell. So began an entertaining tug of war. Once Mavis finally acquiesced and was settled in bed, the nurses slumped into their chairs. I squeezed my eyes shut, hoping they would forget that I had not received my sleeping draught.

Before long, the ward filled with the rumbling snores of the sedated and the whispers of the nurses. Just as they settled down to sip their cups of tea, the hallway outside echoed with running footsteps and shouts.

'Can't be good. We'd better help,' Nurse Bell said.

Nurse Hodge groaned. 'Just once, I'd like to get all the way through a hot cuppa.'

The door was unlocked. Nurse Hodge gave the room a quick scan, and I closed my eyes before her gaze reached my face. I doubted she could see much in the gloom, but I wasn't taking any chances.

Oh, they left the door not only unlocked with keys dangling but ajar, too!

Olivia had told me time and time again that if I was patient and trusted in the good doctors, my time in the asylum would surely end. She was not stuck in this ward, though. Who knew what would become of me? I gulped and decided to risk an escape. If not escape now, then at least a chance to explore the asylum for a suitable path to escape later.

My toes curled at the coldness of the floor as I padded towards the door and peeked out. Doors banged in the distance. I took the keys and crept out. I held the jangle of the keys still and slid my hand along the wall, being able to see very little. Disorientated, I followed the wall in the opposite direction from the noise.

I was in a corridor lined with doors. Even though my heart thumped and blood rushed into my ears, I slowed my breath until my hands were steady and I could try each of the keys until one finally turned in a lock. With any luck, I might follow the corridor, opening doors as I went, until I worked out how to get outside and escape. Then I would need to devise a plan quickly.

My mind roared at me, telling me I was taking far too long to make my way through a maze of corridors and locked doors. Each door took me further into the gloom and abyss of insanity. I stumbled upon rooms where no nurse watched over the inmates, rooms that I had assumed empty until the stench of human waste and clink of chains convinced me otherwise. I slammed those doors shut, remembering too late my need for silence.

At last, a room bathed in moonlight. It seemed to be some kind of library. If it was for the staff, maybe I could unlatch and creep through one of the large windows? In areas for inmates, the windows could not be opened, except for some small windows above them that were too high to reach, let alone squeeze through. Yes! I unlatched the heavy sash window and yanked it up, sucking in my breath at the chill. Once through, I stood gazing out at the moonlit grounds, debating the merits of escaping on such a clear night. On the one hand, I could see where I was going; on the other, I would be easier to spot.

I wiped my sweaty palms on my nightgown and pulled my shawl tighter, glad I had thought to take it from the end of my bed. My ears were tuned to every creak and crack of the asylum and rustle of leaves in the grounds. I made my way along the verandah and slid like a ghost into the crisp night.

Trying to avoid the crunch of the gravel, I skirted the paths, staying on the grass, then sprinted across to the back gate. Huffing and puffing, I fumbled with the gate latch, hoping to find it unlocked. It wasn't. A thump in the field beyond had my heart thudding in my throat. I peered through the crack in the gate.

With a frown, I saw a silhouette of a man. He looked as if he was digging. I bit back my frustration at not being able to continue that way. I watched him a little longer. He stopped digging, then hoisted up what must have been a heavy weight, judging by the groan he made. There was a glint of brass, and I narrowed my eyes, straining hard. Good grief. It was a curtain of auburn hair. Disappearing into the hole in the ground. He was making quick work of adding soil on top of her. I gulped hard, shock making my courage fizz away.

'Just where do you suppose you are going?'

My bounding heart froze.

Matron and Dr Griffiths stood in the shadows. Matron stepped forward and lit her lantern. 'Well?' She turned to the doctor. 'I told you, Seth, that these women were unreliable, and this one is especially cunning.'

Dr Griffiths shook his head. 'It seemed you were progressing nicely.'

I looked up a tree trunk next to the wall.

'Don't even think about it.' The matron gave her lantern to Dr Griffiths and grasped my arm. 'It seems that new treatment will be very well-timed.'

'There's a man out there burying someone,' I said.

'Oh dear, she is in a more dire state than I expected.'

Dr Griffiths took my other arm, and they marched me back into the asylum. They took me along a corridor I had not seen before.

I heard raised voices coming from behind one of the doors. 'Take her back to the cage. She's bitten my finger right through!' a man shouted.

Good grief. They were putting a woman in a cage?

Matron Wright pushed me along, past the door. 'Let's go to the surgery.' She tightened her grip on my arm. 'I hope that Mr Bugwell will take my report of the nurses' misconduct seriously.'

Dr Griffiths sighed. 'We need them. They are dedicated nurses.'

She nodded. 'Then why is this one out?'

A rising howl coming from behind us chilled me to my marrow. I turned to look back down the corridor. The door where the shouting had come from opened and a doctor stumbled out into the hallway. 'I warned them she was only an animal. That she was nearly let loose upon these women. There's no telling what damage she would have done.'

Nurse Bell emerged through the door and stopped dead. 'Mrs Parker? What are you doing wandering about? Come now, back to bed.' She glanced nervously at Matron Wright and took my hand.

'This is not good enough, Nurse Bell. We found her trying to make an escape near the back gate,' Matron Wright said, not quite ready to give up my arm.

'I'm terribly sorry, Matron,' Nurse Bell said, dropping her eyes to the scuffed floor. 'Thankfully, every gate outside is locked and the fences are high.'

'Seclusion might be better for her,' Matron Wright declared.

I gave Dr Griffiths my most pathetic, dejected gaze. He shifted the lamp to his other hand. 'No, she is fine where she is. We'll discuss it more in the morning.'

'Fine, take her back.' Matron released my arm and huffed away. Dr Griffiths sighed and followed her.

As Nurse Bell guided me back to the ward, locking doors behind her, she tutted to herself. 'We would have been in terrible trouble if you had escaped. I do not understand how Nurse Hodge left the keys in the door. Speaking of which?' She put out her hand, and I reluctantly gave the keys back.

This time, I was watched as I swallowed my sleeping concoction.

As I drifted off, my cheeks wet with tears, I felt a gentle touch on my cheek.

'Don't cry. It's much safer here for you in here than out there.'

'There was a woman being buried out in the fields,' I said.

Nurse Bell tutted and stroked my hair. 'There, there. No one was burying anyone. Time to sleep.'

Did she mean that her ward was a sanctuary from the other peculiar rooms I'd seen, or was she referring to the world in general? I did not feel safe in the asylum at all.

TWENTY-ONE

lthough I willed my eyes to open, they remained glued shut. I heard the rustle of sheets, groans, and snorts nearby. My addled brain struggled to clear the fog. Gradually, some clarity sliced through. As I recalled where I was, I heard Nurse Bell's and Dr Griffiths's voices.

'She seemed quite capable and in control of all of her faculties to me,' Nurse Bell said. I sensed a gentle tap at the end of my bed. She had been nothing but kind to me since my escape attempt, and I was grateful.

'Yes, it is a shame she has shown little response to the treatments offered so far,' Dr Griffiths said. 'Her husband has agreed to an operation which I am sure will cure her. She is sorely needed to perform in our Christmas entertainment, so I hope it works. Matron Wright is complaining about what a shambles it all is, yet does not want her back on her ward in the state she was. She wants to ensure Mrs Parker will behave appropriately.'

Nurse Bell tutted. 'Well, she can't have it both ways. I doubt she should have been sent to this ward at all. What does the operation involve?'

'Dr Butcher spent time with the originator of the procedure, Dr Baker Brown, learning to finesse this operation. Dr Baker Brown is an eminent obstetrical surgeon and president of the Medical

Society of London, no less, so I am sure we can trust that he is quite the authority on the nervous diseases of women. He is a true pioneer in the field.'

Even I sensed his evasion.

Nurse Bell sniffed. 'So, you do not know, then?'

'Dr Butcher has good surgical skills. Mrs Parker will be operated on for her hysteria and Miss Hall for her epilepsy, as the operation is a cure for both conditions, among other afflictions. Please ensure Mrs Parker is ready tomorrow.'

I groaned and Nurse Bell touched my hand. 'Time to wake up and have some dinner.'

Dinner? Hadn't I just had breakfast? I blinked and looked around. Dr Griffiths was nowhere to be seen.

Bump ... bump ... bump. 'Is she ready?'

Hands rolled me. I was lifted, carried like a babe in arms.

Thud. I was placed on a table ... I suppose. It was hard beneath me.

There was a scent hanging in the air. I sniffed. Not carbolic, lye soap ... sweeter.

My limbs were cold and heavy. Male voices grumbled nearby.

Something was placed on my face. Darkness. Velvet nothing.

'Oh, Adeline. We must get you out of this place.' Was that Morgan?

'Time to leave now, if you please, Mr Ashton.'

'Thank you, Nurse Talbot. I do not want you to be in any trouble.'

No ... don't leave me here, Morgan.

I sank back into darkness.

'Wake up, sleepy.'

I smiled at the sound of Papa's voice. I sat up in my room, aware I'd been having a string of strange dreams and nightmares. I shook them off, dressed quickly and clattered down the stairs to join him for breakfast.

Papa said, 'How did you go with Mrs Roberts last night? I tried to wait up.' He slurped his tea loudly to annoy Mrs Cook and was rewarded with a scowl.

'That'll be enough of that, or I won't save the porridge from Kitty burning it again,' Mrs Cook said as she huffed off to the kitchen.

I smiled. 'You are worse than a street urchin, with your mischief. Things went well with Mrs Roberts ... in the end. The baby was breech. If only doctors would see sense and let the midwives use some instruments too, think of the time that would be saved in waiting for the men with their forceps. Did you read Dr Playfair's letter in *The Lancet* about one of Dr Radford's cases?'

Papa nodded, and I continued. 'How interesting that in performing a caesarean, he drew the body forth but found the head detained by the uterus, prompting Dr Bedford to lie down the rule of removing the head and shoulders first. All of that quibbling about what parts to remove and where to make an incision. Not that I come across too many women who have had such an operation, but I think that a vertical incision in the upper part of a uterus does not heal well and introduces a risk of rupture. Would it be better to do one in the lower segment?'

Before Papa could answer my question, Mrs Cook returned with two bowls of porridge. 'I wish the two of you wouldn't discuss such matters at the breakfast table. It fair turns my stomach.' She plonked the bowls down and left.

'Ah, nothing wrong with a stimulating conversation to start the day.'

'Couldn't agree more, Papa.'

I frowned as the room darkened. 'Papa?'

'It's time we got you out of here.'

I sighed with relief and opened my eyes. I had dreamt of the past, and now Papa was with me in the present. He had found me.

I was in the asylum infirmary. Papa sat on a stool next to my bed.

'I'm so glad you've come. I was horrified that Spencer put me in such a place.' I sat up and reached for a lukewarm cup of tea left on the bedside table.

Papa rubbed his balding head. 'He is far more devious than I gave him credit for. He cannot wait to get his greedy paws on your inheritance. There would have been far more to keep you comfortable if he had not already drained me.'

He looked at my face and put his gnarled hand on mine. 'Don't you worry, now. I made my choices in good faith, and sometimes people let us down.'

I sighed, the heaviness hard in my stomach. Frowning, I recalled words of an operation. 'So, I am cured now, am I? Is that why you've come?'

He gazed at me with such sorrow I began searching my body for bandages.

'What!' The heat surged through me as I understood where I must have been cut. I patted the sheet down quickly. 'What did they do?' My need to know overtook my humiliation.

His jaw clicked in and out. 'Something unnecessary and very cruel. How they got away with it, I'll never know. They must be stopped.' Papa shook his head. 'You must escape, Addie girl. There is worse than this ...'

A moan in the bed by the door came to me. A dark curl spilled from her bonnet as she rolled towards me. Olivia.

'She needs help,' I said.

I threw the linen back and hobbled over to Olivia, a searing pain shooting through me. I made it to her bedside and slipped. I frowned as I looked at my feet. They were mucky with blood. Olivia's blood.

'Olivia! Someone, please help!' I peeled back her sheets and gasped.

'What are you doing out of bed ... Oh my goodness.' The nurse ran from the room. I heard her thudding footsteps going down the corridor and her screech as she called for a doctor.

Blood pooled on the sheets and floor, pints of it. 'Is it too late, Papa?'

Papa? He had gone. Was he ever there at all? Was my brain now truly addled; was I seeing things that were not there? My heart flickered. Or had Papa's ghost visited me? I sobbed for Olivia and the unknown fate of my papa.

CHAPTER

TWENTY-TWO

It took a little while to fully understand what mutilation had occurred. Once the bandages had been removed and some healing had taken place, my fingers and a looking glass reported the damage.

Ice lodged in my core as I did a double-take. My breath caught as my intellect tried to make sense of what had been done.

Why would a doctor think removing my clitoris would cure me of hysteria? It would *cause* hysteria, rather than cure it. Hysteria that I did not even have in the first place.

I was a ruined woman. My vision darkened, and I sucked in a few breaths.

Before I put the looking glass away, I glimpsed my mottled cheeks. I had moved on from shame. The veins strained against my skin in my neck, and I willed my hands to unclench. I remembered Papa's words. Ghost or not. I must escape, and to do that they had to think I was cured. I tucked the miniature looking glass into my apron.

Still numb from the shock, I was unsure how I would face anyone. I steeled myself as best I could. Some tears were better off well hidden, as once I started mourning for my feminine loss I might never stop. I had not seen Olivia since the night of the infirmary, and even though I was assured she was recovering in a long-term care ward for physical illness unrelated to mood, I worried for her. Coming out from behind the privacy screen for the commode, I pasted on a smile.

Nurse Talbot returned my smile, her equine face transforming with warmth. 'Welcome back. I'm to take you to the hall for rehearsal if you're feeling up to it. Matron Wright is keen to have you back in the play.'

As we walked, she sidled up to me and whispered, 'Mr Ashton has been asking after you. I investigated why you were in the infirmary ... I want you to understand I disagree with that treatment entirely.'

I slowed to a shuffle; my eyes blurred with tears. 'How could they?'

Nurse Talbot took my arm. 'I don't know. It's not for me to question the doctors ...' She blew a breath. 'I shouldn't have said anything.'

I wiped a straggling tear, willing my stomach to hold its contents. 'I won't tell a soul. Thank you.'

We reached our destination and I peered into the hall from the doorway. A backdrop of Scrooge's counting-house, with windows shrouded in fog, was very convincing. In front sat a stool, a coal box, and a table with a lit candle upon it. As I walked in, they began rolling up the backdrop to pull down another. This one a gloomy bedroom. The coal box was replaced with a small, brass bedstead. Edna was directing the stronger women where to move the table. Other women stood by in costume, waiting for the set to be complete.

I looked for a familiar face among them. In costume, with wigs and beards, Leonora and Sophia were hard to tell apart.

Edna spotted me and rushed forward to hug me. 'Thank goodness. Someone with talent. Let's get you in costume. Christmas will be here before we know it.' She then lowered her voice and whispered in my ear, 'It is good to have you back. Do not sink into melancholy, or you will never go beyond these walls.'

Though I wanted to sob into her shoulder, I took a breath and shoved it all down. 'Have you heard how Olivia is doing? When she might be with us again?'

'No, Matron is being tight-lipped about her. We might have to go on a midnight prowl in search of her,' Edna suggested.

I shivered. My last midnight prowl had resulted in an extreme surgical attempt to control me.

Sophia twirled her wig and puffed the pillow under her waistcoat. 'Yo ho, there! Ebenezer!'

Despite myself, I laughed. 'I barely recognised you, Sophia. Or should I say "Old Fezziwig"?'

It was good to be among friends again, even though I sorely missed Charity and Olivia. Good, sweet, Olivia. She had done nothing to deserve such treatment. As if I had been punched, I sucked my breath in. Even if I was well behaved and sweet, these men were doing whatever they pleased to me. They were not interested in my welfare at all.

The doctors and the matron believed I'd been tortured into submission. Now was the time to rebel.

My head was buzzing as I took the dressing-gown, slippers, and nightcap that Edna held out to me.

I knew exactly how I was going to escape.

'What are you lot whispering about? Thick as thieves up to no good.' Prudence ran her hands along the rack of clothes. I edged back into the shadows of the wardrobe room.

'Just ensuring everyone knows where their costumes are. This would be yours, wouldn't it?' Edna asked, holding up a rather drab dress, not much better than the asylum uniform.

Prudence eyed it with a sour pursing of the lips. 'I don't see why I can't be Belle rather than Mrs Dilber. What do I know about being a laundress?' She stroked a burgundy silk waistcoat embroidered with a small leaf pattern Morgan had donated. 'It seems a waste for someone not to wear this. I'd even dress as a gentleman for a chance to wear it. Are you sure it is too fine for Mr Scrooge's taste? Tell me, do you think it would have bothered Mrs Parker that Mr Ashton took to visiting with Sophia Miller while Mrs Parker was stuck with the weak-minded?'

I sucked in a breath as the barb went in. Sophia, who was sitting before a looking glass, stopped brushing her hair and held up her brush as if she'd like to attack Prudence, but Edna held up her hand and she lowered it. Sophia glanced at me as if to defend herself, but, still hiding silently in the shadows, I held a finger up.

'Mr Ashton was not calling on Sophia as a gentleman suitor,' Edna said. 'And it is unkind to deride those who are afflicted with dementia. It is nothing short of tragic that Adeline was put in that ward. We are lucky she was not left there to rot.' Edna threw the drab laundress dress at her. 'No thanks to you.'

Prudence flicked the sleeve of her costume. 'Yes, poor Adeline. Unable to mingle with handsome gentlemen. Her husband is surely handsome enough, yet she fawns over Mr Ashton. No, dementia is not as bad as some things. Hysteria is rather tragic too. Where is the hysterical woman, anyway? Shouldn't she be here by now?'

'Adeline is far from a hysterical woman. She will be here any moment. We have work to do, so get back to yours,' Edna growled. 'I don't think that new elixir is doing you any good. You're the only true lunatic here.'

Prudence laughed as she sauntered away.

'What elixir is that?' Sophia asked as she tucked her hair under the wig.

Edna waved her hand as she turned back to the costumes. 'Dr Griffiths was carrying on about some new elixir he got all the way from Germany. It had some powder made from the leaves of a coca plant in it. He believed it would be good for those with melancholy – not that anyone believes Prudence is melancholic. She suggested he try it for those with epilepsy. The cheek of her, telling a doctor what to do!' She noticed Sophia flinch at the mention of epilepsy and turned to her. 'No need to worry; he told her the elixir was too powerful for those with epilepsy – and besides, you haven't had a fit for years.'

'I know. We all miss Olivia. Come on out, Adeline.'

I did as Edna said and let her help me adjust my costume.

'She's a nasty piece of work, that one. Can't stand that she can't catch Mr Ashton's eye. Imagine the carry-on if this was a London

Season. She'd poke your eyes out without a thought.' Edna snipped a thread on my shirtsleeve.

'Mmm.' I fidgeted with the coat buttons.

Edna gave my back a pat. 'C'mon, lovey. No need to be nervous, either. I'm sure you'll bring the house down and fill the coffers up.'

'Thank you. If you both don't mind, I'd appreciate a moment to prepare in privacy.'

I waited until the room was empty, then put aside the fine burgundy waistcoat, black woollen suit, moustache, and beard. There would not be much time to swap costumes. I sucked in a breath. This had to work.

I crept out of the costume room and looked through a side door into the hall. I was transfixed by its Christmas transformation. At the centre of the hall, a grand Christmas tree stood, at least six feet high. It had been decorated with strands of popcorn, a few beautiful glass balls, ribbons, candies, fruit, and lighted candles. Nearby, a fire roared in the barely used fireplace. More candles burned among mantelpiece decorations of berry-laden holly and pine-cones. The scent of dried orange, pine, cinnamon, and star anise in pot-pourri in bowls spread around the hall was divine.

I ached as the memories of previous family celebrations invaded my brain, casting out snatches of Dickens's dialogue that I was supposed to be performing that night. I was nervous as I watched the crowd trickle in. It was not as if I was going to be on stage at the Adelphi or the Lyceum, I told myself. Surely the patrons and committee members in the audience would not expect much from a group of lunatics or asylum staff. I made my way to where the other 'actors' were waiting.

Once the first words left my lips, I became Scrooge and relaxed. I watched Sophia as she swept on stage. Even in the dress of a young woman working for a milliner, she radiated a confidence I had not seen in her before.

'Here's Martha, Mother!' Sophia said, in character.

As I joined in this performance of a warm though poverty-stricken Christmas family gathering, I felt a wash of sadness that soon I would leave behind this strange new family that had taken me in, and I would become the Ghost of Christmas Past for them.

As we drew around the mock hearth and drinks were poured into tumblers and a custard cup as it was in the novel – no golden goblets to be seen, though – Bob Cratchit (Nurse Talbot) turned to the family and then the audience. 'A Merry Christmas to us all, my dears. God bless us!'

The family echoed the same and drank from their tumblers and cups.

Sophia dropped her tumbler with a clatter. She swayed and collapsed onto the stage.

As her limbs jerked, the actresses scattered. I stood frozen, my useless mouth an O, before I finally dropped to my knees next to her and tried to hold her head steady.

Dr Griffiths rushed forward with two attendants, still in costume. He shoved me aside while the crowd erupted. I was still kneeling when they hoisted Sophia up and whisked her away.

Matron Wright stepped around me and took centre stage. 'I must apologise for this interruption to our entertainment. Miss Miller has epilepsy, but will no doubt recover soon enough. I believe, though, it may be wise to conclude our play for tonight and go on with some carols instead.'

Nurse Talbot hauled me to my feet and guided me to the corridor outside of the hall. 'You are trembling. Go and get changed, and I'll see you get a cup of tea. I'm needed for the carols, but I'll send someone later to check on you.'

She returned to the small group of staff who were singing carols in the hall. An obedient audience was soon joining them in a subdued version of 'O Come, All Ye Faithful'.

I hurried to the costume storage room, but stopped short when I saw Prudence there. She was tucking a bottle under her costume apron.

I barrelled into her. 'What did you do?'

I slipped my hand into her apron and pulled the bottle out. My nose crinkled as we drew apart. She had a familiar sweet scent of jasmine on her.

'It's my elixir. Give it back.' She snatched it from me.

I glowered at her. 'You are not meant to have that with you.'

'And *she* was not meant to drink from that cup. That was supposed to be for *you*.' She sauntered off as I absorbed her words. Clearly, there was more than elixir in the bottle. I was torn. I wanted to check on Sophia, but I needed to change costume while I had the chance.

Once in a secluded area, I ensured my breasts were still bound well and my beard still attached. I added a moustache and pulled on the different waistcoat. I exchanged the silk top hat for a felt bowler hat and put on a dress coat with padded shoulders and boots with lifts for added height. I hoped that would be enough.

I heard Matron Wright coming from the hall. 'This will be our last carol before we ask you to join us in a small supper.'

I needed to get to Morgan before we were sent back to our wards. I made my way down to the Christmas tree.

'Joy to the World' burst from the staff choir, and if I wasn't so nervous it would have seemed quite appropriate.

'Mr Ashton,' I said, 'so good of you to invite me to this fine performance, but I'm afraid the travel has made me weary. Might we leave?'

At first, his eyes popped. Then he looked at the men seated to each side and recovered himself with grace. 'Mr ... uh ... Dalton, of course. Please make our excuses.'

We strode to the door, and it wasn't until we were seated in his coach, galloping away, that I finally breathed a sigh of relief.

'I must admit I am still a little confused – though what a splendid performance, Mr Dalton. I'm sure that surpassed all your onstage efforts.' He clapped his gloved hands.

'I'm thankful you recognised me and responded so quickly to my request for assistance. I understand it is a terrible imposition, but I could not stay in that asylum a moment longer. Nurse Talbot warned me that Dr Butcher was planning to remove my ovaries, Dr Baker Brown style.'

He gasped. 'Surely they wouldn't allow such a thing? I understand there was a harmless minor operation done, but removing ovaries seems a very drastic thing to do.'

My jaw clenched. 'I can assure you that the "minor" operation was neither minor nor harmless. I do not wish to discuss the details. I cannot thank you enough,' I said, taking his offer of a blanket against the chill.

'It must have been quite distressing in there, for you to consider escape. I should have asked more about the treatments at Bloomfield and intervened. I want you to understand you'll be safe with me, and that my intentions are strictly honourable.'

The thrill of my escape thudded like a dropping stone. What had I expected? That he would fall madly in love with me? I chewed my lip, hating the prickle of the moustache above. No, I was no damsel in distress waiting for a white knight. I would hide for a time, and then he would be free of me.

CHAPTER

TWENTY-FOUR

Two weeks. Fourteen days ... three hundred and thirty-six hours. That's how long I had to remain free from those looking for me. The belief was that if a person managed in the outside world for that period, then perhaps they were not as insane as was initially thought. Mind, the people from the nearby village were always on the lookout for escaped lunatics, as they received rewards from the asylum for their trouble. I snuggled back into the warmth of my bedding in a luxurious bedroom.

My suit hung on a stand. The previous night I had decided it would be best for both of us if I remained as Mr Dalton until the two weeks was over. I groaned. If only that did not involve having a beard and moustache. It was much faster for me to dress as a man, but reattaching the facial hair took its time.

I joined Morgan in the breakfast room and admired the view of snow-crusted parkland. As the maid poured my coffee, she examined me, then lit up with a rather flirtatious smile that almost had me in a fit of giggles.

Morgan gave her a pointed look. She blushed and scurried from the room. 'I hadn't considered that possibility,' Morgan said.

'Whatever do you mean?' I asked, mimicking the maid's expression perfectly.

Morgan laughed. 'Best to stay in the library. Even though it's an inconvenience to keep up your ruse, I am sure even those little ears of hers are attached to a big mouth.'

I nodded as I smeared a breakfast roll with marmalade while sniffing the scent of bacon. 'This all looks delicious. Much more exciting than my usual porridge.' I barely talked to him as I scoffed down the bacon, eggs, and a small cake.

'I obviously need to ask more questions about the volume and variety of food available at the asylum,' Morgan commented as he sipped his cup of tea.

I stopped mid-chew and grinned. Once we had finished, I groaned and gave my stomach a pat. 'Remind me to eat more like a lady at dinner. I can't thank you enough for helping me.'

'My pleasure. While I have been satisfied that Bloomfield is a well-run and caring asylum, I do not accept that every woman there is insane. I doubt you suffer from hysteria.'

I cleared my throat. 'Thank you. I can assure you I am completely sane. That it is judged wrong to mourn the loss of a dear baby, as if a woman's heart should not break in the circumstances, is a travesty. And locking an inconvenient wife away and spending the last of her money is a crime.'

Morgan choked on his tea, and I waited while he composed himself. 'I agree,' he said at last. 'Measures should be taken. Far too common a crime, I am sure.'

'I apologise. I forget how to have a polite conversation.' The heat was not just in my cheeks, but my entire body. 'My financial woes are not your concern.'

He smiled. 'It is just as well you are dressed as a gentleman. We can discuss many more topics than would be allowed in polite society otherwise.'

It was wonderful that he welcomed frank discussion.

I smiled and looked around the room. 'This is a lovely manor.' I pointed to a small tapestry on the wall depicting a family at breakfast in this room. 'Is that your family?'

Morgan nodded. 'My ancestors. Ashton Court has changed little in hundreds of years. I am the next in line required to resist altering its Tudor origins. I'll admit that as a child I thought it hideous, but I appreciate the grand old lady now.'

I had always found the Tudor-style steeply pitched gabled roofs and exposed wooden beams between whitewashed walls charming. As I looked through the window, I noticed that the roof on the next wing was thatch, rather than the slate or tile of the Tudor townhouses in London. 'I don't know how you ever found her hideous. Look at those beautiful diamond shapes in the windows! Although, I suppose all the oak panelling might seem drab to a child.'

We both startled at the clang of the front doorbell. Morgan raised an eyebrow but did not move.

'Would you like me to get that?' I asked with a smile.

'Oh, of course. I had forgotten that I sent the butler and footman away.' He leapt to his feet. 'Stay where you are.'

He closed the door behind him.

I fiddled with my moustache while I waited, horrified to find cake crumbs and what was probably egg yolk in it. What would Morgan think of me? I wiped myself clean with a handkerchief, wishing there was a looking glass so I might check that all was well. My behaviour had resembled that of a pig at a trough. I resolved to exercise some restraint at our next meal.

The longer Morgan took at the door, the colder I got. I wriggled in my chair, unsure whether I should exercise caution and hide myself, but I had yet to take a tour of the rambling manor and therefore feared I might get lost.

The grim expression on Morgan's face when he returned did little to reassure me.

'What is it?' I asked, almost tempted to hold my hand up, not wanting any unwelcome news on my first morning with him.

He took in a breath. 'They are searching for you.'

'Oh. I expected Matron Wright and the doctors would be conscious of your concern for my wellbeing, but I did not believe they would go to such lengths as to trouble you at home. I should leave,' I said as I stood.

'No, no. Please sit. There is more.' His solemn manner had me dropping back into my chair.

His broad shoulders slumped as he sat. 'It appears that your lovely friend Miss Miller did not recover from her fit.'

My mind took a while to pull the fragments together. 'Sophia died?'

My throat closed. Fragments of the night replayed in my head. I had hoped Prudence's concoction had caused no major harm and Sophia would recover from her fit. It was clear now that Prudence had meant to cause me more than a cramped stomach or vile fit of vomiting. Why hadn't I shared my fears with anyone?

My lips pressed hard. 'Prudence put something in her cup and poisoned her. It was meant for me. She should be in Newgate, not Bloomfield.'

Morgan's eyes narrowed as he nodded for me to continue.

'It is unclear to me why, but Prudence also threw me down the stairs a few days before you first came to the asylum. I now suspect these were determined attempts to kill me.'

I covered my mouth. Now I did sound certifiable.

Morgan studied me before he spoke. 'Would you tell me what they did to you?'

Shame and a need to share the horror collided. Dressed as a gentleman, I might tell him.

I cleared my dried throat. 'Are you familiar with the work of the President of London's esteemed Medical Society, Dr Baker Brown?'

Morgan shook his head.

I took a breath. 'It appears he believes that many disorders of the female mind, such as hysteria, are directly linked to their ... uh ... intimate areas, and he likes to remove them as a cure. He taught Dr Butcher to do the same.'

I finished the last words in a rush and picked a thread in my jacket.

'He what? He ... oh.'

I did not want to go into further detail.

Morgan sat in silence, turning a shade paler as he absorbed my meaning.

'I will not let them recapture you,' he said at last. 'We must leave here, lest they return. We will go to London.' His mouth was set, but his eyes darted to the door.

'I have already asked too much of you. I will make my way to London and—'

'And what? If you return to your home or any place familiar, they will find you. Prior to my father's passing, I rented a townhouse in London; I am still unknown there, which means we could maintain your cover and remain there until the two weeks have elapsed and they no longer consider you insane.'

Unable to produce a better alternative, I agreed to brave the falling snow and make my way with him to London. I had no idea why Morgan would extend such a kindness to me, but my freedom now depended on it.

TWENTY-FIVE

A s I wiped myself with a flannel in the usual stand-up wash of the morning, a sting registered, followed by a rush of rage. A man's nightshirt was not so different to a lady's nightgown, but having to dress as man and feeling the loss of my womanly parts was disturbing me to the core.

As I poured the dirty water into a slop pail, I was conscious that it reflected how I felt. Dirty and discarded. It reminded me how vulnerable I had felt, lying there, waiting for a doctor to perform heaven knows what. To have lain there and submitted to his will … then there was the operation. It was a far more horrifying treatment than I had ever imagined would be inflicted on an asylum inmate. Midwives' treatment of hysterics might be regarded by some as useless, but telling a woman to pound some caraway seeds, add a small measure of ginger and salt and spread the mixture upon her daily bread and butter seemed a far less harmful remedy.

I was uncertain how I would handle my monthlies when they came, but I'd consider that another time. It was hardly going to be a cheerful celebration of Christmas today.

Morgan had wasted no time whisking us off to his newly leased townhouse in Eaton Square, Belgravia. His terrace was three bays wide, in a classic Regency style. White stucco, palazzo façade with Corinthian-style columns, and a porticoed terrace. Quite grand and tastefully furnished. I guessed it would be more than comfortable for a woman on the run.

After discarding my nightshirt and binding my breasts, I tugged on a vest and pair of drawers, enjoying the warmth of the flannel against the chill. A crisp white shirt, woollen trousers, and waistcoat completed my dress. Incorporating the beard and wig remained somewhat challenging. I did not need to get things perfect, as I would not be under too much scrutiny. Morgan had once again opted to keep a skeleton staff, to stop any chins wagging.

My stomach rumbled as I sat down to a hearty breakfast of eggs, toast, and bacon.

'If I am not careful, these clothes will not fit me for too long,' I greeted Morgan as he joined me.

I flinched at his frown. My doubts flared.

'Good morning to you, Mr Dalton.' He cocked his head to the doorway, beyond which footsteps could be heard approaching..

'Oh. Good morning to you too, my good man.' I had forgotten to speak in my theatre voice, but dropped it now to a deeper tenor as the petite and efficient maid, Mary, entered with our coffee.

We greeted her, then breakfasted in silence as we read the broadsheets. Once things were quieter, we moved to Morgan's study and settled in some comfortable reading chairs.

'I had forgotten how drab and noisy London is,' I said to fill the silence. 'Mind, this is a quiet area, and it is lovely to look out on to a private garden rather than a busy street.'

Morgan nodded his agreement but sat silently, watching the flames in the fireplace.

'What is it? Are you regretting giving me your assistance?' I asked.

'Not at all. Do not dwell on it.' He moved to his desk and withdrew a package from a drawer. As he gave it to me, he wished me a merry Christmas. I groaned. I had nothing to offer him.

'I do not have—'

He waved away my protest. I opened the parcel and found some damson drops and an embroidered handkerchief. Tears fell down my face.

'I did not mean to upset you,' Morgan said.

I shook my head. 'You didn't. Thank you for such beautiful gifts. I am overwhelmed by your generosity.' Instinctively, as I would have with Papa, I drew him close and kissed his cheek.

'Oh, uh 'scuse me. I'll leave these here.' Mary dropped some candles onto a chiffonier and shut the door behind her.

Morgan's brow creased, but his lips were twitching. 'Now they are going to be spreading rumours around all of London as to why I have not taken a wife,' he moaned, while I burst into laughter.

'I must learn to shake your hand. I am—'

His face grew grim. 'While it has been many years since men were hanged for such things, the recent changes to the law have made it easier to punish a man for gross indecency.'

I nodded and gazed at the dancing flames. 'Surely the maid would need to witness more than a peck on the cheek for us to become concerned?'

Morgan shrugged. 'I would hope so. These changes have led to charges, though. I was reading about a foreign sailor in port being given six months' hard labour for such things only last month.'

'I promise I will be more careful.' I was causing him far too much trouble already. I did not want to be the cause of Morgan's coming to any harm.

Morgan had his head tilted to the side, his eyebrows furrowed, reminding me even more that I could not stay. How could I remain here as a glowing ember, poised to ignite?

'I understand I haven't considered my difficult situation much beyond getting away and am not sure what to do after my two weeks' of freedom have expired. I would hardly go back to Spencer and resume life as his wife.' I willed my churning stomach to still. 'I am so worried that Papa is still gravely ill or has died while I was in the asylum.'

Morgan's brow furrowed even more deeply. 'I will endeavour to find out his condition for you. You do not need to concern yourself. I will not abandon you.'

I smiled. 'You are too kind.' Rubbing my forehead, I shrugged. 'I will not impose on you any longer than I need to. I will think upon it.'

Morgan poked an errant log back into the fire. 'I am sure all will be well.'

I tapped the arm of my leather chair as Mary set some biscuits down then scurried from the room. I wished I had some of Morgan's confidence. What would become of an asylum escapee?

With a hand on mine, Morgan spoke in a soothing tone. 'My sincere apologies for the hardships you have faced. I will do whatever I can to help you.'

I squeezed his fingers. They were warm and solid, unlike the feather flutter of my heart.

TWENTY-SIX

I answered the knock at my bedroom door, expecting Mary to be standing there telling me I was late to breakfast. At first, I smiled to see Morgan there instead, until I noticed his grim expression. My mind whirled with possibilities. I had been caught ... he had tired of me and wanted me to leave ... and then I noticed the glimmer of sad sympathy. Papa.

'What is wrong, Morgan?' I asked as I shrugged on my jacket. I closed my eyes for a moment before he stepped into my room.

'I am terribly sorry, Adeline. Your father died just after you were sent to the asylum.' His tone was so gentle that his words comforted even as they cut.

He waited quietly as tears trickled in jagged treks down my cheeks and dripped into the wool of my pants. My emotion so at odds with how I was dressed. I sniffled and wiped my nose on a handkerchief. I sighed and slumped onto the bed. Morgan moved forward and squeezed my shoulder.

A coal of resentment glowed in my centre. Not only had Spencer deprived me of my liberty and tarnished my reputation, but he'd also ensured I was not present to farewell my dear papa.

'Nobody informed me. I was not there for him.'

'It's a terrible blow for you.'

His hand was warm on my shoulder, and I yearned for the tenderness of his embrace.

As if sensing my need, he stepped away. 'I will leave you to your thoughts. Take your time coming down.' He shut the door with care behind him.

I curled into a ball and rocked on the bed. After the spasms of grief and crying had dimmed to sniffles, I got up, washed my face, and reattached my beard.

What the future would hold for me?

Inhaling sharply and lifting my chin, I approached the mirror in the room's corner. I resolved to make sure that the men who had wronged me faced consequences. Somehow, I would bring their wrongs to public attention and seek retribution. I stood tall, looking every inch the confident gentleman.

My mind swirled with possibilities. Given it would be unwise to risk confronting Dr Butcher while on the run from the asylum, I contemplated my next move.

Doctor Baker Brown. The man responsible for inventing that hideous operation and teaching it to others.

A man who had risen through the ranks of mere doctors to head the prestigious Medical Society. Who was obviously well respected and well regarded by his peers, and – even worse – by his patients. I needed to put a chink in that stellar reputation. I tapped the looking glass.

Even if my impatience jeopardised my liberty, I needed to become a man capable of deceiving others.

From the mezzanine near the ground-floor stairway, I strained to hear the male voices rumbling below. Unsure whether I should test my acting ability and disguise or retreat to my room, I was left gripping the mahogany handrail until Morgan moved into view below.

'I'm terribly sorry, Isaac,' Morgan said. 'I remember now that I extended the invitation when I last saw you. I do not have the townhouse ready for company and am yet to complete gathering my staff.'

It was his friend who I had been introduced to at the asylum, the wheelchair man. Mr Walsh.

I did not hide quickly enough. Mr Walsh had come from behind the cast-iron baluster and caught my eye. 'It appears you already have company.'

I did not miss the hurt tone in Mr Walsh's voice.

Morgan's face drained of colour.

'Oh, excuse me,' I said. 'May I introduce myself? I am Mr Dalton, and I have taxed Mr Ashton's generosity, being without accommodation through misfortune.' I came down the stairs and shook his hand. 'If you have made plans together, please do not let me interfere with them.'

Morgan's eyebrows rose, and I gave him a slight nod. I had liked Mr Walsh when I had encountered him at Bloomfield, and while his presence might put my freedom at risk, I did not think he would betray his friend.

'Fine. Mr Walsh, if you can endure minimal service, then you are very welcome to stay as planned.' Morgan picked up one of Isaac's bags. Isaac immediately took it from him and picked up the other.

'I will not be a bother.'

Morgan showed him to his room while I waited in the library. I tested my beard was holding firm.

It wasn't long before Morgan's boots clicked across the polished-oak parquet floor. He gave the door a furtive look. 'Are you certain that you are up to such scrutiny?'

I ran a hand along the marble fireplace mantel and rubbed my hands to free them of the dust. 'I hope so.'

Within hours, I was sure that Isaac's presence was going to be a welcome distraction rather than a concern. His jovial manner lightened our pensive mood considerably, and I was quite entertained by him. I enjoyed watching the two friends trade tales, and Morgan deftly guided Isaac away whenever he turned his curious gaze to me.

It was Mary's sour expression and demeanour over the ensuing days that bothered me more. She seemed quite perturbed to have yet another guest. My first impression was that her displeasure stemmed from having extra work to do with so few others to assist, but then I couldn't help but notice her purse her lips at the clear warmth and humour between Morgan and Isaac.

I felt it was no accident when, one morning, a magazine to which Morgan did not subscribe showed up among the study's newspapers. It was open to a particular article. As I scanned the pages of *Yokel's Perceptor,* my heart caught.

The increase of these monsters in the shape of men … these monsters actually walk the streets the same as whores, looking out for a chance … the Quadrant, Fleet Street, Holborn, the Strand are thronged with them!

…. the neighbourhood of Charing Cross posted bills in windows of several public houses, cautioning the public to 'Beware of Sods!'

Wordlessly, I handed it to Morgan. He took a deep breath. 'Mary?'

I nodded. '*These* are the people subject to hysteria. Mary can obviously read more than a grocery list.'

He thumped the magazine down. 'I will not tolerate that in my house.'

I held his arm before he threw open the door. 'If you dismiss her, it will only add fuel to the fire. Instead, we can impress upon her the need to keep a tidy and clean household and keep her too busy for mischief.'

He grinned. 'Yes, let's exhaust her; then she will be far too tired to meddle.'

Morgan had been considerate in closing off many unused rooms to save on cleaning, but that soon changed. I had little sympathy for Mary the next day when I entered the newly opened main reception room. She huffed as she completed the last of her window cleaning, then she gave me a curt greeting and flounced off.

It was a beautiful room with three full-height sash windows overlooking the garden square. I imagined the view would be both restful and colourful in spring. As I explored the room, I was compelled to examine the delicate scrollwork on a mantel clock.

'That was his mother's,' Isaac said.

I placed the clock back on the mantel and turned to face him. 'Morgan said you—'

His jaw was set, and his arms crossed. 'Mr Ashton is like a brother to me. I do not want his good nature to be taken advantage of. I am aware of the article placed in full view in the library yesterday.'

I fiddled with my cravat. 'I assure you; I have no intention of taking advantage of his hospitality. As for that article ...'

He stepped closer. 'It is clear that you adore the man. I can assure you his interests are not that way inclined.'

I stifled a gasp. It was that clear that I held Morgan close in my affections?

'Is there a problem here, gentlemen?' Morgan asked as he entered the room.

My heart faltered. What had he heard?

Isaac stepped back. 'Not at all.'

CHAPTER

TWENTY-SEVEN

I did not like the way Morgan glowered at Isaac, nor the way Isaac glowered at me. This would never do. It was unfair to ask Morgan to shield me from his most loyal and protective friend.

I closed the door and resumed my usual tone of voice. 'We are already acquainted, Mr Walsh. I will be honest. I *am* taking advantage of Mr Ashton's generosity – far more than you realise.'

Isaac's brows shot up. 'Are you from the West End? Did I meet you at a burlesque ... the Little Duck and the Great Quack?'

I laughed. 'No, I am not one to take on a breeches role. I am no Orpheus or Cherubino.' I was also not one to attend the opera. My only knowledge of it came from Charity's accounts of a string of events that she had been taken to by eager gentleman callers who fed her passion for West End productions.

'We met at Bloomfield Asylum, where you graciously allowed me to ride your wheelchair,' I said, removing my wig but not my facial hair.

'You may remember Mrs Parker?' Morgan said as Isaac reached out to touch my beard.

'Mrs Parker?' he echoed, drawing his hand back. He frowned, then gasped. 'What! Look at you. Why are you dressed as a man, and what are you doing here?'

I replaced my wig. 'I escaped.'

His eyes widened, then he grinned. 'Oh, bully for you. I heard you husband had maliciously placed you there. I will not utter a word, I promise.'

Heartened by his reassurance, I dropped my shoulders. 'You are most kind. I apologise for—'

The men each raised a hand, halting my apology.

'Apart from keeping my silence, what can I do to help?' Isaac asked.

I explained my plan to go in disguise to other doctors of London and question the soundness of Dr Baker Brown's assumptions and operations to 'cure' female maladies. Isaac did not ask for details about these operations, but Morgan let him know he knew and considered them hideous.

While Morgan was cautious about my plans to undermine Dr Baker Brown, Isaac was more daring. He suggested arranging a visit to one of the medical men's gentlemen's clubs. Morgan wanted me to wait until I was no longer being pursued, while Isaac applauded my courage and understood my urgency.

'The longer I wait, the more women will suffer. Not only at his hands, but from the many others who give the procedure any credibility.' I blinked tears from my eyes, and Morgan finally nodded.

'I will not throw myself straight into the lion's den. I will wait until I satisfy you I can handle myself among them.'

I might have been impatient, but I was not foolish.

'Come now, Adeline. You need to hold the bat like so,' Morgan said as he changed my hands into the correct grip. 'It is far too cold to stay out here too long, so let's have one more go at hitting the ball.'

'It's not as if I'll be asked to play a game of cricket,' I said, but maintained the position of my hands.

'It's good to have a thorough understanding of the game,' Isaac said. He moved to the other end of the small rear garden, a rather bare affair in winter, and tossed the ball from hand to hand.

Morgan gave a grin. 'It's a shame the ban on overarm bowling was lifted a couple of years ago. It's much easier to hit an underarm bowl.'

I sniffed at his insinuation that I could not hit an overarm bowl and hit my bat on the ground a couple of times, so he dropped his teasing. Isaac took a few steps, then pitched the ball at me. I kept my eye on it and swung the bat hard. It connected with the ball with a satisfying thunk, and I cheered as it sailed over the fence. The shatter of glass had us running into the townhouse, where we all collapsed with laughter.

Morgan wiped his tears. 'Shot. I'd better go retrieve my ball and offer to pay for the repairs. Jolly good show, Mr Dalton. You'll be set to take on Mr Grace any day now.'

'Hardly! From what you described, he will become quite the cricket hero. I prefer cricket to football, though.' I unbuckled the shin pads and set them on a table.

Morgan left to placate his possibly irate neighbour. Isaac and I settled in the study to read the latest news. Morgan found it surprising that I had always taken an interest in current affairs and had often discussed them in depth with Papa. Sometimes I went on with quite the rant while reading an advertisement or a column in Morgan's presence. Initially, he couldn't understand my outbursts. After a few days, he stopped and listened. Quite a refreshing change from Spencer's icy look that clamped my mouth shut.

'Look at this ... a certain doctor claiming that Dalby's Calmative or Godfrey's Cordial and a whole host of other such products might be useful in calming babies – and then saying that the problem was that women were simply not qualified to give the correct dosage! That administering them should be left to a qualified doctor! Heaven help those poor women, having to wait on a doctor. Oh, those babes I saw that were too tired to suck at the breast. They often became weak and died.'

Isaac's grim face told me he was listening, but I stopped mid-sentence and sat down with a sigh. Sometimes being a midwife had been heartbreaking. But issues like these were not suitable for male conversation.

'Not that I want you to stop talking, Mrs Parker … Adeline. It's just that it reminds me of a tragic loss.'

I leaned forward. 'I did not mean to stir such memories.'

He ran a hand through his wavy hair. 'It is not *my* tragic loss. It is Morgan's. His mother suffered the loss of many early pregnancies, and when one of them came finally to term, the baby was born too small. The little one died a few months later. Morgan's mother was distraught, and Mr Ashton Senior placed her in an asylum. Morgan was sent away to boarding school soon after. We were both young, and he begged his father to let me go with him. He never saw his mother again. He has pieced this together over the years through talking with servants and an aunt. I am grateful Morgan's father had heart enough to agree to keep us together.'

An image of my blue marble babe filled my mind. I pictured a small boy, an outsider to his mother's grief. There being no space for him, being sent away. He was without his mother, father, nurse, and home. I let the tears dribble of their own accord.

Now I understood his sympathy for my plight. Where he might have so easily hardened his heart, he had kept it open. He was a rare man indeed.

CHAPTER

TWENTY-EIGHT

Isaac had been making enquiries among my father's colleagues and his own acquaintances. Many of the Medical Society of London frequented Lettsom's, one of the private gentlemen's clubs. He had secured an introduction, even though Morgan still wanted me to wait until we were sure the asylum had stopped searching for me.

'Before we go to the club, we should walk the streets. I will walk some distance behind and observe,' Morgan said.

My mind was quickly bombarded with the 'rules' of male etiquette. Rules such as tipping my hat, moving to the street side for any lady passing, and retrieving any items she might have dropped.

Once we had donned our black coats and hats, we set out from Eaton Square, and I moved to the east of the square, past St Peter's Church with its six-columned portico and classic style, which might have inspired the building of the terraces in Eaton Square. I shook my head, having already lost concentration on ensuring my stride was long and my shoulders back. The air was tinged with ice and soon numbed my cheeks.

I made my way to Green Park. There were few people walking about, and in such a quiet area of London, I sensed little a challenge. I told Morgan as much when he caught up to me.

'Would it be better if we went to an area I am more familiar with, and where people might even know me? I could go to our old apothecary on Harley St, just down from where my father lived and worked. Mr Murray has known me since I was child and has been a wonderful friend to my family. If he is fooled, then all is well.' I tugged my hat down as it jiggled in the ice-tinged breeze.

Morgan rubbed his nose, which was reddened by the cold. Before he could disagree, I flagged down the omnibus clopping behind us. Riding on the knife-board atop the coach was far better than being confined inside with the scent of musty hay. I had not ridden on top like this since I was a girl, unencumbered by a long skirt. I almost giggled at the look of trepidation on Morgan's face before realising that of course young men do not giggle and that Morgan rarely travelled in such middle-class 'splendour'.

'Hold tight,' I warned him as I grabbed the nearest rail.

He gripped a rail just in time, as the horses jerked to a start. 'Good grief, we may be pitched straight onto the road.'

As we made our way to Marylebone, a wave of grief-tinged nostalgia left my chest tight. Most of us rattling and swaying on top of the omnibus had tears dribbling down our cheeks from the icy air. I let my grief mingle with my own tainted tears.

We reached our destination and, as we climbed down the ladder, Morgan raised a hand to assist me. I glared at him. Upon noticing his mistake, he turned away.

'It seems being a gentleman is well ingrained in you,' I commented, as I led the way to the apothecary.

'Yes, you'd expect by now I'd be accustomed to your most entertaining presence, Mr Dalton, instead of the lovely Adeline's,' Morgan said.

I stopped walking so suddenly that the man trudging behind landed straight into me.

'Oh, I apologise, sir,' he said.

'Oh. Please forgive me. I stopped far too sudden,' I said as I recovered my senses. I smiled as the stout man continued, but I was glowing. Morgan thought I was lovely.

'Whatever is the matter? Are we there?' Morgan asked.

'No, but not far.' I strode onwards. I took a deep breath and returned my focus to the task at hand. We entered the apothecary's shop with the tinkle of a bell. Standing in front of the polished mahogany shelves and gleaming jars, I sniffed deeply the familiar laurel and liquorice scent of myrrh, and lavender and camphor. A neatly dressed but reedy-looking man approached us.

'We would like to speak to Mr Murray, please, as Mr Ashton has a rather delicate matter he would like to address,' I said, ignoring Morgan's sputtering cough.

The apprentice appraised us and, with a sniff, flicked back a curtain, which gave a glimpse of Mr Murray working with a brass pestle and mortar at his dispensary bench. With a murmur, he came through the curtains.

'How might I help you fine gentlemen today?' he asked, wiping his hand on an apron.

I bit my lip as his wizened eyes met mine. They seemed to flicker with recognition, but after a slight shake of his head, he turned his attention to Morgan. I desperately wanted to ask news of so many people. We had always shared information, not gossip, and he was an avid supporter of the midwives in the area, often giving us ingredients for a much-reduced cost. In the silence I realised I had better come up with a problem needing remedy.

'I have heard that bismuth salts are a much more effective treatment than calomel,' I began.

Mr Murray nodded. 'Yes, far better than many treatments, even Fowler's Solution. I will be back shortly.'

Morgan frowned. 'Pray what malady have you assigned me?'

A smile twitched. 'Oh, the pox is a wretch of a thing.'

Morgan's face paled, then became flushed, his mouth opening in protest, but clamming shut as Mr Murray returned.

' Oh, and I should mention, these are not recommended should you have blood in your stool.'

I nodded solemnly as Mr Murray continued to give Morgan instructions on the dosage and payment was completed.

Once outside, I laughed. 'I am sorry. I should have named a disease of a less personal nature, but my mind jumped straight to the last conversation Mr Murray had with my father. We had been discussing the plight of some of my women with pox. On a positive note, Mr Murray did not recognise me.' I twirled the chain on my fob watch in triumph.

'Now, what will I do with this package? I have no use for it.' Morgan was holding the small box with its paper-wrapped powder as if it were a tooth-baring rat.

'Oh, I shouldn't have wasted your—' I slammed straight into a petite woman. 'Oh, I'm awfully sorry.' I gripped her elbow to steady her.

She turned to face me. 'No harm done.'

'Charity!' I hugged her hard.

'Unhand me, sir!'

She landed a kick on my shin, and I released her instantly.

'Mr Dalton, we should move on,' Morgan said.

I shook his hand from my arm. 'Charity, it's me ... Adeline.'

She gasped.

Maybe I was making a mistake, but I'd missed my closest friend.

TWENTY-NINE

'I would never have believed it was you,' Charity said as she stroked my beard. 'Isn't this itchy?'

I nodded. 'Very. The concoction I use to glue the moustache on can be hard to fully remove at night, too.'

We both sat back in our armchairs in the parlour with a sigh. Morgan had stepped in when we'd collided in the street and handed Charity a card with an invitation to tea the next day. He had instructed the only two servants he had – Mary and a cook I had yet to see – and a rather curious Isaac to leave us in peace once we had been served tea.

I had given a wide-eyed Charity a full rundown of my time in Bloomfield House and the predicament I was in. She stopped twisting one of her stray curls, the auburn strands now quite tangled.

'I doubted Clara Hughes and her unpleasant gossip, but she was telling the truth. You were indeed locked away in an asylum and deserted by your awful husband. I looked everywhere for you and feared the worst.' Charity gripped my hand. 'I even stood by as they recovered one of the poor souls from the Thames, to ensure it wasn't you.'

My vision blurred as I offered a quivery smile. 'I have missed you too.'

Charity dropped my hand and looked around the sparsely furnished room. 'Even though the room is elegant, it could do with a woman's touch.'

She was obviously comparing it to my Georgian townhouse in Devonshire Place.

'I can hardly be caught by the servants adding some pretty wallpaper or a framed sampler though, can I?'

I stroked my sleek men's waistcoat, and Charity laughed. 'You make a fine-looking gentleman. Imagine if you turned up at Devonshire Place. I wonder what Spencer would make of it. Of course, he'd be more than likely to ship you back to the asylum. Now, back to the problem at hand. I am aware of this so-called harmless operation and have seen the result of such in at least three of the women I have birthed. Thankfully, it did not stop the women bearing children, but I have heard of some becoming quite ill. Others have come to me unable to bear the shame.' Charity's eyes became more like flint with every word.

I sighed and shook my head. 'I was unaware of it, but I am now very concerned that this Dr Baker Brown truly believes he can cure many female maladies with such an operation and is on a path to convince other doctors to take it up. What woman at the end of his hot iron or scissors would ever agree that they have been cured of anything? As learned men think they are far superior to women, my best option is to find other doctors who do not support him and encourage *them* to raise opposition. As to Dr Butcher ... preying upon those locked away in asylums ... and my treacherous husband, who demanded the operation—'

Charity placed her teacup down with a clatter. 'I agree with your actions and find it amusing that you might infiltrate the men's club, but I am concerned for your safety. What if you are caught or your disguise is discovered? These men won't take too kindly to being deceived.'

'Morgan – uh, Mr Ashton – has already raised these objections. I will not sit idly by while more women suffer. Hopefully, I will achieve my aim and then lie low for a while.' I tried to stop my eyes from blinking too much.

'Don't deny you are scared. I would be terrified. It is very kind of Mr Ashton to take you under his wing. I will go back to those women and ask for more detail. If there is anything else I can help with, let me know.'

It was as if all the knots in my stomach unravelled into a tingling warmth. The realisation that Charity hadn't questioned my sanity, and that her friendship remained strong, was such a blessing.

'Thank you.'

I noticed a twinkle in her eye as she studied a portrait of Morgan with his father over the mantel. 'No,' I said. 'He is being the perfect gentleman. No doubt made very easy by me being dressed in this garb. He is a most compassionate man.'

Charity made a tutting sound. 'What a shame. I was sure he regarded you with more than sympathy for your difficult situation. His friend is rather charming too.'

I waggled a finger at her, even though my heart ached for her to be right. 'None of that. I have been burned once by a handsome face, and it will not happen again.'

On saying the words 'handsome face', something clicked in my memory. Prudence had said *Her husband is surely handsome enough.* How did she know my husband was handsome?

When I had bumped into her in the costume room, I had smelt jasmine. I groaned.

'What is it?' Charity asked.

'Maybe I am getting overwrought with it all, but I suspect my husband knew the woman who attacked me. For a start, she inadvertently told me she knew my husband was handsome. But what's more revealing is that he often used to come home smelling of jasmine. The same scent *she* wore to the Christmas performance in the asylum.'

Charity frowned. 'That hornswoggler! He put on such a show of caring for you. He said that he had arranged for you to have a wonderful retreat in the country, and I was not to concern myself. To entrap you, agree to your mutilation, and then let this woman attack you! You do not deserve such treatment; you've done nothing but be a good wife.'

My throat closed as we sat in silence. 'I do not understand either. I guess gambling can make a man lose his soul.'

'Certainly, his senses. To treat you so.' Charity slumped back in her chair with a pout.

I shook my head. 'I have no idea how I can ever trust a man again.'

'Therefore, it is much better to remain a midwife and live the spinster life. Mind, it doesn't have to be without the odd dalliance here and there,' Charity said.

I leaned forward. 'Oooh, you've turned as pink as your dress. He must be special. Tell me all.'

A bittersweet twinge came to me as we gossiped. A warmth that my friend was back in my life, but an ache that I would never marry again. Even if I trusted my heart, would I be too ashamed of my ruined body for intimacy?

THIRTY

I tugged a wad of extra padding into place on my bust and stomach and stretched a mauve ready-to-wear crinolette dress over my now-ample figure. I added a brunette wig set in a pompadour, using some rats to fluff out the sides. Charity had chosen well with the funds that Morgan had generously provided. While I was not familiar with the women Charity had invited to her townhouse on Charlotte Street, we wanted to err on the side of caution and ensure I was not recognised.

Charity sat at an escritoire in the room's corner to take notes after she had welcomed and explained to the women what this rather clandestine meeting was about. Even though Charity had been a midwife to all these women, I had expected them to be hesitant to share their experiences of Dr Baker Brown's operation, especially in company, so I led the conversation with candour. Enveloped in the cheerful butter-coloured parlour with its matching burgundy drapes, new walnut balloon-backed chairs, and Persian rug, the three women shared their woes.

Mrs Bateman, though soft in her body and manner, was the first to pluck up the courage to share her journey. She adjusted her spectacles and began. 'I was admitted in May last year. From the tender age of fourteen, I have been attacked by fits. I would get one a week and often had headaches. That doctor told my husband that even though I acknowledged I had had no pleasure with him, I was in constant state of peripheral excitation, as evidenced by my dilated pupils, hot skin, and moist palms.' Though her doughy neck mottled with colour, she continued. 'I did not know about this discussion with my husband until later, and so I was terribly shocked by what that surgeon did to me. My fits recurred, yet he declared they were now slight. Now my bladder leaks, and it is excruciating to pass water. My husband ... it was so terribly sore, I screamed, and he has not touched me since. I am sure he has a woman in St John's Wood now.'

We all murmured in sympathy. Many men had mistresses in villas there.

Mrs Hill was much younger in years than Mrs Bateman. Her china-blue eyes filled with tears as she began. 'I saw Dr Baker Brown after I suffered pain in my right leg. The situation worsened so severely that ambulation and even sitting were beyond me, and I was limited to a spinal couch.' She smoothed her dark hair. 'After ... I was in far more pain in areas I had never known to hurt, that I attempted to leave my husband immediately. It took over a month to walk out of his home. My spinal irritation, sciatica, was not cured. It was not until I met Miss Evans here,'—she nodded at Charity—'and she suggested moving my body a certain way and applied some geranium oil, that I improved. We are both sure that Dr Baker Brown's operation caused my first labour to be far longer than it needed to be.'

She wiped a tear and delicately blew her button nose. We turned to the last woman, Mrs Biley. She was an elegant woman, wearing one of the slimmer skirts of the latest fashion I had noticed on the streets. Although she was of a higher class than the others, she seemed just as relieved to share her burden. 'I have experienced such shame since the operation.'

My heart swelled with compassion, and I hoped she felt it flowing towards her.

'I have complete trust in Miss Evans that this information will be wisely used. If I can stop another woman from this travesty, I will.'

Charity looked up from her note-taking and nodded.

'I saw Dr Baker Brown a few years ago, when I was twenty-one. I had been bleeding every day. Despite over five visits to the hospital, I was uncured. In constant pain and quite anaemic ... I was quite desperate. He told my father there was irritation in my right ovary and evidence of long-continued peripheral irritation that required surgery. I can assure you, there was none of that.'

I nodded; her tone made her opinion of masturbation clear.

She sniffed and continued. 'I left the surgical home with less blood, and still bleeding, and the problem returned worse than ever until Miss Evans treated me with labour tea.'

'Extracts of ergot,' Charity explained. 'I use it for women bleeding a lot after they've had their babies.'

Mrs Biley smiled, revealing a slight gap in her fine teeth. 'Yes. My father was informed of the operation's specifics, and he considered it a triumph. My niece, Nurse Finch, has recently taken up a position at the surgery, and I dread she will discover what has happened to me there. Since Miss Evans's treatment finally made marriage possible, I worried more about the future. I wondered whether to tell my future husband. I found I could not say the words.'

I took a gulp of lukewarm tea. How do you explain such a situation?

'You see, it was not the physical act that became the problem. He had very little interest or care that it caused me discomfort, so he did not examine things too closely. It is more that I am reduced to cowering at the removal of my clothing. I still cannot sleep at night, being plagued by terrible nightmares, and I all but prickle at the slightest touch. I wonder if I am not better off with the hysterical women in an asylum?'

I gasped at her words, and Charity put a finger to her lip, trying to assure me that Mrs Biley meant no harm. She did not seem to direct these words at me as she stared blankly into the fireplace. I took a deep breath as Mrs Hill and Mrs Bateman admitted to sharing such fears. How many women were suffering because of this Dr Baker Brown?

Once alone with Charity, I sagged into my chair. 'Do you believe these medical men will care a jot for what agony has befallen us?'

Charity sat opposite me, a thoughtful expression on her face. 'Whether the men do or not, *I* care for what has befallen all of you.'

She lifted a hand as if to touch me, then lowered it and stroked the chair's arm instead. No matter how much she wished to offer me sympathy, I was grateful she had restrained herself. The afternoon had been harrowing.

'I think I cannot deal with this matter properly until I meet the culprit himself.'

Charity jolted upright. 'No, you must not risk it.'

'We need more ... records and such. I wonder if Nurse Finch might be of assistance?'

As my chin jutted forward, she sighed. 'You are far too stubborn for your own good, Adeline.'

THIRTY-ONE

'We'll be there in a few minutes. What a long-winded name. The London Surgical Home for the Reception of Gentlewomen and Females of Respectability Suffering from Curable Surgical Diseases,' I said to Charity.

She looked down the road towards Dr Baker Brown's Notting Hill surgery, better known as the London Surgical Home for Women. 'I understand we agreed I would help you collect evidence … but I wonder if Mr Ashton is right. A meeting with him could be quite perilous.'

I flicked away her concern with my hand. 'No one will see me. A quick ride in a carriage and a visit to the fiend. You have already contacted Nurse Finch. It is important I distract him while you peruse his records. I am still hoping he will listen to reason.'

She bit her lip.

'If not, and if he is indeed a madman determined to continue to defile women based on some ridiculous notion that masturbation causes a woman to go insane, *I* will ensure the medical men will doubt his theory has any merit at all.' I wiped some spittle from my mouth, horrified I had raised my voice so, but I was tired of being meek in the face of horror.

Charity ran a hand through her hair. 'I apologise. I have not endured such an operation, and it is not my place to tell you what to do.' She re-pinned her hat.

'No, I apologise. I am aware you share my passion for preventing Dr Baker Brown and his followers from succeeding.' I inhaled sharply, wincing at the pain in my heart. 'You don't understand ... I need to stop him.'

She touched my arm. 'There is more to this need, isn't there?'

I swallowed hard. 'Yes. Remember when Ma was heavily pregnant, so she sent me to do my first birth without her? I was terrified of all the possible problems, but she reassured me I was ready. Sure enough, she was right.'

Charity waited, quiet among the clop of horses' hooves and shouts of hawkers on the street.

'As exhausted as I was afterwards, I ran home to tell Ma all about it, but when I arrived, Papa was pacing. I felt something was wrong. He told me had called in the accoucheur. When I burst into the room, Ma pleaded with me with her eyes. The baby needed turning, and my hands were small enough to do so manually, but the accoucheur shoved me aside and told me to leave so he could do his work privately. I refused ... so I had to watch the horror of him shoving some metal contraption inside her. He was not careful. He crushed the baby's skull and tore something inside of Ma. There was so much blood. We lost them both. I had not tried hard enough to make him to listen.'

I pinched my lips tight to stop them quivering. 'Don't tell me it wasn't my fault. Papa told me that many times. When she needed me most, I failed her.'

'Why didn't you ever tell me? We are a fine pair.'

Charity's words were so quiet I almost didn't register them. 'What do you mean?'

'After I was born, my mother suffered. Childhood rickets had left her with a narrow pelvis, so the labour was lengthy. She did not recover well. After enduring much pain, she took her own life. My father deflected all blame to me – and, as a child, I took his word for it. As soon as I was able, I ran away. That's when your ma and pa got Mrs Becker to take me in.'

I winced. What a burden to lie at a child's feet. I had believed Charity and I had bared our souls many times over. How was it these stories had never left our lips?

'Oh, Charity. It seems we have both carried burdens I am sure our mothers would not have wished us to carry.'

Charity raised her eyebrows. 'If only it were easy to shed our burdens. But we cannot.'

'Then you understand why I must do more to help the women who have suffered as I have.'

She nodded. 'You have my full support, as always.'

'Miss Charity Evans, you are the most wonderful friend a woman has ever had.'

I listened to the scratch of the fountain pen as Dr Baker Brown recorded some notes. He dipped and tapped it in the inkwell and continued, his florid face the picture of concentration, as I stared at his thinning hair on the top of his tipped head. He was seated at a large mahogany desk and I in a comfortable chair, reminding me of my time in Bloomfield House.

It struck me as rather odd to be talking with him in such a manner. It reminded me how much I preferred to be the one asking such personal details. As a midwife and a woman, I was usually welcomed into the house of my patients, who I typically knew well enough. We would have tea and discuss life in general before delving into what was happening with their bodies. My advice would usually be a mix of practical and herbal remedy, based on the knowledge of generations of women before me. Certainly, over time, better solutions might be offered, but none so brutal as those offered by these new medical men.

I had come here certain I would loathe the man who was responsible for the invention and sharing of his 'harmless' operation. He had not bothered with any chit-chat, being very brusque in his manner and far too direct with his questions, but underneath it all I sensed warm intelligence. He actually believed his method would cure me and relieve me of menorrhagia. Where I would have suggested that a woman take chaste tree drops, shepherd's purse or yarrow, this doctor would assume she had indulged in masturbation, thus overstimulating herself, which he believed necessitated the removal of her clitoris.

'I assure you, Mrs Dalton. Once I perform a simple operation to destroy the nerve causing irritation, you will be cured of any further problems.' His manner was sincere and now slightly arrogant.

'What would such an operation involve?' I asked, wondering if he would become as slippery as a Thames eel.

He set his pen down and steepled his fingers, looking down his nose at me. 'Oh, it's very minor. I will require you to stay here for a few days to ensure all is well. I will need to examine you now.' He opened the door and called for Nurse Finch. He cut me off as I asked questions.

So, he had decided on his course of treatment before he'd even had a look. I followed Nurse Finch to another room, where I was given a gown and told to undress and lie on a table with a sheet over me. She was brisk, and I stood still as she unbuttoned the back of my dress. She then left me to it. It was a plain room, with only a table, screen, and hooks on the wall to hang my clothes on. I shivered as I lay on the table. What would he think when he saw the result of my little operation?

From what I had gathered from the patients Charity had already spoken to, Dr Baker Brown had little to do with the women's aftercare. The nurses ensured the dressings were changed and bleeding monitored for the days following, and then the women returned to their homes.

Nurse Finch checked I was ready, and then Dr Baker Brown came in. He told me to bend my knees, and he lifted the sheet.

He gasped and coughed. 'Uh, Mrs Dalton ... you did not mention ...'

I kept my eyes on the ceiling. 'Mention what?'

'It seems you have some deformity or—'

'Deformity?' I echoed. Heat coursed through me, and I closed my legs with a snap. I sat up and glared at him. 'That deformity is your fault. I assure you, if you had not encouraged other doctors to take up such a horrific operation, I would be perfectly fine.'

He had obviously never seen the long-term damage caused by his butchering.

'I don't understand,' he stammered, stepping back.

I swung my legs off the table and stood, my finger pointing at him, wanting to jab him hard in the chest. 'I do not know where you came up with such a ridiculous idea that you can see if a woman has any so-called peripheral excitement of the pudic nerve, let alone that it would be a good idea to remove the cause of such excitement, or that such an operation would cure her of all manner of ills. Your idea is a falsehood – and it is far from harmless!'

He frowned and blustered at me. 'Now, see here. I will not tolerate the likes of you challenging my expertise. Who sent you? I have so many jealous colleagues, I cannot even begin to guess.'

I put my hands on my hips, not caring about my flimsy attire. 'I came of my accord, but I can see you will not listen to reason. I had hoped you would be shocked and be willing to listen.'

His lips pressed tight as his face reddened. 'I have had enough ridicule from other medical men. I will not stand for it from an ignorant woman. You will leave at once.'

He strode from the room, slamming the door. If there had been any object to throw at the door, I would gladly have thrown it. I tugged the gown off and dressed as rapidly as possible. Nurse Finch slipped in, and I allowed her to button me up.

'I've never seen the doctor so angry,' she muttered. 'Mind, I have not long been working here and at first did not know what devilment he was up to. It *is* wrong, isn't it?'

I turned to face her, noticing a smattering of freckles on her upturned nose. They reminded me of Sophia.

'Yes, very wrong. I am – or was – a midwife and can assure you he does not have any inkling of how to treat a woman for rather ordinary women's issues, let alone for any more complicated ones.' I softened my tone. 'This is not the place for a Nightingale.'

She raised an eyebrow. 'How did you figure that out?'

I smiled. 'From the condition of your hands, I can see you wash them frequently, and this room is in a state of cleanliness and order that I have only seen when I've encountered a Nightingale.'

Nurse Finch blushed. At first I thought it was with pride, until her gaze dropped to the floor. 'I did not take well to the Liverpool Workhouse Infirmary. But my aunt has been so supportive of my hopeless ambition, as my mother likes to call it. I hope I have given your friend, Miss Evans, enough information to assist you.'

'I am sure any hospital would welcome you.' I finished tying my boots. 'Thank you so much for your support. I hope that Dr Baker Brown will not be in business for too much longer.'

'Good luck to you, Mrs Dalton.'

I left the London Surgical Home without a backward glance, more determined than ever. Dr Baker Brown would wish that he had never raised a cautery iron to a woman by the time I was done.

THIRTY-TWO

Charity shared further information with me about Dr Baker Brown's victims of the so-called 'harmless operation'. What Dr Baker Brown considered a cured patient and thus a success was more likely to be a terrified, damaged woman who complied with his orders, just to avoid further, more dangerous experimental treatment. Upon further enquiry, she learned that many of their husbands were equally horrified once they were aware of the damage, and that Dr Baker Brown had charged them a very large fee for the 'privilege'.

I wondered what angle to take in discussing this with others in his profession. Would they care that a woman was ill-informed, that her husband was equally ill-informed? Would they consider the operation to be barbaric? An extreme measure to take for a melancholic mood or hysterical outburst?

Isaac secured us a dinner invitation at Lettsom's. He assured me there would be no debauchery there, so I would not be shocked by the display of men falling into temptation with women or gambling – and, like many clubs, Lettsom's had banned smoking, so I would not suffer the offering of a cigar. My mind whirled and my stomach tumbled.

Once we finally made our way inside what had seemed a rather ordinary-looking house in St James on the outside, it became obvious this was no ordinary townhouse. It was a land of gilt-framed oil paintings, mahogany tables, rich oak panelling, heavy burgundy drapery, and leather armchairs. My heart gave an extra thump as I bumped a marble bust, and I smiled my thanks to Morgan as he steadied it.

'Ready?' Isaac asked.

I nodded, though my throat felt as if a hand clutched it.

Although I was introduced as a surgeon specialising in women's issues, I explained that I mostly aided the destitute in the roughest neighbourhoods of London (where most men wouldn't dare to go). I felt awkward shaking the hands of so many gentlemen. Was I applying enough pressure or too much?

Once we settled to a delicious roast beef dinner in the formal dining room, I relaxed and listened to the surrounding gossip, only offering an opinion on the cholera epidemic the previous year when asked by Dr West seated next to me. It was a heart-sore topic for me, given cholera had caused Papa's death. We agreed on Mr Snow's assertion that it was caused by something in the water, not in the miasma. It was not until we had moved to smaller groups into a reading room that Morgan began the conversation we had come here for.

'Dr West. I have recently taken an interest in St Bartholomew's Hospital, where, I understand, you trained and have since lectured in midwifery. Since recently assuming my father's position on the Visiting Committee at Bloomfield House, I wonder if I could trouble you for your opinion. I have become aware of Dr Baker Brown's operation being performed by Dr Butcher on women there to cure hysteria. As you are an expert on women's issues, are you aware of such an operation? And what are your thoughts?'

Dr West placed his rum onto a small table, and his lip curled as if the rum was bitter. His deep-set grey eyes, flint-grey hair, and mutton-chops were saved from dullness by his dignified manner and a blade-like nose.

'Yes, Mr Ashton, I have lectured at Bart's, and yes, I am aware of this experimental operation. I do not support Dr Baker Brown's work, nor the publicity he seeks to ensure he gains patrons. You would do better spending your time and money on other endeavours at Bart's or even on my pet project, the Hospital for Sick Children. If you require further reassurance, Mr Haden is in the billiards room. He is a fine surgeon and a fellow of the Obstetrical Society. He has more than once told me that such an operation is barbaric and only a form of quackery.'

We thanked him and moved on to Mr Haden, who generously halted his game and gave us his attention. His robust body matched his opinions. Mr Haden was horrified that Dr Baker Brown was not only performing the clitoridectomy, but encouraging other doctors to do so. I held my arms steady but found I wanted to hug these men in thanks. Surely it would be possible to prevent Dr Baker Brown from continuing with his sordid activities.

Mr Haden nodded, setting his jowly chin a-wobble. 'It does not seem to me that an affliction of overexcitement requires the removal of part of the body. What will he do next, removed the offending fingers? It differs from cutting off a diseased limb.'

'Even if diseased, some limbs might be kept with the right attention,' I said. 'My father was a surgeon in the Crimean War, and the experience soured him to the practice of amputation, but I remember as a child much debate between my parents about when to cut. I was always in trouble for reading his medical books and applying his instruments on some poor, unsuspecting fruit or such. He drew the line when I found a stray cat to practise on.'

I was rewarded with a chuckle. 'Well, you are young yet. Never too late to try your hand again. There are many more helpful operations for women than those of Dr Baker Brown's that you might try,' Mr Haden said.

Our conversation had drawn some attention. I recognised one man, Dr Greenhalgh, as a surgeon who had a practice on Harley Street near my father's, but he was not one of my father's colleagues. It seemed he was, however, one of Dr Baker Brown's.

'It is my understanding,' Dr Greenhalgh began, 'that Dr Baker Brown is offering a remedy for some of the most distressing cases of illness, especially hysteria, epilepsy, and catalepsy, among women. It's believed that any sexual act without reproductive intent squanders a woman's finite sexual energy. I agree that an operation such as Dr Baker Brown's serves a similar purpose in preventing boys becoming overly excited. It is a mere circumcision. And with his other new surgical techniques, such as treatments for a prolapsed uterus, he is a true pioneer.'

Dr West joined us. 'I hardly think so. I am not sure he is correct in his diagnosis of many patients. As an example, I saw a forty-year-old woman who had much swelling and irritation at the perineum and vulva with adhesions between the two surfaces of clitoris and nymphae.'

I nearly felt the heat of Morgan's embarrassment as he listened, so I angled myself away from his flushed cheeks.

Dr West was oblivious to Morgan's lack of medical training and continued on. 'She was in severe pain. Dr Baker Brown wanted to charge an enormous fee for a clitoridectomy. But it is absurd to think she would have been touching this painful area. Observing head and eye pain, and a facial rash, I believe it was a case of chronic eczema, best handled by an apothecary. Apart from this, I say his operation is an *alleged* cure only.'

Dr Greenhalgh snorted. 'So says the man who applies caustics to a clitoris and considers himself more humane.'

I winced; a ripple of pain resonated in my intimate area. Neither of those curative options seemed at all appealing.

As the words bounced around me, so did my emotions, until the stiffness in my neck became unbearable. I unclenched my fists and anchored my legs, which were twitching to walk out.

It was the conviction of these doctors that the clitoris held little importance for the average woman, rendering its absence inconsequential. They also, however, considered it capable of harming a woman's health because of the 'known' link between self-gratification and mental illness.

I pried my lips apart. 'I must agree with Dr West. Even though I may work with women of the lower class, I have never seen hysteria, epilepsy, or idiocy be induced by masturbation. Apart from this, Dr Greenhalgh, are you not concerned that many women are ignorant of the scope and nature of the operation before it is undertaken, as are their families?' I had to discover a point of view on the debate to which they would all subscribe.

Dr Greenhalgh's brow furrowed. 'I have visited the London Surgical Home many times, and Dr Baker Brown has always been accommodating. I have found nothing untoward there. In fact, he will soon publish a text on his case studies to encourage more doctors ...'

No doubt he saw a glimmer of horror in my eyes. I needed to be more manly about it. 'I have it on good authority from discussions with some of his previous clients, their families, and midwives that he has often performed the operation with minimal information and with absolutely no consent. Mr Ashton is aware of such cases at Bloomfield House.'

Morgan touched my elbow to steady me, so I took a breath and sat back with a squeak into the folds of the leather armchair. In the background, the clatter of billiards balls and the murmuring of players filled in the silence as Mr Greenhalgh considered what I was saying.

He ran a hand through his hair and his rather long, wiry beard. 'If what you are saying is founded on truth, then I would also have to agree this manner of operating is unacceptable, and I would not be associated with such unethical conduct. I will investigate the matter further and ensure all ethical protocol is being followed. If not, the doctor will be held accountable.'

By now, many of the doctors were nodding agreement.

I trusted that Mr Haden would be true to his word, and as we departed Lettsom's, I felt a sense of relief. Perhaps those who did not accept that madness stemmed from masturbation would assert themselves, and those who continued to advocate such treatments might find themselves unsupported – or at the very least, a woman's informed agreement to submit to such torment might be sought.

Isaac took up the invitation to stay in the accommodation at Lettsom's for the night, as a few of the medical men wanted to meet with him to discuss his self-propelled wheelchair. As we tumbled into the carriage, Morgan's eyes glittered in the dim light.

'Dr Winslow, a man of great influence in medical circles, will be more than happy to disparage the work of Dr Baker Brown publicly. He is of the opinion, as you are, that the disturbance in most cases starts in the head, not the vagina.'

'Oh, you are very pleased with yourself. You didn't even blush when you used the word "vagina",' I teased.

His face dropped, as did his shoulders. 'No, no. *You* have done brilliantly. Thank you.'

I hadn't meant to dim his spark, and I closed in for an embrace. 'I mean it. I cannot comprehend how I would have coped these last few days without you.'

'Uh, your beard is tickling my chin. The things women must find irritating about us—'

Retracting my arms, I pulled back as if he had thrown a flaming log from the fireplace at me. 'I did not intend to irritate.'

I turned away before he could observe the tears welling. I tried to fight the sway of the carriage jostling my body against his.

'I meant nothing ... I apologise, Adeline. I forget how difficult it must be for you to remain in disguise,' Morgan said, holding my arm to turn me back to him. I shrugged his hand away.

I bit my lip. How was he to know that the most troublesome part of my day was not wearing a man's clothes, but knowing that my feelings for him were so much as odds with his for me? He was unaware of how captivating I found our discussions, how thankful I was for his compassion and warmth and, most importantly, how he ignited such passion inside me. I idly dwelled on his tapered fingers and what they might feel like running along my stomach; I stared at his full lips and imagined them devouring mine.

If only the glint in his beaming eyes was for me. Just for the sight of me when he returned from London's clamour. If only I could be his refuge from it all. It was impossible to let him know my feelings. Surely, he would laugh, and I'd shrivel from the embarrassment – and, as I would not be able to face him again, I'd have to run.

I chided myself, moved to the seat across from him, and forced myself to talk. 'No, I forget how much of an imposition I must be. Surely, you have much to do other than watch over an escaped lunatic.' I almost spat the last word, and he flinched.

'You are no lunatic. You are the most intelligent, steady, and capable woman I know.' Morgan sounded sincere. 'I am honoured to support you in your cause and stop this man who has disfigured you so.'

We came to a halt, and the tears I had held back broke. 'Yes, I am ruined for any man.'

I bolted from the carriage.

'Adeline, I did not mean—'

I threw myself on my bed. After a good, womanly sob, I rose and tore off my clothes, removed my horrid beard and wig and bindings, then stood naked with my hair falling down my back. I had cut it shorter to sit better in the wig, but it was still long enough to appear feminine. Yes, my poor breasts bore indents from their strapping, but they were full. I had little to say regarding the operation's impact, an impact that was not readily apparent, given the anatomy involved. But there was little point to having an attractive body now.

'Oh, I'm sorry,' Morgan stuttered as he stood in the doorway.

I remained still. 'Do you still see me as man?'

Morgan slowly opened the door wider and stepped into the room. 'I never did. I did not want you to suppose I was assisting you just so I could help myself.' Morgan stepped towards me and touched a tendril of hair, wrapping it around his finger.

'I do not question your honour.' I would not smother what I wanted to ignite.

I turned away, and he moved to face me and embraced me.

We both stiffened at the squeak of a floorboard in the hallway. Was someone there? What had they seen? At most, Morgan's back and my arms around his neck, I hoped.

He backed away. 'I will leave you to dress.'

Upon later becoming aware of a knock on the door, I hoped Morgan had returned.

'Mr Dalton, are you in there?'

'Oh. Uh. Mary. Yes, I am, but I am not in a state to answer the door. What is it?' I struggled to lower my voice to its usual Mr Dalton timbre.

'Mr Ashton asked me to inform you he will not be present for breakfast tomorrow, as he has an early meeting in town.'

'Thank you, Mary.'

I smothered my sobs in the pillow.

CHAPTER

THIRTY-FOUR

After my lonely breakfast, Mary delivered a message addressed to me. Our dinner at Lettsom's must have been a success, as a Dr Russell was inviting to meet to further discuss my thoughts on Dr Baker Brown's procedure. Knowing I should decline it, I accepted. I only had a limited time to impress on these men that the operation was unsuitable and dangerous. I did not want to sit waiting for Morgan to return.

As soon as I had been welcomed into Dr Russell's simple parlour, regret washed over me. How was I to hold my own with this doctor? My ruse might be discovered at any moment. With effort, I reminded myself not to become too heated with frustration at the things these medical men held sacred.

I was trying to digest yet another difficult belief that Dr Russell had expressed. I swallowed hard and took a breath. 'So, you uphold the common assumption that women do not feel any sexual desire at all?' My mind filled with the many flickers of desire I had been squashing since meeting Morgan. I looked at Dr Russell's smooth cheeks and his earnest expression. He was young. There might be hope. 'But as *I* see it, if a woman expresses a natural desire, a man becomes fearful. He thinks she is becoming a wanton woman with uncontrollable lust – which may be judged unbecoming in a wife, but not in a mistress.'

Dr Russell gave a cough, and I realised I had hit the mark. Of course, he had a mistress and enjoyed her lustful attention.

I shook my head. 'Surely, sexual desire is natural to both men and women, as designed by God to ensure we continue to produce children?' He opened his mouth to protest, but I cut him off. 'I know, yes, women will continue to be with child whether or not it is a happy union. But it is the men who miss out when they treat their wives as is if they have no desire for their husbands.'

He placed a hand on his mouth and rested his chin on his elbows, deep in thought. I sat forward in my chair across from him. 'Wouldn't it be far more inviting to come home to a woman who speaks of more than household management, is far more engaged with *him* than with her needlepoint or charity work, and lights up at his touch in the bedroom? It is we, in our set ways, who stifle her – more than the whalebone corset.' I sat back, wondering if I had gone too far.

Dr Russell's sea-green eyes sparkled. 'While that picture is rather appealing, it is far-fetched, but I will grant you I question the cause of a woman's mental disease being an over-stimulated clitoris.'

I bowed my head. 'I am thankful that you have been open-minded enough to consider that the operation is unnecessary. I deem it quite damaging to those it is inflicted upon.'

'Oh, yes. I will not be recommending it to any of my patients or peers.' He sniffed. 'What are your thoughts on Dr West's alternative?'

I groaned. 'Should my understanding be accurate, and he elects to apply strong caustics to this so-called peripheral irritation, then his assessment of a woman's mental imbalance is also flawed, and this is far from a satisfactory treatment. Of course, this is between you and me, as I am sure he has far more experience than either of us. I find, though, that with the poor women I have treated, there is much benefit in a stroll in the park, simple regular meals, and a kind ear to listen to her troubles. Mind, many of the women I visit find these things hard to come by, overworked as they are. But these remedies are also inaccessible to many women of the upper classes, who are judged too weak to exercise or are prevented from engaging in what society sees as unladylike behaviour. A life of few heartfelt choices is bleak indeed.'

Dr Russell rocked in his chair, its leather squeaking as he moved. 'You seem most taken with a woman's lot in life. I have seldom encountered such insights. You must have a strong wife?'

I bit my lip. I was not the only woman who would have baulked at this conversation. Women did not want to be seen as weak or useless. I gave an uncomfortable chuckle. 'Oh no, I have not had the fortune to find a woman who will bear with me.'

Dr Russell offered a look almost of condolence. 'The poor women of London are fortunate to have you. Are you considering Mr Walsh's suggestion of taking up as a man midwife? He appeared to believe you were frequently needed for such services in Whitechapel.'

I hadn't realised Isaac's cheeky suggestion – or any of our discussion at Lettsom's – had been overheard.

He seemed to mistake my hesitation for embarrassment. 'I do not look upon it as a lowly position at all. My father was one. His old bag full of his instruments is over there.' He pointed to a battered leather bag in the corner, next to a coat rack. 'You had such an interesting discussion with Mr Walsh about the design of forceps. I was unaware of the risks to the mother and baby.'

I took a breath as I realised I was enjoying this conversation with Dr Russell. To be treated as an intelligent man was refreshing.

'Yes. I am considering providing my occasional service as an accoucheur. I think it will be invaluable. Mr Walsh and I believe that if the forceps had no angle between the shanks and the blades, and a sliding lock, then they might be suitable to provide rotation when the baby's head is tilted to the side. The pelvic curve of the blades would stay the same.'

He nodded, though I saw he didn't understand, so with his leave I found his father's forceps and illustrated my meaning.

Dr Russell was most impressed. 'How clever. My wife is currently in labour above us. I hope she will have no need for such an instrument.'

I gasped. How was it possible for a man to be so nonchalant about such an important event as to be holding a meeting in a downstairs office while it occurred?

Before I could construct a suitable response, there was a knock at the door.

'Ah, perhaps time for the big announcement.'

Dr Russell was mistaken. The maid was huffing with exertion, obviously having run. 'Beg pardon, sirs. The midwife has dropped on the floor, with Mrs Russell taking so long. She needs to see a doctor.'

CHAPTER

THIRTY-FIVE

Without being asked, I followed the maid and doctor to his wife's lying-in room. The midwife was still lying in a muddle on the floor. The room was stifling.

'Open the window,' I ordered. 'It's meant to be comfortably warm, not hot.' The maid did as I asked. The earthy scent of horse manure from the street mingled with the tang of sweat in the room.

Mrs Russell lay in a dejected form on a low-lying bed, sweat pouring from her brow and lank brown hair, which had come loose from a night-time plait. Her eyes opened at the sound of her husband's voice as he checked in on the midwife.

'Give your wife some comfort while we look after the midwife,' I told him.

He looked alarmed. 'What if she gives birth? I have no business here.'

I gave his shoulder a pat. 'Once the midwife is settled in a maid's bed to recover, I will return, and you can leave. She is having a hard time of it.'

His alarm gave way to concern, and he moved to his wife's side. 'Oh, my love.'

I guessed the midwife was overheated and had taken no food or tea for some time. I helped her out of the room and scolded the maid, who assured me she would watch over her.

Once on my own with Mrs Russell, I put on the doctor's apron that Dr Russell had given me and left the man-midwifery bag at the door. I did not bother with a modesty sheet as a true man midwife would, but examined her without it, hoping she was too exhausted to care that a man was attending to her.

'I understand you are exhausted,' I said as I wiped her brow. The room had cooled and was much more comfortable. I was concerned that the baby seemed to be large, and, looking at the forceps I had dumped onto a small side table, hoped there would be no need to make use of them. I searched the bag and found a hook, perforator, and several glass jars. I pulled out one of the glass stoppers and determined that the label of brandy was correct. Another jar held ergotamine, and the last an opium tincture.

Opting for the opium tincture, I offered Mrs Russell a small dose once a powerful contraction was completed.

'Now, let's get you off your back and ...' I realised she was too exhausted to stand and lean against the window, so I helped her into a kneeling position on the floor. 'There, that will help get things moving again.'

I knelt beside her, grateful for a soft rug under our knees. I rubbed her lower back as she puffed and panted. 'All is well, all is well.'

I breathed through the contractions with her as they grew in intensity and frequency. 'Not long now.'

I stoked the fire back up, and even though the air was bitterly cold, I left the window a fraction open.

There, finally, the sound she was making became more guttural.

'Have no fear, you can do this. You are not dying,' I reassured her, remembering how I had felt at this stage of labour.

She nodded her head in disbelief. 'Oh, I am burning.'

I made a quick inspection. 'Ah, the baby's head. Keep bearing down, as if you are on the privy.'

I ignored a splash of blood and mucous, then explored the area around the baby's neck. 'Oh, wait. No more pushing. Pant, pant, pant. Wait until I tell you.'

'Ohhhh, I can't,' she moaned, head rocking with her body.

'You must.' I worked my slender fingers hard, finding space to untangle the cord around the baby's tiny neck. 'You may push now.'

She groaned with relief.

'The head is out! Go again.' I held the tiny, slippery head as the next contraction eased out the shoulders, and the rest of the body slid into my hands.

The babe did not utter a sound at first.

A mewl, like a kitten.

'You have a sweet baby girl,' I said as I cut the cord. I rubbed the baby down and wrapped her in a muslin cloth. 'The placenta will be along soon.'

I placed the wrapped baby at her eye level on the bed, and they gazed solemnly at each other. Lost in a world of their own, oblivious of the rumble of wheels and clatter of hooves coming from outside the window. Relief washed over me, along with the bittersweet emotions of loss and joy. I had missed this work terribly.

With a speed born of well-known habit, I completed the cleanup and soon had Mrs Russell washed, settled, and nursing. She did not question my expertise in this matter.

'I am most grateful ... we have not been introduced,' she said, looking up from her baby.

'Uh, Dr Dalton, at your service,' I said, wiping up the last of the blood from the wooden floor next to the rug. 'I'm afraid the rug is ruined. I should have covered it.'

Mrs Russell waved a hand. 'It does not matter. Before you go, fix that moustache.'

My hand flung to my upper lip. My sweat must have interfered with the paste, as a corner had come loose. 'Oh.'

'I believed I was addled by the labour,' she said. 'You move and care much like a woman. I've never met a doctor who cleans up after himself. Do not trouble yourself; your secret is safe. If it is not too much, I would ask what your name is ... only your first.' Her face was glowing with kindness.

I was confident I could trust her. 'I did not mean to deceive anyone, and I assure you I have my reasons. My name is Adeline. I must attend to this.' I reached for a tiny pot in my pocket, dabbed on Edna's paste, and reattached the moustache.

'What happened to the midwife?' she asked.

'Oh, I had better check. She collapsed because of the heat; I will pass on the good news and organise the caudle.'

When Mrs Russell was ready, an excitable puppy of a husband followed me in.

'Please meet your daughter, Rose Adeline,' Mrs Russell said, offering the sleeping bundle. Through a blink of tears, I showed him how to hold the baby, and then I made my farewells, ignoring Dr Russell's offer of payment. Maybe I would stay a man and become a man midwife who had every tool at his disposal.

As I left his house on Harley Street, I willed my feet not to return to Papa's, nor wander past my home with Spencer. I had spent far too long out and needed to leave this area immediately. With the emergency purse Morgan had given me, I hailed a hansom cab and climbed aboard. As the horse gathered speed, a face on the street turned towards the cab and chilled my innards. Was that Prudence?

I had barely entered the foyer when Morgan stormed towards me. 'Are you trying to get caught?'

I took off my Inverness cape, avoiding his stern gaze. 'No, of course not. I considered it important to discuss—'

He took the cape from me. 'No. What is important is that you remain hidden until you are free. And did you contemplate what might become of my reputation if you are discovered here?'

I looked down at my muddy boots, only now noticing the footprints I had left on the scrubbed floor.

'You are behaving like an errant child. I need to go about my business without concerning myself that ... are you crying?' he dropped the volume of his voice.

I blinked hard. 'I apologise for my careless behaviour. I will lie down in my room for a while and be no further trouble to you.'

I stumbled up the stairs, not caring about any muddy boots.

'That was harsh, wouldn't you agree?' I heard Isaac say.

Morgan was right. I had been thoughtless. Collapsing onto my bed, my body trembled, and I ignored the tapping on my door.

First, Mary knocked and told me she had set a tray outside with supper.

Then Isaac knocked; he was more determined and refused to leave me be until he had seen for himself that I was in good spirits.

I allowed him in, and he waved a box at me. 'The finest sweets there are. Join me in a humbug?'

He looked at me expectantly, with a childlike grin. 'Go on, say it ... Morgan said you were ever so good on stage.'

I rolled my eyes. 'Bah, humbug.'

Isaac held the box close. 'Say it with flair.'

I managed a smile. 'Bah, humbug.'

'There, that wasn't so hard, was it?' Isaac gave me one of the mint-flavoured toffees.

'Thank you.' I sucked the toffee, trying not to chew, knowing it would stick my teeth together.

Isaac put the box on my nightstand. 'He gets cantankerous when he cares.'

'Morgan was right to be angry. He has risked much, and I have been too concerned about my cause.' I wiped a bit of dribble before it got into my beard.

Isaac chomped for a bit. 'We will both be out early tomorrow, so do not think he is punishing you by being absent. Give him some time.'

Time. How long would Morgan take before he thawed, and I was in his good graces again?

THIRTY-SIX

Although I expected a chilly and isolated breakfast, I was astonished to find the table unlaid and no fire in the hearth. Frowning, I called and searched for Mary, even going down to the kitchen. Not a soul to be found. No cook batting pots and pans about, no scent of bacon in the air. Not even a brew of tea or coffee. Everything was scrubbed and in order and abandoned.

I clomped my way up to the maid's room and knocked on her door. When she failed to answer, I swung it open, only to find her packing a spare uniform and pair of boots into a carpetbag. The look she shot me chilled me in its malevolence.

'I'll not be stayin' in the devil's pit,' she said as she shoved past me.

'What are you on about?' I concentrated on keeping my voice low, though I was very alarmed.

'He'll 'ave been thrown in the clink with that other bloke by now, and soon they'll be comin' for you,' she warned. 'I saw you together, you molly boy.'

My mouth had not closed by the time she slammed the door. She had peeked through the door, seen our embrace, and now doomed Morgan and Isaac to gaol. I cursed myself for putting him in such a position.

There was nothing for it. I would have to reveal my identity and get them out of gaol. As I did when things got difficult during a labour, I slowed my breath down and then my thoughts. If I threw myself at the mercy of the gaolers, I might not be of any help. The image of Papa's solicitor and friend, Mr Starkey, came to mind. Number one Wardrobe Place, Doctors' Commons. I needed to make haste.

It did not seem that the powers that be agreed with my urgency. I was dismayed to find the Doctors' Commons deserted; I was told that the building would be demolished, the society having had their last meeting. Once again in my disguise as a man, I traipsed around an increasingly unfamiliar London until I found Mr Starkey in a new building on a developing street. I was surprised to see that in the short time I had been locked up, Five Foot Lane, Dove Court, and White Bear Alley had all been demolished to make way for this new thoroughfare. The world carried on and changed regardless, making me feel even more the urgency of my mission.

Mr Starkey's new abode was a classically styled Portland stone building of four storeys, with grand pilasters to the upper floors. I used Papa's name to gain admittance. Highlighting the matter was urgent.

'Mr Starkey, good to see you,' I greeted the solicitor as he looked at me warily.

'Dr Ward.' His faded grey eyes matched his flowing beard, his collar-length hair a snowier white. He paused for a moment and took my outstretched hand. 'Please follow me.'

We entered a study, and he directed me to sit. I admired the diamond-and-button pattern on a Chesterfield chair before I sat on its comfortable leather cushions. The vanilla aroma of dusty tomes on bookshelves that lined the walls gave the room an old-world scent, while the new oak floorboards gave a sense of freshness.

With a glint of curiosity in his eye, Mr Starkey peered at me, then in a gruff manner started the meeting. 'I know my friend Dr Ward is no longer with us. I hope you have a reason for pilfering his good name.'

I swallowed. 'I apologise for my deceit. I am his daughter, Adeline.'

His bushy eyebrows shot up, and he waved me to continue. I summarised the predicament I was in and what had befallen Morgan and Isaac.

He stroked his beard once I had finished. 'So, this allegation of sodomy is false. I will ensure it is framed as fraudulent and, if need be, an attempt at extortion by a disgruntled maid.'

I sat back. 'You believe me.'

He nodded. 'When I used to dine with your father, I'll admit I found it odd that he encouraged you to converse at the table with us. He rightly admired your acuity of mind. You are going to great lengths and risking recapture to put things to rights. I have no reason to question your character. I will not betray your trust, as you are clearly not insane.'

I almost wept at the kindness shining from his eyes, but settled for a grateful smile. 'I am most relieved. Thank you.'

He waved away my thanks. 'I had wondered why you did not heed my summons when your papa died. He gave explicit instructions I was not to discuss certain matters with your husband.' He moved to a large mahogany cabinet and withdrew some papers.

I leaned towards him when he sat with a slight groan again. 'Dr Ward had taken me in confidence regarding his concern for your welfare. A well-founded one, to be sure. He placed a substantial amount of funds in my care, to be used only by you at your discretion, should you find yourself in trouble.'

'Is such an arrangement within the law?' I asked.

He shrugged. 'He saved my life more than once. What matters is that you are obviously in need.'

I left Mr Sparkey with a blend of shiny optimism that he would ensure Morgan and Isaac's expedient release from gaol and numbness, knowing that I now had the funds to be an independent woman. I might choose to leave London, to be far from Spencer and his greedy clutches. If I did not wish to leave London, I had the funds to divorce him. This would be a much more difficult path, as I would have to prove him to be cruel and adulterous. It would not matter that I would lose claim to any property, as the property was already lost.

I caught an omnibus to Charity's to share my news. As it clopped along, I noticed a familiar figure strutting along the street, whistling and tipping his hat jauntily at an attractive lady, and I almost leapt off. I stopped and gathered my wits. I had no desire to be one of the many who found themselves under the wheels of a passing cart. I kept my eye on the figure and dismounted at the next stop, relieved to have him still in view.

I was sure the man was Spencer.

I ignored the twinge that told me to leave well enough alone. Why risk discovery? But an ember within burned to know what he was doing. Why was he so cheerfully walking the streets of London, with his suffering wife trapped in an asylum? Perhaps it was folly to follow him. What would I discover? A new gambling den, a mistress, a brothel?

I needed to find out.

THIRTY-SEVEN

I followed Spencer down a street near the Haymarket as the afternoon dimmed into twilight. It was crowded, despite the light drizzle, with plenty of hawkers and barrow-boys plying their mishmash of goods. I darted down the cobbled street, among the scent of roasting meat, sandalwood perfume, and a touch of wood-smoke. I continued to shadow him as he eventually made his way to Cleveland Street. It was not the most dangerous of areas that I had ever travelled in as a midwife, but it was unfamiliar. I made more of an effort to keep up with Spencer. It had been such a shock to spot him strolling along that I had followed him despite the danger, certain he would not recognise me disguised as a man.

I waited at the mouth of a laneway, unsure of whether to risk going into the tavern he had entered. I slipped a beggar woman some coin, and she gave a gummy smile as she went into the tavern. The open door spilled out chatter, music, and light.

My breath caught as a man stumbled into the old woman as she entered, as he looked slightly familiar. But it was not Spencer.

Then my breath hitched again as another man came into view. This time it was Spencer.

'I don't have a clue what caper is going on here,' a voice came from behind me.

I turned to see the soot-stained face of a street urchin. 'What do you mean?' I asked.

With a skinny finger, he pointed. 'You're spying on 'im. He's followin' *that* fella, and just down there ... *she's* watchin' *you*.'

I looked at where his finger pointed, and there, lurking in the shadows of the street, was a woman. As she stepped into the lamplight, a tendril of blonde hair glowed. Prudence! She gave me a pointed stare, then melted back into the shadows. How did she figure out it was me? Surely I looked like any other gentleman of London?

She had seen me in character as Mr Scrooge, I realised in dismay, so she was more familiar with me dressed as a man. I looked down. My shoulders sagged. Oh! I was wearing the burgundy waistcoat she had admired long ago in the costume room.

I almost sensed the stickiness of the web I was caught in brush my face. This would not end well.

My eyes opened as the candle guttered, leaving me in the gloom of my midnight-dark room. I felt around for the lucifers I'd brought from a little girl near the tavern – brothel – and lit up another candle. A terrible waste of beeswax. My mind kept torturing me with images of Prudence's twisted smile. With a sigh, for the fifth time that night, I took my candleholder to each corner of my room to check she did not lie in wait.

I was far more rattled to have seen her free on the streets of London than I would have been to see her at the asylum. I turned my thoughts to Spencer and the man he was following. Who was he? As my eyes drooped, I snapped awake. I *knew* I had recognised the man! I had met him once at the club that Morgan had taken me to. He was an earl. My memory strained. It was his daughter that I'd seen Spencer flirting with at the archery meeting.

Why would Spencer be following him? Perhaps to dig up any secrets so he might persuade the earl to share his good fortune and title, for the earl would certainly want to keep any depravity a secret. So, the whisper of the rumour I recalled at the archery meeting may have been correct. That his sexual appetite included young boys.

Satisfied that I now understood what Spencer was up to, I wondered if Prudence was also aware of his interest in Lady Elizabeth Telford. If so, then his new love and I were both in danger.

It was with much relief that I welcomed Morgan and Isaac back. Morgan seemed to have forgiven me.

'I hope I have not overstepped,' I said. 'With the cook and maid both gone, I have asked my father's former, most trustworthy servants to step in. If you are not content with this arrangement, I will find them a position elsewhere. Spencer interfered with Papa's wishes and left them to the workhouse.' Charity had made enquiries, and we had both been horrified to learn of their fate. They were apparently just as concerned when Charity revealed my perilous situation.

Morgan nodded. 'Of course. After a night in New Prison, I have a new appreciation for life's comforts.'

Isaac's laugh was booming. As we ate a late breakfast, he seemed to consider the whole thing fodder for an entertaining tale.

Kitty was nervous about having been promoted from a scullery maid to a parlourmaid. She kept apologising as she slopped tea into saucers and dropped tongues of bacon.

Before her tears fell, I held up a hand. 'Please, Kitty. We are quite capable of serving ourselves.'

She twitched and gave a bob. 'Yes, sir ... ma'am ... miss. Oh.'

Isaac burst out laughing, spraying his eggs onto the table. Morgan gave Kitty a sympathetic smile. I sighed, observing her difficulty accepting my new clothing and identity.

Kitty wiped her hands on her apron. 'I am very grateful to Miss Evans for finding us and to you for taking us on. To you both, Mr Ashton and ... uh, Mr Dalton.'

'It is my pleasure, Miss Kitty,' Morgan said as her cheeks flamed.

Kitty nodded and scampered from the room.

'Oh, I hope I have not made an error,' I said. 'She is a lovely girl.'

Morgan threw his napkin on the table and rubbed his belly. 'She will be fine. And Mrs Cook certainly lives up to her name. I do not need to have her impress me any further with pickled oysters, salmon *au bleu* or *oeufs cocottes* for breakfast. Breakfast rolls, sausages, eggs, and cakes will suffice, or I will need a new tailor.'

Isaac was devouring a beef rib. 'I appreciate a morning banquet.'

As Morgan sighed, Isaac added, 'Of course, that is too much work for two women.'

As I was about to share more of my visit with Mr Sharkey, a distant but loud retch sliced through the air.

'Perhaps Kitty's nerves got the better of her,' I said. I made my way to the kitchen and found Kitty in quite a state. Mrs Cook looked far from impressed at the pool of vomit on the floor.

I administered some herbs, cleaned her up, and sent her to bed despite her protests.

Once she was more settled, I examined her to determine what might have disrupted her digestion.

'I drank some of the cocoa. Perhaps it were too rich for me?' she said. She held her stomach as it cramped again. 'I thought it grainy and bitter compared to the Cadbury's new Cocoa Essence that you gave to us last night. Ohhhhhh.' More cramps.

I waited for further cramps to pass, which they did, thankfully without any further expulsion of fluid. 'Have you cleaned the chocolate pot and moulinet?' I asked.

She nodded. 'Mrs Cook said there's no need for a moulinet for Cadbury's.'

I had hoped the little stirring stick might reveal some evidence of the tampering that I was now suspecting. 'Where is the chocolate?'

I found the tin of cocoa powder next to the white-and-gold porcelain chocolate pot in the kitchen.

After asking about Kitty's welfare, Mrs Cook got on and scrubbed the pots with brick dust. Maybe I was just rattled by thoughts of Prudence and over-reacting, but I thought I would rather be sure. She did not ask what I was doing as I heated the cocoa powder and milk then sniffed deeply.

Yes, under the bitter scent of cocoa was a distinct odour of garlic. It was arsenic.

'Don't drink or serve anymore of this,' I warned Mrs Cook. 'It's been laced with poison.'

I was sure my face was as pallid as hers.

Was this Prudence's doing? Why was she following me? Why was she still determined, not just to maim me, but to kill me?

CHAPTER

THIRTY-EIGHT

organ's face turned a blanched-almond colour as I gave him the details of my exploits and discoveries while he had been in gaol. Neither of us mentioned him bursting in on me naked.

'You must not go wandering about London until the two weeks is done, Adeline. It's only two days away.' He rubbed his chin, his breakfast forgotten. 'It is vital that Spencer is not alerted to your newfound wealth, or your father's protection will come to naught.'

The gloom of the bruised clouds outside did not entice me out for any further adventures, anyway. 'I promise I will remain here ... though, it is clear that Prudence is aware not only of my disguise but also my whereabouts.' I tapped the side of my teacup. Kitty was still ill, so I had served the meal myself. 'Perhaps I need to ...'

I did not know where I would go. I could not impose on Charity, as surely that would put her in danger.

The thud of the front door knocker jolted me out of my thoughts. Morgan gave me a concerned look as he went to answer it. I heard a rumble of voices and Morgan's boom of protest. Four men burst into the room, as Morgan tried to block their path. Two of them were police constables. So, Prudence had ensured that if I was not poisoned, then at least I would be recaptured.

A squat gentleman pushed past Morgan. 'Out of my way, sir! I am a doctor. I am here for Mrs Parker.'

'I assure you that Mrs Parker is not here!' Morgan said. 'Only Dr Dalton. Yes, I met him at the asylum Christmas performance and took pity on his change in circumstances that left him without accommodation.'

'Then I am sorry, Mr Ashcroft,' said the squat gentleman with the doctor's bag. 'You have been duped by a very cunning woman, as this Dr Dalton is indeed Mrs Parker in disguise.'

I rose from the table, ready to defend my good character, but the squat man was having none of it. He strode towards me and ripped off my moustache. I gasped and rubbed my stinging skin. With another tug, my wig and beard came free.

'Ah, there you have it. Please escort Mrs Parker to the carriage, Constable Peterson.'

Morgan took my arm, but the policemen shoved him aside.

Tugged free of Morgan's hands, I was loaded, screaming, into a wagon.

The doctor retrieved laudanum from a bag and measured a dose. The administering doctor's serious demeanour and his attendant's powerful grip on my arms suppressed my resistance, though my muscles twitched. With a firm grip, the attendant squeezed my jaw until I opened my mouth. I spat the laudanum out.

The doctor turned a shade of purple and dug back in his bag, and withdrew a silver plunger with a glass tube and a sharp silver tip. I drew back into the corner, not caring that I was cringing into the smelly armpit of the attendant.

'I will take the laudanum,' I said. 'There's no need for a needle.'

'Morphia should do it,' he said.

I was too petrified to move as the metal tip plunged in. They ignored my scream. I rubbed my arm. Did the man understand where the needle should go or the amount of morphia he'd given me?

'Now that you are settled, Mrs Parker, allow me to introduce myself. We have actually met, though you were not conscious at the time. I am Dr Butcher. You really should have made the most of the convalescent wards in Bloomfield. You'll be out the back with me in the refractory ward now, and I'll be having no trouble from you.' I winced as he ripped the last of the moustache from my face and uttered his disapproval. 'Fancy taking advantage of one of our esteemed committee members. Mr Ashcroft will no doubt endorse any treatment I see fit.'

It's Ashton, not Ashcroft, I was ready to tell him. With one look at his thunderous expression, I found myself silent. Too numb to think or feel, I turned to watch Belgrave fade, trying to avoid further scrutiny from his ice-blue eyes. If only I had not had such false confidence in my ability to roam London undetected ... had waited before I challenged the doctors at the club. The dullness in my chest matched the dullness in my brain, and I succumbed to the drowsiness, wishing Spencer had never set his sights on me. I had been far happier without him.

Some obedient but distant part of me followed an unfamiliar asylum surgeon's instructions as he examined me in a tiny, airless room. He exclaimed with horror when examining the site of my harmless operation, then advised me he did not endorse the latest procedure, but I was floating away. As each door in the refractory wing was clanged shut and locked behind me, I lost a bit more of a feathery hope that this was not truly happening.

I was led to a tiny cell with a horsehair mattress set on a plank and covered in the thinnest of blankets. I shivered in the blast of winter air leaking in from the tiny, barred window above. I sat with a thud on a wooden stool.

'It'll be dark soon. Don't bother screaming and crying for help or the like, because we only open the door at first light,' the surly attendant muttered as she slammed the door shut.

It was the darkest, coldest night I had ever had. So bereft that even tears failed to escape.

After a very meagre breakfast, I was led with some other women into the yard. Unlike the lovely gardens I had strolled through with fellow recovering patients during my last stay, the refractory yard was dreadful, enclosed by tall stone walls topped with sharp iron spikes much like those I imagined would be found in London's most wretched prisons.

'What 'ave we got 'ere?' A hand roughly spun me around, and I gagged on the woman's breath. 'Too good for the likes of us, eh?'

She wiggled a rotted tooth at me, while another woman stood watching with a sneer. One was as stout as the other was rail-thin. Both had lank, greasy hair and pockmarked skin. Other women glanced at me, then away.

'Whattaya think, Mabel? Isn't she a pretty one?' Beady eyes travelled over my body, and stubby fingers jabbed at the buttons of my dress.

'What? No!' That was all I was able to say before she tugged at and ripped the dress.

As the other gripped my hair and yanked my petticoats off, I screamed. Tears streamed down my face as a chunk of hair was torn out. I fell to the ground and received a solid boot into my stomach. I curled into an icy ball.

'Stop! That will be all, Miss Webster.' A hand hauled me off the ground. 'I mean it! Go on with you, Kate.' When they eyed her boldly, she stood her ground. 'Off to seclusion for you, then.'

Kate threw a tuft of my golden hair at me.

After the women were escorted away, the wards woman smoothed down her uniform and handed me my torn clothing.

'How are women like that able to be at Bloomfield? They belong at Newgate or Broadmoor,' I protested.

She shook her head. 'You're probably right, but money talks. Not that I know where the likes of them gets any. You need to toughen up, or you won't last long in the ward.'

Wiping tears and blood from my mouth, I tugged the smelly, tattered gown back over my head. My scalp bled from a small bald patch. I dabbed it with a handkerchief before covering it with the remnants of a straw bonnet with a faded blue ribbon.

'Few of the women who find themselves here will harm you. I'd be more worried if I was one of their husbands or children.'

I blinked fast. 'Their children?'

'Oh. I thought with you having been a midwife and all, you'd be aware that too many children and a drunken husband can lead to desperate measures.' She nodded towards a slender young woman. 'That one threw herself and her baby onto the lime used to mend the roads. It was rather shocking for all who witnessed it.'

I peered at the woman; she had angry red welts on her face. She caught me staring and turned away. The heat rose in my cheeks.

As I was later passed a pewter bowl of something resembling beef stew and brown bread, I thought of Spencer, sitting in his soft leather reading chair by the cosy fire, sipping brandy. I swear I heard something deep within me crack. I imagined my fingers curling around his thick, sweaty neck and squeezing so hard he turned blue.

THIRTY-NINE

Until Dr Butcher had time to decide on my treatment, it seemed I would spend my days scrubbing and polishing. There would be limited leisure time for reading, playing parlour games and the like until I proved I was a well-behaved lady. I traced the check of my gingham dress as I ordered myself to deepen my breathing and still my fidgeting fingers. For all intents and purposes, I would be a model patient.

I was anxious about Morgan's fate. Was it their assessment that a clever lunatic had deceived him, or were they making him also suffer for his participation in my escape?

As I sat picking at my steamed pudding in the dining room, I saw no friendly faces. Although there was one familiar one. Nurse Talbot used her imposing height to ensure no inmate would dare to tangle with her and was sharper in her manner than she had been in the convalescent ward.

There was no banter or conversation like I had had with Olivia and Edna. It made for many a dreary day. Mama and Papa had long ago impressed on me how important it was to learn people's names and address them by those names, not to be tempted to talk of them as their disease or as cases. I would have hated to be addressed as 'that hysterical woman', so I tried to remember the names in the wards – though I will admit that after meeting so many women, they became a blur.

As the attendants gathered up our cutlery, there were only murmurs of talk, until one woman flew with the pointy end of the spoon at another. She grabbed her hair, and they rolled on the floor, covered in pudding, until attendants got them in hand. I kept my face a blank mask, but inside I trembled.

The dayroom for this ward was a small, simple affair. The wooden chairs were bolted to the floor, and there were no comfortable armchair options. There was still plenty of light from large windows, but on the lower levels, bars blocked free access to the glass. Only a few women were seated within: two playing cards, one tinkling at the pianoforte, and another, who sat listening, with her feet tapping. One woman near the back of the room held the most bizarre position. She was hunched in the back, standing on one leg, with her arm held out, fingers splayed. Her face was contorted. She did not utter a word or blink.

'Stay away from that one,' Nurse Talbot said, with a nod in the woman's direction. 'Poor Eliza will stay like that for hours, not moving a muscle. Then, without warning, if you're within reach, she'll grab any part of you she can and bite down. Her jaw becomes locked, and it's not a simple thing to get her to release you.'

I crossed my arms around me.

The woman listening to the music stood and pointed at me. 'Lady Talbot, why have I not been introduced? I cannot abide having strangers in my court.'

Nurse Talbot smiled at the haughty attitude of the woman. On closer inspection, I noticed she was the only woman I had seen in the asylum wearing any form of colour on her cheeks and lips. She had fashioned some sort of crown of twigs and browning roses and set it upon her tangled brown hair. I guessed her to be forty years old, as her waist had thickened and bosom dropped. Her startling green eyes bored into me; her expression clarified that she did not expect me to meet her eyes with such directness.

'There's always one in every asylum,' Nurse Talbot said. 'She's quite harmless, with no access to alcohol. Miss Victoria Smith bears the same Christian name as our queen, but she knows no more of the royal protocols than we do.' She took my arm and guided me to stand in front of Victoria. 'Please forgive me, Your Majesty. May I present the lovely Lady Adeline of Devonshire.'

Nurse Talbot curtseyed then whispered to me as she rose again, 'The day goes more smoothly if you play along.'

So I followed suit, bowed my head, and curtseyed too.

'Ah. Welcome, Lady Adeline. I hope you are here to provide some entertainment on this beautiful morning. Do you sing?'

I rose, and Nurse Talbot nodded. 'She doesn't care whether you sing woefully or well. Every new person to her court must pass the test.'

Before I could answer, the woman at the piano began a familiar tune. So, with a shrug, I sang. When I finished the last sweet note, everyone clapped, and it seemed Her Majesty was thrilled.

'You will sing another,' she commanded. 'Nellie, play again.'

The woman at the pianoforte nodded. 'If it pleases Your Majesty.'

My humour faded, as the next song was Papa's favourite. I had the wisp of a memory of my mother singing it with him, so I raised my voice to the heavens and sang 'By the Sad Sea Waves'.

By the sad sea waves, I listen while they moan,

A lament o'er graves of hope and pleasure gone.
I am young, I was fair,
I had once not a care
From the rise of the morn to the setting of the sun.
Yet I pine like a slave, by the sad sea wave.
Come again, bright days of hope and pleasure gone.

I continued on to the next verse and did not wipe the tears that dribbled down my cheeks. It seemed my melancholy was contagious, as sniffs echoed mine and tears were wiped on other cheeks. The woman who had held her awkward position softened and sat on the floorboards, curled in a ball but looking at me.

'That will be all for today. I expect you here tomorrow.' With that, the Asylum Queen left the dayroom.

'You have a beautiful voice, Mrs Parker,' Nurse Talbot said.

'Please call me Adeline.' I wiped my tears with my handkerchief and took one of the few novels from a table. I settled as best I was able in a chair by the window, hoping the novel would offer some escape.

A skeletal slip of a girl sidled up to me. 'That was so sad. Have you lost a babe, too?'

My heart jolted. The song had been about loss, though not of a child. 'Ah, yes, I have.'

'I thought so. We can lose so many people, but why do men not understand what it is to lose a baby? How sad it is? I lost four of mine.' Her skin was so thin, it was if she were translucent. I would have doubted she could ever carry a baby to term, let alone birth one.

'Did you lose them before you were able to birth them?' I asked as she sat across the small card table from me.

Her doe eyes dimmed. 'I birthed them all, but none lived to reach the age of two.'

My throat closed, but I managed to say, 'I am very sorry for your loss.'

'Oh, thank you. I am hoping *this* one stays with its mama a long time.' She stroked a very flat belly with a dreamy look on her face. 'How I look forward to stroking that soft cheek and downy hair again.'

'Rosetta, it's time for your bath.' A nurse I didn't recognise led her away.

When Nurse Talbot came back into the room, I couldn't resist asking her about Rosetta. 'Does she suffer from puerperal psychosis?'

Nurse Talbot looked around and saw no one was listening. 'Not that I should discuss other inmates with you, but yes, I have no doubt she does.'

I shook my head. 'It's so sad to lose four babies and then think she is having another.'

Nurse Talbot raised an eyebrow. 'No, what's sad is her taking a knife to them. She cut the throat of one and was caught pinning her twenty-month-old between her knees and holding a knife above her. A newborn was also found suffocated beneath the blankets in the bedroom. And she's not the only woman here who should be in Broadmoor.'

A tingle ran down my spine. The paint-flaked walls closed in. I needed to get out of here.

CHAPTER

FORTY

A gentle touch on my shoulder woke me in the night. Nurse Talbot stood by my bed with a candle. She motioned for me to follow her, so I slipped from my bed and wrapped my shawl around me, and we tiptoed from the room.

'I hope you were telling the truth when you said you were once a midwife?' she whispered.

I nodded. 'I was.'

'Follow me to the infirmary. The patient, Clara, believed she had stomach pains, but I am sure she is in labour. I have not assisted in many births in my training.' For a tall, solid woman, she looked awfully worried. It seemed that since spending a few more months with me, Nurse Talbot deemed me worthy of her trust. I glowed with the thought.

Clara was curled in a moaning ball on the bed, her brown braid wet with sweat.

'May I?' I asked as I stepped closer. Clara's face grimaced, but she nodded. I placed my hands on her nightdress and felt a familiar firm bulge. As gently as possible, I lifted her hem and slipped her undergarments down.

Clara's wide-set eyes shifted as the pain eased. 'It was the mutton.'

'I don't think so, Clara.' I probed her belly, checking for the baby's position. 'Nurse Talbot. Would you bring some boiled water, rags, and scissors? Some lavender water and sweet almond oil too, if you have some.' I would have to do my best without the supplies I usually had on hand at a birth.

'Clara, I need to put my hand inside you to confirm where the baby's head is.' She was so young and petite, and unfortunately had narrow hips. Our ill-fitting asylum dresses had easily hidden her swollen belly. What I didn't understand was how she had come to be in such a state.

Nurse Talbot had gathered the supplies hastily, and I rubbed the almond oil over my hands before slipping my hand into Clara's body, searching for the V of the baby's scalp. 'Yes, Clara, there is definitely a baby on its way. Nothing to do with the mutton at dinner. I can feel the baby.' I removed my hand and wiped it on a towel that Nurse Talbot offered. 'How long have you had the pains?'

'A couple of days, on and off, but not like this. These have been since bedtime.' Clara gasped as another contraction gripped her.

Observing her flushed face and fatigued state, and noting the time, I made my calculations. 'All being well, this baby should arrive within a couple of hours.'

With a moan, Clara's face rippled, then settled. 'I don't understand. How can I be having a baby? I have not—I mean, I am not married.'

Nurse Talbot and I exchanged a glance. 'Let's focus on getting the baby safely delivered.'

She dropped her head back on the bed.

'I hope we do not need to call an accoucheur in,' Nurse Talbot said as she wiped Clara's brow with a wet rag.

'No, there should be no need for forceps. Many think women like Clara are too weak for a healthy birth, but I do not think mere weakness is the problem. My experience shows that lying down with legs raised does little to help the delivery. If I had my mother's birth stool with me, I would make effective use of it. Let's see if raising her up and getting her to squat gets things moving along.'

Thankfully, Nurse Talbot deferred to my experience and was strong enough to help me move Clara into position. Clara's pain immediately came in stronger waves more frequently. We gave words of encouragement.

I washed my hands in lavender water and re-oiled them with almond oil, rubbing some into her belly and on to her perineum. 'Not long now, Clara.'

Clara moved from the squat and rocked on her knees as I told her to, then dropped her head into the pile of pillows Nurse Talbot had made for her. Rocking, moaning, then falling into silence, on she laboured. Then I noticed the shift. A change in noise and a tightening in her legs. I tapped Nurse Talbot's arm and held a lantern to Clara. I smiled when I saw the baby's head.

'Can you feel that, Clara? You're nearly there.' I grabbed some rags, mopped up the blood, and threw them on the floor.

'Should we lie her down?' Nurse Talbot asked.

'No, she'll be more comfortable this way, and I can manage.'

After much whimpering that she was surely dying and much encouragement from us, a baby was finally expelled into my hands. 'It's a girl. She looks fine.'

I tied off the cord, gave the baby a quick rub and cleanse, then swaddled her up. Nurse Talbot held her as I waited for the afterbirth, cleaned Clara and the bedding up, then got her in position to hold her tiny babe.

After the tiniest of squeaks from the baby, I showed Clara how to attach her to the breast to feed. Clara looked both astonished and besotted as she nestled her daughter to her.

I sighed with contentment, feeling the calm that usually followed my elation after a good birth. With Mrs Russell and now Clara, I realised that my fear of losing my midwifery skill in the abyss of married life was unfounded. If it were possible for me to shield my heart from the loss of infants, then perhaps after my release, I might be able to practise again.

Nurse Talbot was less content. 'Now, what are we supposed to do with her? They'll no doubt take the baby and send it to the Foundling Home, and find some way of keeping her quiet.'

My contentment dissipated. 'How did she ...?'

Nurse Talbot poked her head out of the infirmary door, then shut it. 'Dr Griffiths is involved. This is not the first time.'

'I would not have thought ... she never said a word.'

Nurse Talbot snorted. 'She wouldn't. She thought he loved her.' She rolled her eyes. 'For Clara's sake, I hope we can trust in your discretion.'

'Of course.'

I was surprised at the wobble of emotion in Nurse Talbot's voice. 'Are you feeling well?'

Nurse Talbot leaned against the wall, almost dropping the candle. 'It was not for epilepsy that Miss Olivia was given the same operation you had. Matron found them in an unsavoury position, and he said he was seduced by her. Said she had nymphomania. He said the same of others, and Matron accepted his statement. Not all of them think he loves them; I have seen a haunted look on some of them coming out of his treatment room.'

My hand went to my mouth as Nurse Talbot kept talking. 'I saw that look often on girls at the Poor Law Infirmary in Burmantofts. I knew things were going on there, but I was able to do little to protect the poor souls. When I could not care for my younger sister at home any longer, she ended up in the workhouse and then the infirmary ... there was a doctor there. He took advantage of her.'

I gasped. 'He raped her?'

'Yes.'

I waited for her to gather herself before she continued.

After a few sniffles, she did. 'While I was not sure about many of the men there, I did trust this one handsome doctor – at first. He had said he understood what it was like to be poor and wanted to help. He told me he had had a comfortable life until his father ended up in Newgate after being unable to pay his debts. But it soon became apparent that he lacked pity for the needy. It's my feeling that he loathed them.'

'Really? It seems reasonable that he would show more understanding,' I pondered.

Nurse Talbot shook her head vehemently, and the tears trickled. 'No, he was desperate to rise in society and was taking any opportunity available. Molly was so ill; she was in and out of that horrid place. When her condition became obvious, he did his best to get rid of it. She bled to death. I failed her.' Nurse Talbot slid to the floor, and I sat next to her, placing the candle between us. 'How I wish she had had someone like you in there to help her.'

I was lost for words. I leaned into her as she sniffed away some tears.

She wiped her face and sighed. 'I'd best get you back.'

As she closed the door to my cell, I heard her whisper, 'Thank you.'

For once, the refractory ward did not seem as lonely.

FORTY-ONE

A few days later, Nurse Talbot led me to a cosy room attached to the convalescent wing. She wouldn't tell me why, but a smile tugged on her usually grim lips.

I let the plush cushion of an armchair and the warmth of the cheerful fire crackling in the hearth comfort me. I savoured a hot tea loaded with sugar, much more to my liking than the lukewarm, diluted ones I'd have of late. The scent of dried roses was also a welcome change to the tang of urine. Even though there were no doctors on duty and Matron Wright was at the church service, Nurse Talbot was taking a risk to offer me some luxury as a thank you.

The weak winter sun filtered through the tall arched windows, dappling the turkey rug with light. I sighed in contentment. How often I had taken such moments of comfort for granted in the past.

'Looking quite the lady of leisure there,' a cheerful voice said behind me.

I leapt to my feet, splashing tea on my better dress. 'Charity!'

We embraced. Nurse Talbot grinned, then left us to it.

Charity and I sat down, and I almost laughed as she babbled, neither of us sure of how much time we would have together.

'I have been petitioning to visit ever since I found out what happened. Morgan has been distraught at being forbidden to see you. The administration deemed it unwise at the current time, given he is apparently too gullible to be in the company of a lunatic.' She covered her mouth as she saw my expression. 'Not that you are a lunatic, of course. Now, I wish we had some champagne, as we need to celebrate your success. Morgan has the finest Perrier-Jouet Cuvee K champagne waiting for you.'

'What are you talking about?'

'Dr Baker Brown published his book of case studies, *On the Curability of Certain Forms of Insanity, Catalepsy and Hysteria in Females*. He wrote he was convinced that peripheral excitement of the pudic nerve was at the root of it all and that removing it would cure all. Once all the gory details were published, it seems any doctor associated with such brutality became rather coy about it. Yes, they carried out the operation; no, they did not want the details to be discovered.'

I failed to grasp why they would ever have considered it at all.

Charity seemed irritated about that, too. She flicked a nail so hard it pinged into the wall beyond us. 'He actually named men who had adopted his views and treatment with gratitude. I do not think they appreciated his said gratitude. Drs Savage, Routh, and Rogers of London, to name a few, and even his own son. Dr Boyer Brown was taking it to the colony of New South Wales. Those poor convict women.'

I crossed my legs and leaned forward. 'It sounds like he had a lot of support.'

'No! That's the exciting thing! Instead of garnering him more credibility, it provoked objections ... even Dr Greenhalgh, who once supported him, remembered your visit and started speaking up in protest. Those who already considered it quackery spoke even louder. They were horrified to find that women and their caretakers were unfamiliar with the operation's full scale. I took up the opportunity to press more papers on to Mr Haden. It seems Dr Baker Brown was falsifying records at the surgical home. He was expelled from the Obstetric Society. His practice is a shambles!'

I managed a small smile and accepted her touch of her teacup against mine, as if it were a champagne glass. 'Thank you for helping me gather all the notes and for sharing what the women and families had to say.'

She beamed with radiance. 'Happy to oblige a worthy cause. You should be thrilled with that result.'

Charity was right: I should be happy. But still I felt unsatisfied.

I gulped down some tea. 'Did it not bother you it was not the efficacy of performing the operation that got Dr Baker Brown expelled, but the circumstances? It seems the medical men do not object to the procedure itself, but only to the fact that it was being done without the consent of their natural protectors.'

Charity set her cup down. 'You are determined to spoil this, aren't you? Yes, I agree. I do not understand why Mr Haden did not present *our* papers to the council or why they were not more concerned about the operation itself, but I doubt that any doctor will have the assurance to resume performing it, regardless.'

'I am still rankled by these medical men and their debates,' I said. 'I read of one man writing to the *British Medical Journal* pondering the value of women being subjected to this mutilation. He had heard of unmarried men avoiding young women who had visited physicians that insisted on digital examinations for *all* illnesses ...' the words had been seared into my memory when I'd read them. I could not tell whether it was the warmth of anger or tea rushing through me.

Charity refilled both of our cups and nodded. 'How dare these men think they can't marry such a woman? She would not have expected or welcomed the fingers of a doctor in her private parts. You've done your part to help woman who might have fallen into Dr Baker Brown's clutches.'

Yes, I had done everything within my power to prevent Dr Baker Brown from sharing his technique and others from adopting the clitoridectomy. Yet, here I was, still trapped by the likes of Dr Butcher, who was more than happy to take up another mad doctor's idea of cure.

FORTY-TWO

Charity fell silent, and I sensed her brain whirring to find a topic to cheer me. 'Oh, remember that woman that Spencer was most irritated with?'

I raised my eyebrows. 'You may have to narrow that down for me.'

She grinned. 'Miss Garrett, the one who aspired to be a doctor. She did it. Sat the apothecary exam and has opened her own practice in Upper Berkeley Street.'

I was cheered. 'How wonderful! I am sure she will not be a party to any of the procedures these men are doing.'

'At least Dr Baker Brown has been stopped. It is unfortunate that Morgan was unable to join us to celebrate,' Charity said.

Now gloom overcame me. Perhaps Morgan was lost to me now.

'Thank you for coming so far to visit me. I know it was a long journey.'

She waved my thanks away. 'You should not be in this asylum at all.' She stopped when she saw my set lips. 'Anyway ...' She stooped down and undid her boot, removing an envelope. 'I apologise for the state this is in. I wasn't sure if my person would be searched. Morgan is very concerned that Spencer will keep you locked up indefinitely.'

My heart lightened that Morgan still cared. I took the letter and held it to my chest. Then her last words scudded in like clouds. What if I was to spend the rest of my days here?

'Do you believe there is *any* hope that Spencer may step forward and secure my release?' I failed to hide the desperate note in my voice, and her eyes flooded with sympathy. 'I am wasting away in here.'

'We are working on it. He is adamant that you are hysterical, and since you've escaped once, you're seen as perhaps dangerous, so it is that much harder. He is, however, growing a reputation for being a rake and in debt because of his gambling habit, so his word may soon hold little stock. Not that it should have ever held more than yours.' Charity's cheer finally flagged.

I studied her face and her flicking, now-broken nail. 'There's more ... tell me.'

She closed her eyes for a moment. 'He's had to sell both townhouses.'

I gasped. 'Both? Papa's as well?'

'Yes.'

The silence hung between us.

'He cannot find out about Papa's hidden money.'

Charity pasted on a determined face. 'He won't. Behave as if you have no money left at all. Perhaps when you are released, you can return to midwifery?'

'I believed I could, though I still don't know if I can. It was always a struggle for me when a babe died, even before ...' I shrugged, but my mind immediately wandered and opened a long-sealed door. Wisps of memory formed a solid picture.

The dormer windows of 13 Archer Street in Soho jutted out of the clay-tiled roof. Thirteen and 14 Archer St were little artisan cottages that seemed to have been forgotten in time among the other newer-built Regency shopfronts embellished with cast-iron guardrails and patterned fanlights. I made my way to the upper floor, which was humming with activity.

Women sat at spinning wheels, wicker baskets at their feet in the workshop, making trimming for the upholstery. In the corner, on a pile of rags, was the woman I had been called for.

'Emily! What are you doing still working?' I scolded. The sight of her sweaty, scarlet face and the moan that erupted from her quieted me. Time for that later. A couple of women looked torn whether to stay or get back to work. I asked one to fetch me a stool.

'Mr Benson will not want her doing that here. She'll stain the floor,' the woman said as she handed me the stool then wiped her hands on her apron. She may have sounded gruff, but her eyes showed sympathy and concern.

Another woman spoke up. 'Emily is a good worker. I'm sure he'll forgive her. My name's Mrs Croydon.'

By now I had checked Emily over and gathered, from another groan and an utterance that she was in hell, that it was far too late to move her.

'Well, Mrs Croydon. Let's make sure Mr Benson does not come up those stairs, as this baby is coming any minute.'

Before I even had to ask, Mrs Croydon got behind Emily and propped her up, supporting her against her ample bosom.

'I've been there for a few births in my time,' Mrs Croydon said as she leaned over and wiped Emily's brow with a handkerchief.

Spinning wheels were abandoned as the other two workers gathered in. I rewashed my hands with lavender water and smiled at a young girl, who handed me a square of linen.

'For the babe,' she whispered, keeping her eye on Emily's contorted face.

'That's it, the head's out. One more push,' I said, guiding the baby into my hands as Emily arced her back and the rest of the baby slithered out.

'Oh,' was whispered, with a covering of mouths. The baby was tiny and blue. So still. I rubbed the little one with the linen, trying to get it moving. Without bothering about the blood, mess, cutting the cord, or worrying about the afterbirth, I focused on that baby. I puffed tiny puffs of air into its mouth and rubbed its chest as I had seen my mother do many times, but I had been called to do on few occasions, but the baby remained marble in my hands.

A hand touched my shoulder, and Mrs Croydon gently took the baby from me and handed it to Emily. 'There, Emily. Say goodbye to the little 'un.'

When tears trickled down the women's cheeks, my numbness broke, and torrents of tears bubbled over. With Emily taken care of by the other women, Mrs Croydon bustled me downstairs to the kitchen and plied me with tea. She waited until I had cleaned myself up and hovered when I gave a gentle hiccup.

'Now then, don't take it so hard, or you'll not be long in this business,' she said, handing me a biscuit.

'I am so sorry. I have made a complete spectacle of myself. I have birthed many babies, but still find this breaks my heart.'

I had not told Charity the toll it took on me, much preferring to share the lightness of handing a new little life to the waiting arms of an exhausted but relieved mother. I was unwilling to disappoint Charity, because we collaborated in our small midwifery practice.

The worry lines on Mrs Croydon's forehead deepened. 'Now, now. I've upset you. Emily has always spoken highly of you, as has any woman I have encountered who knows you. You must continue on.'

I gave a grateful smile. 'Thank you. I understand this is part of being a midwife, and there are many losses. You are right, I must not let this stop me when I can help so many women.'

Mrs Croydon's grey curls bobbed as she shook her head. 'Mercy, I was worried we had turned you from your calling. Ah, loss happens to us all, and it will always break our hearts, even if we don't tell a soul how much.'

I left the cottage far heavier of heart than I had arrived.

'Of course, and with now having lost your own baby ...' Charity's voice jolted me back to the present moment. 'First, we have to get you out of here.'

I nodded and slumped along with her. 'I'm aware there are worse asylums out there,' I said. 'If Spencer has gambled away all our funds, he will probably want me to be moved to one. Some wards here are quite lovely, and the intention is good, but so many women who are held here do not need to be. How wonderful it would be to have a *real* retreat for women who need care, especially those with a heavy heart, having lost a baby. Or a place of true refuge from the damages a man can inflict.'

'Now that would be wonderful,' Charity agreed. 'You just need to get out of here, get your money, and find a few wealthy patrons with a heart. I'm familiar with one.'

'Stop that mischief. I am sure Morgan ... Mr Ashton is quite done with this damsel in distress.' My heart ached to admit it. 'He will not want to spend his money on the likes of us.'

'No, he is not done with you at all. He is most sympathetic to the women in the asylum and feels many are not insane at all. It is a shame that you fell into Spencer's clutches first, as Mr Ashton is quite taken with you.'

I did not meet her eye, becoming rather interested in the pattern of peacocks on my porcelain teacup instead.

Charity was sensitive enough to change topics. 'Did you notice that the nurse who brought me in had the same accent as Spencer does when he is drunk?'

I scoured my mind. 'Why yes, he sounds like Nurse Talbot when he is drunk or angry. He told me once that his tutor came from Leeds, and he must have picked the accent up as a boy. It is strange that it comes and goes like that.'

As if her name had been spoken, Nurse Talbot came into the room, and we both sighed.

'I will visit as soon as I can, provided I am given permission, of course,' Charity promised. 'Do not let it all get you down. You will be free soon enough.'

I gave her a watery smile and bit my lip, unable to utter any words. It was all I could do to hold in my sobs as she left the room.

FORTY-THREE

Dearest Adeline,

I must apologise for being a poor protector in your hour of need. I should have taken you further afield than London. I am racked with many regrets. One of those is that I turned my back on you, which I now realise you have perceived as a rejection.

I assure you, I have always seen you as a beautiful woman and only did not want you to think I was taking advantage of your trust. I am not reckless, and considering your marriage and hardships, I chose to neglect my own requirements so I could be the supporter I believed you needed. I understand now it wasn't financial assistance you required. Neither was it appropriate for me to make you a project that would ease my conscience.

My father placed my mother in an asylum many years ago, and I never saw her again. I had accepted his reasoning and thought she was safe until my aunt told me otherwise at my father's funeral. I joined the Visiting Committee to reassure myself that my father was correct. Bloomfield House looked every inch the peaceful retreat for a troubled soul. Yet, once I learned of the operation you endured and how desperate your measures were to escape, I knew there were more shadows in the corners of the asylum than I had been privy to.

I will not treat you as a cause, but promise to continue working on yours. Yes, Dr Baker Brown will not be troubling another woman with his awful operation. Of course, it may take time to bring the other doctors who perform it to their senses. I will ask those opposed to continue their objections.

I intend to do as much as I can to secure your release. Not only because I'm unconvinced you should be in the asylum, but for my own selfish reasons. I long to spend more time with you. I am uncertain what the future holds for us, but for now I want you to hold on to hope.

Yours with much affection,

Morgan.

I folded the letter and tucked it into one of my novels, which Nurse Talbot had brought me from a small trunk packed and stored for me upon my admittance. She told me I had not been given any personal items upon my first admission in case they caused an adverse reaction. When I was re-admitted, they did not seem to be concerned about whether my belongings would evoke painful feelings.

They were right about personal items provoking a reaction. The sight of a cherished novel that I had once read in my comfortable sitting room evoked bittersweet emotions. I sniffed the vanilla scent of the pages, then placed it on a mostly bare shelf. Lost in a memory, I knocked the other novel from the shelf. It tumbled to the floor, and I groaned when I saw the spine crack. I picked up something that had fluttered to the floor from its pages, then groaned again.

Spencer had placed a wedding portrait of us within the pages. It did not invoke in me any tenderness. I wanted to poke the serene woman and tell her she'd made a terrible mistake. To run.

The chill of the cell penetrated my aching bones. My breath came in short gasps as the room seemed to shrink. With a hiccup,

I stumbled out, grateful that it was morning and I was able to make my way to the dayroom.

A new inmate sat hunched in a ball at the back of the room, still in her nightgown, scratching at her ratty hair. With a yelp, she slapped at her arms and legs. 'Get them off me! Get them off!'

Nurse Talbot raised an eyebrow. 'She imagines beetles consuming her skin.'

I grimaced. 'How horrendous.'

'She sees people too, she says. They haunt her day and night. Whisper terrible things in her ear. Dr Griffiths is at his wits' end, as he doesn't like to admit incurables too often. She's apparently done quite the tour of the different wards here.'

I was relieved that even though I was in this more challenging ward, I must still be considered curable.

Nurse Talbot responded to the Asylum Queen's bidding and presented herself for her daily audience. While she was distracted, I frowned at the slapping woman. Her face seemed a little familiar. Ah, I had helped at the birth one of her children ... Mrs Clarke.

She stopped slapping at that moment and stared at me with grey, vacant eyes long enough to draw a shudder.

'You! Come here,' she ordered.

I made a few tentative steps.

'I'm acquainted with you. Put my Beatrice to the breast when my Charles wanted me to use a wet nurse like the Queen.'

The Asylum Queen raised her head and nodded to us. 'Oh yes, breastfeeding is for the animals, so the wet nurse is the necessary cow.'

It was uncanny that the Asylum Queen spoke much like the authentic Queen Victoria.

'As a midwife,' I said, 'I assure you breastfeeding is a natural and hygienic thing to do. While it can indeed be done by a wet nurse, I consider it useful for proper bonding and even preventing the births of a quick succession of little ones.'

Considering their blank faces and Nurse Talbot's amused expression, I realised I was wasting my rational argument.

'Time for a song, Lady Adeline.' Obviously, the Asylum Queen did not want to engage in any further debate.

After I had finished my daily singing performance for the Asylum Queen, rather than clap, she frowned. Eliza had, as usual, dropped from a bizarre pose to a ball on the floor. I swear she was looking at me with more intelligence than blankness these days.

'Lady Adeline, it would please me if I ask more of you. Is it possible that you perform in plays?'

'Mmm. I could perform parts of *A Christmas Carol* if that would please Your Majesty.' It was the only play I was familiar with. She nodded, and I began, switching from role to role as best I could remember, and it wasn't long before all in the dayroom were gathered to watch.

My chest tightened as I remembered performing at the Christmas fundraiser. Words became lost to me. The room remained silent, all eyes on my burning cheeks, until the Queen clapped her gloved hands.

'That was wonderful. How I wish we could dance.'

On the other side of the window, a gust of wind blew leaves of muddy yellow and red. How would that be, to be free to dance in the autumn air? My morning panic resurfaced. How was it autumn once more?

I had been patient and done my time in the ward, but it had been months. Dr Butcher seemed to have forgotten all about me, leaving me with no treatment or hope.

A spark of mischief burned the melancholy away, and I stood in front of the Queen, miming a gentleman asking a lady to dance. I swapped sides and mimed having a fan fluttering at my face. I took on a feline grace as I flirted with the gentleman. I switched to the man's role and added a familiar military preciseness in my movement and clipped speech. Nurse Talbot put her hand to her mouth as she sniggered, and the Queen grinned. Mrs Clarke clapped and jumped up to join in, dancing with her own imaginary partner (or, in her case, perhaps one only we couldn't see), and Nellie moved back to the piano to play a jaunty tune.

We all collapsed into giggles at the end.

'Settle now, ladies,' Nurse Talbot said. I retreated to the corner and opened my novel. Eliza shuffled over to the wall, a small distance behind me, taking up a guard pose that would have done the Queen's Beefeaters proud.

Mrs Clarke also gravitated towards me and sat on the floor. 'Be good. Be good or be buried. Be good or be buried.'

I slammed my novel shut and leaned over to listen to her mutter.

'Be good or be buried,' she repeated as she slapped at her legs again.

'What do you mean Mrs Clarke? Amelia, what do you mean by that?' I asked. 'What ward did they bring you from?'

'The dungeon. This castle has a dungeon. Be good ... or be buried.' She would not speak another word, no matter how hard I prompted her, and I gave up with a heavy sigh.

Finally, she stopped slapping and looked up at me. 'Oh ... they bury the bad ones.'

I had given up on telling anyone about witnessing the man burying a woman in the fields. She knew.

FORTY-FOUR

I flicked through a couple of editions of *The London Illustrated News* that Nurse Talbot had given me. One was from last October. The only passage that caught my eye was among the birth statistics that I read from habit. One infant had died from swallowing a splinter of wood that had been in a little sugar, causing perforation of the bowels and peritonitis.

I swallowed a bubble of grief. What a terrible way for a baby to die. Such pain it would have been in. Though the article did not say, the implication was that the baby had been murdered. How sad that I had not been blessed with a live baby, when so many women who had them found them a burden. Maybe if I was living in a hovel surrounded by seven hungry mouths, my opinion would change.

Nurse Talbot wandered past, looking a tad bored. 'Anything to report?'

I looked at the edition. 'Old news in this one. It's from October.'

She shrugged. 'I don't have time to keep up with current events, so I don't mind if it's from last year.'

'Oh, this sounds interesting. From New York, no less. A Captain Wirtz is charged with conspiring with other southern leaders to murder federal prisoners. Charges of horrible cruelty have been made against him. He sent bloodhounds after them and injected them with poison. The gaol he kept them in was a hotbed of filth and pestilence, and not less than two-and-a-half thousand of them were sick with scurvy, gangrene, and other diseases,' I read to her.

Nurse Talbot, slightly pale, raised a hand. 'I am sorry I asked. Now I understand why I avoid it. Captain Wirtz sounds like some men who run the workhouse in Leeds. I'll leave you to it.'

I perused the latest edition of February and found my stomach gripping. How much my life had changed as these editions had rolled out. I resembled a child in an engraving picture I saw in the newspaper titled 'Caught Napping'. A boy lay with his head on a desk as a schoolmaster stood by with leathers ready to strike the oblivious boy from his slumber, while a group of others watched with expressions ranging from indifference to amusement or distaste. Like that boy, I felt as if I were sleeping, in a nightmare from which I could not wake. Never knowing what punishment these medical men would inflict next.

'We meet again, Adeline.'

I cringed at the familiar voice. Prudence laughed as she strode towards me. What on earth was she doing here in the refractory ward? She had come into the asylum voluntarily and left when she pleased, so there could be no reason to come into this ward under that arrangement. Although I had few comforts in this ward, I had at least believed myself to be safe from Prudence. As she approached, Eliza, in her usual spot near me, grunted strangely.

Prudence scanned Eliza and dismissed her with a flick of her head. 'They are getting stranger every time I come back.' Her eyes narrowed. 'You are becoming a very troublesome presence in my life. I came back to finish what I started.'

I gulped. I folded the papers, leaving black ink on my clammy hands.

'Since you were found with another man and all, I am sure Spencer could file for divorce.' Prudence sat on the wooden chair next to me and leaned in, so close I was sure she could hear my thudding heart. 'But I could save him the expense.'

I mustered up some courage and snorted. 'You realise he's already pursuing someone else. Someone with both wealth and title.'

'You're lying.' The pulse in her neck was beating fast.

'No, I am not. You saw him follow that man. He was collecting mud to use for blackmailing the father of a rather wealthy young lady. I know he is courting this lady and will marry her once he is free of me. No doubt he intends to drain her finances. Then I am quite sure she will be driven to hysteria. The poor man has no luck with women, it seems. We are all too delicate in nature.' I stood up as tall as I could and held my chin up.

She raised her head, a haughty smile upon her lips. She sauntered over to dazzle Nurse Talbot with her charm, and I released a breath.

'Oooh. You are in serious trouble with that one,' Nellie murmured to me. 'That look on her face. I've only seen it once before in here. Have you ever seen the caged woman?'

I frowned. 'What? A *caged* woman?' I had thought I knew enough of the dark recesses of Bloomfield.

Nellie nodded. 'Yes. When the asylum first opened, she came here in the carriage with me as one of the original inmates. Agnes. She'd caught her husband with another woman ... not unusual, but she didn't let on she knew. She made friends with the woman and all. Invited her over for dinner one night and when her guest asked what delicious meat they were eating, she said she'd slaughtered the husband and cooked him up. She'd fed the woman his, ah, man parts.'

I gagged.

Nellie gave a solemn nod. 'She should have been hanged, or at least put on the last transport to Australia, but she ended up here. Had a very wealthy father. She was so dangerous they ended up putting her in a cage. I only saw her once, when I collected the linen, but I've never forgotten the look she gave me when I told her I couldn't steal the key and let her out. Gave me the shivers.'

Nellie moved to the piano. 'Of course it's awful she's in a cage, but I can't help feeling safer for it. I would not want such a monster wandering among us.' She started playing a rather ominous tune.

How I wished Prudence was in a cage. As if she had heard me, she sidled up, ready to taunt me further. I made ready to retreat to my room.

'Where are you going, Mrs Parker? You really should remain comfortable, as you are going to be here for a *very, very* long time.' With a toss of her shiny curls, she made to grab my arm.

'Ow, let go!' Prudence shrieked.

Eliza held Prudence's outstretched arm tighter, her knuckles whitening as she held on. No matter how Prudence tugged, Eliza was immovable. As Nurse Talbot rushed to her aid, Eliza looked at me, and I swear she winked. She locked her teeth around Prudence's arm, and her shriek became a howl.

Nellie decided the unfolding drama needed a musical score, and the scene became a farce. She grinned at me as I escaped the room. I'll admit I was chuckling to myself as I thought of those teeth locked onto Prudence's delicate arm.

FORTY-FIVE

'She's going to kill me.'

Dr Butcher gave a solemn nod. 'Mmm. Nurse Talbot informed me of your fears. Miss Shaw should not even be in this ward, as she is quite stable after her treatment, but she assured me you needed some extra comfort.'

'Why would you give any credence to her words?' I squawked.

He shifted in his chair, a bloom of pink filling his cheeks. 'Now, now. We take it upon ourselves to ensure our patients receive the best treatment, and as you were close in previous times—'

'We were never close,' I protested. 'She is in cahoots with my husband, and they both want me dead so they can continue on their merry way.'

His office was far pokier and more cluttered than Dr Griffiths's. I ran a finger through the dust on the arm of my chair.

He shook his balding head. 'I would hardly think so. Miss Shaw is free to come and go, which I admit is not the experience of most women here, but she finds the asylum agreeable.' Of course. Prudence came from a wealthy family. Why else would she have such freedom in an asylum? He consulted his paperwork. 'I had thought you were settling into the ward very well, so was leaving treatment until it was necessary. Obviously, though, with this type of thinking …' He pushed his fingers together in a steeple on his desk as he peered at me through his spectacles.

'I assure you I am quite sane and am in imminent danger.' Even I heard the rise in my voice. I took a deep breath and mustered a calm demeanour. 'I am not hysterical.'

His brow puckered. 'Oh dear. I beg to differ. As you have already had one operation, I must look toward other measures.'

My frustration chilled to dread, and any protest froze on my lips. Expressing my fear of Prudence and begging for protection had only made matters worse.

'No, no. I promise I am fine. Perhaps I misunderstood Miss Shaw's words.' I swallowed the sour taste in my mouth.

He stood, and I made to leave the room.

'Just a minute, Mrs Parker. I think it best I gather the other doctors to consider your case.' He motioned to an attendant seated behind me, and her meaty fingers gripped me. 'Please escort Mrs Parker to the examination room, prepare her, and gather the other doctors.'

'As you know, Dr Griffiths and I are staunch supporters of Dr Baker Brown's procedure for curing hysteria, even though it is currently under debate in medical circles. As Mrs Parker has undertaken this operation and appears to be returning to her hysterical ways, we all need to examine her to discuss whether enough tissue was removed,' Dr Butcher said to the gathered doctors.

My face must have reflected my horror as I stepped back.

'Oh, it is all in the interest of medicine and offering the best care to women, Mrs Parker,' Dr Butcher said as he indicated for me to lie on the table in the centre of the room.

I licked my dry lips and dragged myself onto the table. There was no point in resisting. They had removed my dress and replaced it with a flimsy night shift. As I lay on the cold table under a sheet, tears trickled down my cheeks. Sickly sweet and stringent scents of carbolic soap, chloroform, and vinegar mingled in my nose, turning my already roiling stomach.

Dr Butcher wasted no time gathering the surrounding men. He asked me to bend my knees up and, whipping away the sheet, he left my intimate parts on chilly display. I focused on the wisp of a spider web flitting in the ceiling's corner. Not listening or looking at them, I did not respond when they poked about. I floated above them.

Through the fog, Dr Butcher instructed me to dress. I was left alone to do this while Nurse Talbot hovered just outside the door.

As I tugged on my clothes, Nurse Talbot's voice came to me through the door. 'I warned you it would be a bad idea to discuss Miss Shaw,' she said.

'Don't you think these doctors are more insane than any woman here? Why should they be considered the expert on—' I broke off as Dr Butcher came into the room.

Dr Butcher gave me a grin. His tobacco-stained teeth did not enhance his bloated face. 'There now, Mrs Parker. I think we may have decided upon a suitable treatment. I'll need to perform a further operation to my first—'

I flew at him, clawing at his beady pig eyes.

Before I could do any actual damage, Nurse Talbot's arms encircled me and she lifted me off the floor, holding me like a vice as I snarled and thrashed. No more civilised than an alley cat.

'Sedate her and take her to seclusion.'

When I regained consciousness hours later, perhaps I should have felt a sense of remorse. I had made things for myself much more difficult. Now I was trapped in a tiny cell of a room. I had heard they used restraint as an absolute last resort. It seemed I had reached that point. My hands and legs were shackled to the chair, and my head was held by some contraption that resembled a birdcage.

A pair of beady pig eyes watched me through the viewing hole. I struggled against the bindings. 'Ah, Mrs Parker. Perhaps this will make you think twice before attacking me again.'

Dr Butcher slammed the metal view cover shut.

I would ensure any further attack was worth the effort.

CHAPTER

FORTY-SIX

I had tugged and stretched my various restraints to no avail; my ankles and wrists were now chafed and aching. My shoulders knotted under the weight of the cage on my head. No matter how I shifted, I could not find a comfortable position, which I guessed was the point of my punishment. Dr Butcher wouldn't care that my bottom ached and the ridges of the wooden chair dug into my bony back.

While the room was gloomy and the chill seeped into my marrow, that was not the worst of it. No, worst of all was the pressure on my bladder. I held on for as long as I could, then released it with shame. Sitting in my urine and ... oh ... I had held it for so long. Faeces. I could not own that the stench was mine.

I had screamed until my throat was raw. Pleading for anyone to help. Begging for any liquid or food. I had cried until there were no more tears to be shed, not even a drizzle of snot to run from my nose.

Left with only the moan of the pathetic, I sat. When a nurse finally creaked open the door, I could not look her in the eye. I heard her retch. She placed a cup of tea near my feet. So tentative and watchful. A bowl of porridge was next.

'If you behave, I can take off the cage so you can eat.'

I nodded. The cage was carefully removed, as were my restraints on my wrists. I rolled and rubbed them. 'Thank you.'

She jumped when I spoke. I looked at her then. A young woman with dark pools for eyes.

'I won't bite,' I said as I clutched my cup of lukewarm tea. I had intended to sip it but gulped it down. 'Is there any more?'

She glanced to the hallway, debate in her eyes.

'Please.' I would ask, not beg.

I tipped the porridge down as best I could without a spoon while she got more tea. Some dribbled down my chin and onto the stained nightdress I was clad in. I wiped my mouth on its sleeve as she came back in. I gulped down the next cup, too.

'I suppose a bath and a change of clothes is out of the question.' While I would rather have had no witnesses to my state, I was keen for her to stay and talk to me.

The idea that I wasn't a dangerous lunatic about to attack her allowed a sliver of sympathy to show on her face. 'Not yet.'

'How long am I to be left like this?'

I shouldn't have asked.

She shrugged. 'I don't know. I'd best get on.'

I could not stop my breath hitching or the tears rolling as I complied with her orders to sit and allow myself to be tethered again.

Back to the strain and pain. It was not long before my lips were chapped and my throat parched yet again. How much time ticked by before this nurse returned, I did not know, but each time she did my heart leapt with hope. That I would be set free. No. The cage was replaced.

The relentless chair and cage dug in and bruised every part of me they touched. There was no way to relieve the pressure. At first, my mind was consumed with the sensations in my body. It was if I was on fire. Wanting to burst forth from my skin to escape its torture.

Then my mind floated. Wisps of memories had me crying for Ma, then Pa. Then Charity and Morgan. Anyone who had ever cared. The list was shorter than I would have liked. Then it locked onto Spencer ... to Dr Butcher. I cracked and withered. One kernel of life sprouted from the misery. Filled me with purpose and strength. Revenge.

I would live through this. I would get my revenge.

CHAPTER

FORTY-SEVEN

I was obviously not showing Dr Butcher enough remorse for my attack on his person. No longer in an isolated cell, I had been placed with the caged woman. Despite the chill, sweat dripped into my eyes as she growled at me and tried to grip my skirt. It was only just beyond her reach, and being still chained to a bolted chair, I could do little to protect myself.

In the room's gloom, I could barely see her features beyond matted hair and tatty clothes. I saw her skeletal fingers reach at me again and tried not to yelp. I blocked my nose to the stench. As my eyes adjusted, I saw the cage was only tall enough to allow her to sit and barely large enough for her to lie lengthwise on a threadbare mat without touching the overflowing pot in one corner. There was only enough space for someone to enter the cell and move around beyond our reach.

'Hello, Agnes,' I whispered. I hoped I had remembered her name correctly.

Agnes giggled. At first, I was reassured that she had responded well, then grew more disconcerted as the maniacal sound vibrated against the stone walls. She halted at the clink of keys in the door and withdrew into a corner of her cage.

Dr Butcher entered the room with the scent of peppermint oil about him, perhaps either to ease inflamed tissue or to mask the stench. Another man hesitated in the doorway and then, at Dr Butcher's impatient nod, stumbled in, putting his handkerchief to his nose. I squinted against the brightness of the lamp.

'Dr Granville, come now. I know this is most unpleasant. As you are to work with me in the more progressive surgeries required, you must see what we are up against. I know it seems abhorrent to place a woman in a cage.' He shrugged his shoulders. 'In some cases, the gentler treatment the Quakers promote is far from helpful. There is no hope for temperance, industry, self-control, or decorum in this patient at all.'

As if to agree, Agnes snarled at him. Dr Granville jumped, and Agnes cackled.

'Dr Butcher,' I began. 'I really don't think that it is appropriate I be left in such a device and in such company.' Oh, the struggle to speak a civilised sentence to a man I loathed.

He held up a hand. 'We are not here to address your treatment or concerns.' He turned back to his companion. 'As I was saying, Mrs Wainwright has no hope of any form of recovery, and her family has run out of funds to secure her place here, so they have given permission for whatever treatment we see fit.'

Dr Granville was a tall, slightly built man. Beside Dr Butcher's hulk, the man looked as if he would be whisked away in the slightest of breezes. He wiped sweat from his upper his lip as he watched Agnes bite her fingernails and spit the torn ends in his direction.

'She certainly seems chronically disordered,' Dr Granville stammered. 'Is she not far beyond hysterical? What was the cause? Suppressed menstruation? Disappointment in love? Reading sentimental romances or a chronic inflammation of the womb?'

Agnes paused mid-chew, eyed him, then pulled up her big toe to chew upon it, ensuring her soiled skirts were fully lifted.

'Oh my,' Dr Granville managed.

Dr Butcher kept a neutral face, but even in the dim light I saw his eyes glitter. 'Stop that at once, you wicked beast.' He put down the lamp, grabbed an iron bar near the door and banged it on the cage bars. Dr Granville and I seemed far more disturbed by the racket than Agnes was.

When he was finished, Dr Butcher dropped the bar and said, 'I believe the cause to be inflammation of the womb. Mrs Wainwright has already had the same operation as Mrs Parker here. It appears we need to extend the removal of further female parts – ovaries ... perhaps a full hysterectomy. That should cure her of her devious and conniving ways.'

I gasped and rattled the cage contraption on my head. Agnes started whistling as if she were a bird.

I glared at her. 'You would unsex her?'

With a small huff, Dr Butcher continued his conversation. 'Such women are capricious in their character. Mrs Wainwright murdered her poor husband in the most terrible manner, and by rights should be at rotting at Broadmoor. Mrs Parker attacked her husband and used devious means to escape the asylum. I can tolerate those whimsical in their conduct, whether they be frivolous or excitable, but obstinate and violent I will not.'

Dr Granville nodded. 'We must help these poor suffering women.'

'How is locking a woman in a cage, either upon her shoulders or around her body, to alleviate her suffering? To take a scalpel to her delicate parts ... remove the essence of her as a woman ... how does that cure a woman and make her more refined and less morally flawed?' I all but screamed the words.

Dr Butcher frowned. 'As you can see, Mrs Parker has become quite agitated and overly excited. You must remember the uterus is the controlling organ in the female body. It is wise, with women like these, to remove the seat of hysteria. I will speak with Dr Parker to see if he concurs with my thoughts.'

My body shook with agitation as they slammed the door behind them. I could not form any further words. Yes, I was agitated. I was furious that I was – like Agnes – to be little more than a science experiment. I would have given anything to return to a horrid wet-towel wrap for treatment now.

I ranted aloud about what I thought of Dr Butcher until I was exhausted.

As my head hung, Agnes clapped. 'I didn't do it,' she whispered. She started to keen and rock, curled in the corner of her cage.

Many days of listening to Agnes's growls and silent stares led me to believe my civility would soon vanish. As my filth grew and layered upon my body, I lost more of myself.

One day, desperate to distract myself from my bleak predicament I hummed then sang a lullaby. As Eliza had done in the refractory ward, Agnes slowly stopped rocking and unfolded her legs. Her face glistened with tears. 'My ma used to sing that cradle song to me.' Her words were husky and hesitant, as if she could barely remember how to form words.

'Mine too.' I sang it again as Agnes swayed.

'He was cruel, but I never killed him,' Agnes muttered.

'I believe you.'

She whacked the bars, and I shrank from her. She gave a shrug of apology. 'I could kill that Dr Butcher.'

I nodded, trying not to shiver at her stained-teeth grin. 'When a woman is mistreated by a man, such a desire hides deep within her soul's shadow.'

'My soul must be all shadow then,' Agnes whispered.

CHAPTER

FORTY-EIGHT

Even though I stood in my new room on the convalescent ward freshly washed before him, Dr Butcher curled his lip as if I were a disgusting farm pig swilling in its own filth. Perhaps a few hours ago, when first released from my restraints, I had indeed smelt like one. I was still stunned that they had left me with no option but to soil myself. It was beyond mortifying.

'Mrs Parker. I hope you now realise that we do not take violent outbursts here lightly, and I hope time in seclusion has tempered this violence.'

I lowered my eyes and kept my posture meek. 'Yes, sir.'

'I know the public considers the use of restraint to be beyond the pale, but I will do what it takes to protect myself, the staff, and other patients. Do you understand, Mrs Parker?' His commanding tone had me nodding my head before he had completed his sentence.

I looked behind him at Nurse Talbot, standing in the gallery beyond my door. Far from seeing a reflection of his stern expression, I noted a flicker of sympathy crossing her face.

'Yes, Dr Butcher. I understand.'

He gave a sigh. 'If only the operation had been successful. I hate to see women like you suffer from such outbursts. I have heard that you believe hysteria is not related to the female anatomy but originates in the brain, perhaps?'

I frowned. Was he considering that I might have a valid opinion? Was he reconsidering his earlier position that the womb was at fault and needed to be removed? 'Perhaps.'

He sniffed. 'I have reviewed my earlier thoughts, as I recently received some interesting correspondence. I have colleagues both in London and Switzerland who are considering this is a possibility. They propose that other mental disorders might also originate in the brain.'

Hope bubbled within me. 'So, there may be no need for further surgery ... the removal of the uterus or ovaries?' If I behaved well, he might not contact Spencer, and the rest of my body would remain intact.

'I will delay until I know more.' He regarded me as if I were some interesting bug that had landed on a bored schoolboy's desk. His studied expression increased the tension in my aching neck.

He pursed his lips. 'I suspect it will not be long before they trial their theories on some asylum inmates. If slicing into a scalp and using the metal shaft and spike of a trephine to poke into the brain's dura matter will ease such suffering, I am fully in support of such measures.'

He would *what*! Slice into my head and spike my brain? I gulped and leaned against the wall as my legs wobbled.

'I would require your husband's permission, of course. Now, I am sure we will not have to disturb him, will we? On the other hand, if you behave like a young lady, I can inform him of our success, and you can begin the road to recovery and hopefully release.'

Still reeling from his barely veiled threat of yet more horrifying surgery, I ignored his farewell. Why did I believe he expected me to lose my temper again?

Nurse Talbot's eyes were still wide. 'Don't let him frighten you. I am sure no one would return to such an ancient practice to rid a person of evil.'

She gripped my swaying body by the arm and lowered me to my mattress. She slipped a biscuit to me and locked the door behind her.

I lay my stiff bones down, my wrists and ankles still bearing the indents of my struggle against my restraints. Perhaps Dr Butcher was old-school and thought I had been taught a powerful lesson that would induce exemplary behaviour. But he could not see beyond the docile cow eyes, the hung head, and slumped shoulders. Deep within was a woman not beaten into submission.

Once I had released some kinks in my body, the restless urge to move about after being held in position for so long had me up and pacing. Eventually, I leaned against the door, its bolts digging into my back. I frowned as the scent of jasmine wafted through the viewing hole.

'How wonderful to have you back. I think Dr Parker would be most interested in curing his poor, violent wife of her ills with such an operation. I must let him know.'

I hit the solid oak door with my hand, but Prudence had moved on, her cackle echoing down the hallway. I slid down the door, curled over, and rocked in place. My throat ached, and I finally released my tears. Maybe it would have been better if Nurse Talbot had not caught me tumbling down the stairs.

I needed to do things differently. Stop behaving like some demented, independent bluestocking and be more like the delicate, demure woman who posed no threat. Would they believe I could be such a creature?

FORTY-NINE

Even though there was a bite in the air that hinted of snow, I was content to follow Nurse Talbot's suggestion of a brisk walk in the airing court on the new tarred track (well, new to me since my time in seclusion). I settled on a seat in a quiet corner and closed my eyes to the weak sun above.

'Morning, Adeline.'

I blinked hard to ensure I had not drifted into a dream. Morgan's handsome face remained before me. 'Morgan! You have no idea how happy I am to see you.'

Morgan gave me a warm smile. 'It is wonderful to see you, too.' He sat beside me. 'I have had a devil of a time trying to get permission to speak to you. Nurse Talbot's was the only sympathetic ear I could bend, and no doubt she is risking much in permitting this meeting.' He scanned the surrounding yard. 'While I do not want to raise the ire of Matron Wright, I needed to see all was well with you. We don't have long.'

I gave a dry laugh. 'I am alive. As for well ...'

He dropped his head. 'I know it has been months, but please don't lose heart. I am doing as much as I can to secure your release.'

A glossy black crow hopped along the brick wall, watching us with avid interest.

I blinked hard. 'I have been enough bother to you.'

He tapped his gloved fingers on his knees. 'It is no bother. I may have hidden my fondness for you, as I did not want you to think ...'

'Fondness?' I wanted to be very clear where my heart stood. My elation at seeing Morgan again, the tingling within me and the desire to share every part of me with him indicated a sentiment much more powerful than the lukewarm touch of fondness.

He cleared his throat and tipped my chin up. 'More than fondness. Love, then.'

He leaned forward and gave me the most tender of kisses.

I answered hungrily.

Despite my predicament, a sense of lightness came over me, something I hadn't experienced in months. When we parted breathlessly, I said, 'I return your affections.'

'I wish we had longer together.'

I clenched my hands as he gave me another quick kiss, then left me.

I watched the crow creep closer. 'I wish I had wings like you.'

The crow bobbed its head from side to side, its muddy brown eyes unblinking. It seemed to agree that wings were very much needed, and with a coarse caw, flew off.

Thoughts swirled in my head. Should I have told Morgan about my time in seclusion, the horror of the threats made by Dr Butcher, my fears of Prudence? No. He said he was acting on my behalf. I would have to be patient and hope that no harm would come to me. If it did, I knew Morgan would turn every stone to uncover the truth.

I touched a glove to my chapped lips. How different this was to my previous limited experience of men. I had scoffed at women who believed in love and romance over practicality. I had considered *not* getting married, since I could support myself as a midwife; I had done it only to please Papa, who was well aware that tides could turn and wanted me to be secure. But he was wrong; Spencer had left me far from secure.

What if I was mistaken about Morgan? He would face many challenges in choosing to love me. If I were free, I would be no longer content to be the London wife; I wanted to continue to help women in whatever manner I could. Nor would I be silenced about my views or dismissed any longer.

However, I experienced a greater sense of being seen and heard in Morgan's presence than I had with anyone else besides Charity, and, more recently, Edna. Although I had more than enough funds to support myself, it was not an independent life I craved. I wanted to share it with someone who cared deeply for me, and who I cared for in return. I had no doubt of my desire for Morgan. I did not know if my mutilation would leave me too sullied to contemplate a loving act with him (although I ached at the thought). If he linked his life to mine, his social status would drop to who knows what level.

I laughed at myself. Did I really believe it would be simple? To leave this asylum, be free of Spencer and live a happy life? I wiggled my numb toes and began walking back to the dayroom. Even if it was unlikely, that was the vision of the future to which I was clinging. It was far more hopeful than the nightmares I suffered most nights.

I was more than pleased to be back in the convalescent ward. They needed to believe I had learned my lesson and was a changed woman. Even though Nurse Talbot could not risk any further visits from Morgan, she informed me he had other wealthy friends who took an interest in conditions at the asylum and in my welfare. Even though their influence did not seem to extend to my release, I took their interest as a positive sign.

'When you are done sweeping the floor, Matron wants you to polish the door plaques and brass handles. Then you may continue reading your novel in the dayroom, Mrs Parker,' Nurse Talbot said, then coughed violently into her handkerchief.

I slammed my novel shut and stood up from the stair I'd been sitting on. Edna stopped sweeping the hallway and stepped back. Most of the staff and patients had been taken ill with influenza.

'Mrs Parker was keeping me entertained while I swept. She's not feeling the best herself,' Edna said, winking at me. I gave few dry coughs for good measure.

'Perhaps a cup of tea would do you the world of good, Nurse Talbot,' I suggested.

She blew her reddened nose and sighed. 'I would love one, but I can't leave you.'

'I can sweep and polish without getting into mischief,' Edna said, brushing with extra zeal.

I took the jar of brass-polishing paste from the cleaning bucket and nodded. 'I'm well enough to polish. We'll be done in no time.'

She gave each of us a thoughtful look. 'I won't be long.'

Edna gave a cheerful wave, then kept sweeping. I started on the super's plaque, wrinkling my nose at the scent of turpentine. When I touched the doorknob, the door opened. I couldn't resist; I stepped inside. Edna had told me that Olivia had not returned from whatever ward she was supposed to be recovering in. It had been months.

Dr Bugwell's room was gloomy but as orderly as he was. I set down the piece of leather and jar of paste. I perused the shelf of medical tomes, running my fingers along their spines. One lay open upon his desk. I flicked the pages and noted I had landed on instructions for performing a castration. From the handwritten notes, it appeared that mutilating women was not enough to satisfy him. He was considering castration as an option for men being incarcerated for gross indecency. I shuddered at the thought.

'What are you up to?'

My heart leapt. I looked up into Edna's sparkling eyes. She put the broom by the door, glanced over the pages I had been reading, then ripped a page from the book and pocketed it, ignoring my gasp. She flicked a few pages forward to hide the tear. 'I like to collect useful information.'

'I hardly think ...' I began as she moved to the casebook cabinet and tested the drawer. It was unlocked. What would *my* book say? Would I be able to find where Olivia was?

'Now, there's plenty of useful information in here.' She raised an eyebrow at me, and I nodded. I couldn't resist.

'I'll get back to it, then.'

My fingers fumbled, and I bit my lip as I flicked through the books. A clock on the mantel ticked, each tick louder than the last.

I could not find Olivia's casebook, but I found mine. I dug it out and flipped it open on the desk. I scanned the notes that contained a physical description, details of my 'hysteria' and treatments given. In neat copperplate, it stated that my diminished reproductive capabilities were because of excessive mental stimulation. Spencer had told them of my enjoyment of reading and discussing medical journal contents. That while he had encouraged me to renounce all professional ambitions and was opposed to my intellectual pursuits, in his eyes his wife had not adapted well to domestic life and did not have domination over her emotions.

My fingers twitched as I flicked to the next page. I ignored the pounding in my ears and read on, gasping as I came to the last few words. He was going to let them do whatever they deemed suitable. I replaced the casebook.

'Oh, Uncle Cecil. I thought you were too ill to come in.' I jolted at the sound of Nurse Talbot's voice coming from the hallway.

'Nurse Talbot,' a voice snapped sternly, 'you know our family connection is not to be spoken of.'

'Of course, Mr Bugwell, I am so sorry! Miss Hall's mother has written again, no doubt prompted by her son, who used to visit. I have searched—'

'Nurse Talbot. Please leave such business to me. Mrs Hall does not need to be corresponding with you personally, so redirect her to the appropriate channels. Miss Hall is receiving special treatment, and it is of no concern to you on the convalescent ward.'

I slid the drawer shut and tiptoed to retrieve the polishing paste and leather strip. I peeked from the doorway. They were at the end of the hallway, and he had his back to me.

'In my haste to leave yesterday,' the superintendent was saying, 'I was not sure I locked everything, so I just came to check. But while I have you here, there is something I want to discuss. I know you have developed a soft spot for Mrs Parker. It has not escaped my notice how much she resembles Molly. For this reason, out of compassion I have indulged you, but I can't keep moving you around to her ward every time she moves. Although, with any luck she will be cured and leave us.'

'How will that happen? I do not think the last operation—'

'Now, you will be pleased to know that her husband is so concerned for her recovery that he has given permission for the most progressive of surgeries. Dr Parker will meet with me next week to discuss the detail of the operation. As he will stay nearby for a few days after the Lunatics' Ball, he has requested to observe the procedure and, given his scientific interest, I have agreed. The ball will display those we have operated on, so our benefactors can see for themselves the wonderful work we are doing here and allow the program to expand. A wonderful way to secure funds for the New Year.'

I heard the intake of her breath, which led to a coughing fit.

'Oh dear. You must take your bed. Come now.'

I slipped out of the room and skittered down the hallway behind Edna.

'I will once I've escorted the women to the dayroom,' Nurse Talbot said.

Mr Bugwell turned. 'Oh, I didn't realise. Fine, then.' He gave a quick nod and, noting that his door was indeed unlocked, went into his office.

Nurse Talbot raised an eyebrow at me.

'Yes, I heard everything.'

Edna heard the tremor in my voice and placed a hand on my shoulder.

I told her what I had learned. 'What am I going to do? Spencer has really got me this time.'

Nurse Talbot looked as wretched as I felt. 'When he comes, we must convince him not to go ahead with it.'

The flutter of hope at her kind use of the word 'we' soon dissipated. 'He has no heart and no use for me,' I whispered.

'Then we will have to find you a way out of here. I will not be party to what would surely maim or kill you.'

Despite my pounding heart, I sensed the steady hold of her promise. I had escaped once; I could do it again.

'Time to go, ladies.' Nurse Talbot said as she turned back to the dayroom.

Edna passed me the torn page as we walked. 'I think this would be too good for your husband.'

Nurse Talbot had looked back just as I took the sheet and stopped in her stride, almost causing me to collide into her.

'What is that?' Nurse Talbot asked.

I showed her the page bearing a detailed description of castration. 'Edna thinks Spencer deserves some treatment of his own.'

Edna cackled. 'If only ...'

'Oh, you are making my head ache even more. No more of that nonsense.' Nurse Talbot picked up the novel I had left on the stair and handed it to me. Something fluttered from it and landed at her feet. 'Your wedding portrait.'

I went to take it from her, but her hand held it tight. 'Nurse Talbot?'

'Is this your husband?'

I frowned at her tone. 'Yes, that's Spencer.'

She shook her head. 'That man is not Dr Spencer Parker.'

'What?' Edna and I said in unison.

She released the portrait and looked me in the eye. 'That is the man who hurt my sister at the workhouse infirmary in Leeds. Dr Leycroft.'

My mind whirled as her eyes darkened.

She drew herself up to her full, imposing height. 'He will pay for what he did.'

As we walked across the foyer, dappled with colour from the stained glass in the afternoon sun, I saw our lengthened shadows merge. Spencer, or whoever he was, would regret ever sending me to Bloomfield House.

CHAPTER

FIFTY-ONE

I had followed Nurse Talbot's midnight bidding, fully expecting to be asked to assist with another birth. She did not guide me to the infirmary, though. We seemed to take many twists and turns, her with determined strides. Me scuttling along as fast as I could. I swore I could smell rosewater and checked behind me for Edna.

When we arrived at the surgery, I blinked in confusion. There was no woman groaning and writhing on the floor in need of aid. There was, however, an unconscious man lying naked on the table.

I stepped closer to examine him in the dim lamplight, then gasped. 'What have you done to Spencer?'

Nurse Talbot ignored me and rattled around, gathering instruments. She placed a scalpel in my hand. 'I know you studied that torn-out page. He deserves this, and only you can do it.'

I choked. 'You want me to castrate him?'

'Of course. Now, get on or he will wake up.'

I looked from her granite features to the blade in my hand. Yes, he deserved this.

My fingers trembled as I poked the scalpel's point into Spencer's shrivelled scrotum. His fluttering eyes popped wide open.

242

'Ah. Good evening, Spencer.' He took in the dingy surrounds of the surgery and the gleam of the scalpel in the lamplight. We were alone; Nurse Talbot had slipped out to guard the door.

'Don't move. I'd hate for this thing to slip.'

He gasped. 'What are you doing? Is that you, Adeline?'

Despite my instruction, he wrestled with the straps at his arms and legs. I poked a little further, and he groaned.

'I warned you to stay still. I will not stand for you ruining my life. You will arrange for my release, or I promise I will escape and kill you. Perhaps, after I do this, you will wish I had.'

'I promise I will get you out. Let me go, please, Adeline. I'm begging you.' He choked on the last words as a tear dribbled down to his ear.

I sighed, then remembered not to breathe in too deeply, as the sweet stench of chloroform hung in the musty air. I waited for my inner debate to resolve. Should I finally carry through my fantasised revenge or leave it at scaring him? Where was the niggle of doubt a kind-hearted woman should have?

No, not an ounce of kindness left.

'Don't hurt me. I will leave you alone,' he repeated. 'I will leave the country. I will—'

I poured more chloroform onto a cloth as I held my breath. Then I placed it on his face, hoping I was using the correct amount. My heart had softened enough to perform this punishment without his screams of agony.

Once his head lolled to one side and his breathing was steady, I adjusted the lamps and began. A deft slice here, a tug there. I mopped up the blood and continued.

Plop. His useless organ was dumped into a bowl. I wiped the sweat from my brow, blinking against the sting in my eyes, and finished. There, the man was now un-manned.

I stitched, gauzed, and bandaged. Done.

Spencer lay there, oblivious to my wickedness. I waited for the spike of guilt ... of any feeling.

Only numbness.

I washed my hands in lavender water and removed my blood-splattered apron.

The door squeaked open, and Nurse Talbot, who had been guarding the door, nodded in satisfaction. She moved aside as Edna made her way in.

'Nurse Talbot caught me outside following you,' Edna said. 'She said you were helping her with ... who is that? Not your husband, is it? What did you do?'

I gave Spencer's arm a pat. 'Just something many wives would love to do to those husbands dipping their wicks too often in the pleasure gardens. When he wakes, I will tell him he endured only a harmless little operation.'

Edna took in the unconscious body and touched his face. 'Are you sure he's alive?'

'Of course.' I quickly checked his breath with my hand.

Peering into the bowl, she recoiled. 'Is that ... is that his ...?'

I nodded.

Edna's shoulders shuddered. Had I lost a loyal friend with one slice of a scalpel?

I frowned as a strangled muffle came from her.

She was giggling. 'This is terrible. You are an evil woman ... but oh, how many men deserve this? Spencer most certainly. I cannot believe that you went through with it.'

She poked at his penis, then picked up the whole lot, the weight of the testicles threatening to tear the thread of skin and drop with a mess on the floor. 'Are you sure this is not his brain? As he sure liked to think with it.'

'Ew. Put that down.' My stomach roiled as the reality set in.

Even Nurse Talbot turned away.

Edna waggled the penis at me.

'Stop that, Edna.' I gazed down at Spencer. 'I don't think he is going to take this very well. He may retaliate.'

Edna shook her head. 'No. I'm sure he'll be terrified of what you can do with a sharp implement.'

I should have been mortified, caught at my worst. Instead, I saw the sparkle in her eye, and we laughed. Spencer knew me better than I thought. It appears I was indeed a lunatic, after all.

'Is it done?' Nurse Talbot's question stirred me from my vivid flight of fancy. The images had been so detailed and real that I needed to gather my bearings. A mixture of chloroform and the woody scent of Spencer's hair filled the air. The small windows set high in the walls rattled as the wind and rain buffeted against them. My fingers, numb with cold, were almost insensitive to the scalpel's heft. I looked down at Spencer. I had inflicted no harm, and his eyes remained closed; his head lolled to one side.

I shook my head and placed the scalpel down. 'I can't go through with it.'

She frowned.

'If I did what was done to me, then my soul would be as stained as his. He would not understand the message. No doubt he would be so livid he would aim to destroy many more women than he already has. I cannot be as cruel as the men here.' I placed a sheet over Spencer. 'I know you went to a lot of trouble for us to exact revenge, but my heart is not in it.'

For a moment, her fingers trembled. Would she hack into his nether regions herself? 'Nurse Talbot?'

As if shaking off evil thoughts, she trembled bodily, then slowly nodded. 'You are right. I lost my head. If we move him to the infirmary, he will think he drank too much whiskey with Mr Bugwell and had a terrible dream. I hope I was not too enthusiastic with the sleeping draught.'

We dressed him with much effort and dumped him into Isaac's wheelchair. After securing him in a bed, I returned to my ward.

'We will not speak of this again,' I reassured her.

Spencer would wake with a pounding head and a birdseed mouth. No idea how fortunate he was to greet the morning with his manhood intact. I hoped my soul shone fractionally brighter for having triumphed in the face of such a challenge.

FIFTY-TWO

I stood just outside of the infirmary door, unsure it was a wise thing to do. I wanted to know if Spencer had any recollection of the night before or what had almost become of him.

'Doctor Parker, I hope this will not become a habit. These beds are needed for our patients,' Matron Wright admonished.

'Though I have no memory of how I came to be in your infirmary, I apologise.'

'Fine. I'll let Dr Butcher know you are ready to meet with him once you are dressed.'

I backed into the shadows as Matron Wright left the room and headed down the corridor. All was well.

I slipped into the infirmary. Spencer was sitting on a bed, propped up with pillows, drinking from a cup of a tea. His eyes widened as he saw me come closer. He put the cup on a set of drawers next to the bed, sloshing tea into the saucer.

'If you think I am letting you out of here, you are sorely mistaken.' Spencer's eyes glittered with hate. 'I remember very well how you threatened me last night, and I have a slight nick on the skin in a sensitive place to tell me that what I had initially thought was a nightmare, was, in fact real.'

I did not remember drawing any blood with my scalpel. Though my throat ran dry, I stood firm. 'It seems my mercy was wasted.'

He shook his head. 'You would never have gone through with it. You are far too soft.'

Prudence stepped into the infirmary and stood beside me. 'Yes, she is too kind-hearted. It is time you got her out of our way.'

Spencer's face drained of colour as she sashayed to his side. 'What are you doing here?'

'Helping you be rid of her, of course.' She frowned as he refused to touch her hand.

His mouth opened and closed a few times, leaving me confused. Was he worried I knew of his plot and Prudence's role in it?

'As I have told you *many* times, it does not matter how much you follow me, beg me, or interfere with my life. I will not marry you! This has got to stop. This is exactly where you belong, you lunatic. I will ensure *both* of you are dealt with.' He scrambled from the bed and shoved her away. He then stalked out of the room, throwing a fearful glance over his shoulder as he turned the corner.

Prudence folded her arms and leaned against the wall. 'Mmm. He really is so confused. Of course, we will be together once you are dead.'

I could barely comprehend her words.

Spencer had *not* sent Prudence to kill me.

She pursed her pretty lips. 'We will make quite the team. I will continue to recommend him to those in our circle, and he will continue to prescribe cocoa as a soothing tonic before bedtime for so many of his elderly patients.' She gave a sly grin. 'I know so many things about so many people ... why else would I have let him go after the likes of you?'

'My family is not wealthy.'

She shook her head. 'So you say.'

I did not know what else to say. I wanted to ask her more, but was not sure I could believe anything from her spiteful mouth. She laughed and left me none the wiser.

When I told Edna of the encounter, she was horrified. 'We need to get you out of harm's way.'

'I don't want to risk getting anyone else into trouble. I'll find a way.' My outward confidence far surpassed my inward state. My mind was a swirl of ideas quickly dismissed as I considered the obstacles. I could not form a plan that guaranteed me freedom.

'Thinking like that will get you nowhere. This is a time to lean on others. Those that love you will accept the risk.'

I could no longer see Edna's sweet face.

'Come, wipe those tears. My perspective on the matter might have been more positive if he were a eunuch; at least then you'd have gotten your revenge.'

I wiped my tears and shrugged. 'I think revenge can make for a satisfying fantasy. In reality, what would it have changed? I would still be mutilated, be trapped here and worse ... have lost something vital.'

Edna grumbled as we walked to breakfast. 'So would he. What's so vital for you?'

'My heart? My soul? I don't think I could have lived with myself if I had done it.' I sat down at our table with no appetite at all.

Edna snorted. 'I guess.' She sat across from me. 'Do not be afraid of your own shadows, Adeline. Within our darkness is also our gold.'

I had no idea what she meant. Even holding the scalpel at Spencer, I had sensed the flicker of darkness within me. It wanted to consume me. Even in threatening to take his precious testicles, I had stirred something even deeper in Spencer: the wrath of a truly wicked man.

FIFTY-THREE

'Wake up, Addie. You're having a nightmare.'

Edna's gentle voice and touch penetrated, and I awoke, dripping in sweat. Wisps of the dream remained, and I ran a hand over my scalp. No, I was not once again encased in Dr Butcher's birdcage contraption with its sharp, metal spikes piercing my skull until I drowned in rivulets of blood. No, Olivia was not with me, bashing against some kind of coffin.

'Oh, it was terrifying,' I admitted. 'With the likes of Dr Butcher here, it could even come true.'

At the wobble in my voice, Edna held me in her bony arms. 'There, there, child. I do not want to raise your hopes, but I can contact Lily if there is a dire need, and I believed there is. She could contact Mr Ashton and warn him of Dr Parker's plans. Between us all, I believe he can be stopped.'

I took a breath to slow the thudding of my heart. 'We must find Olivia.'

Even though Edna was concerned for my welfare, I was more determined to worry about Olivia's. We developed an avid interest in ensuring the area near the medical men's offices was kept spotless. I would never have thought myself capable of stooping to blackmail, but I was desperate. Nurse Talbot willingly assisted. Locked offices became strangely unlocked.

We had dug about Mr Bugwell, and Dr Griffiths's offices and found nothing on Olivia.

'Her casebook must be with Dr Butcher then,' I said.

His office was in far more disarray than the other men's. I shivered at the curios he had collected in a cabinet near the window. Insects trapped in amber, tiny skeletons, and ... surely, that was not a shrunken head. I turned back to rummaging through the casebooks on his desk.

Edna threw her hands up. 'Nothing. Where is her casebook?'

I sighed and kicked a panel in the wall. 'We've got to help her.'

Edna pointed to the panel. 'Now we're for it. You've ruined the wall.'

I noticed the wood had come away and stooped to shove it back into place. 'There's a cavity here!'

We tugged the veneer away and pulled out the contents. Casebooks. As we read, Edna gasped. 'There is a whole hidden ward of "failed" operations. Some women were my friends. I stupidly believed the staff when they said they had died or left the asylum cured. I will not let you become one of them,' Edna said, her voice rising in determination.

'What do you think we can do?' I asked, ducking behind the desk as footsteps clonked past. I picked up the last couple of books. Olivia's was one.

Edna crouched down next to me. 'I don't know.'

My brain began whirring. 'If we can get into that ward, we will get Oliva out. You know, I think the ball could be a genuine revelation of the wonders of Bloomfield.'

Edna gave my hand a squeeze. 'That is a wonderful idea. It might put a stop to Dr Butcher's experiments. That bastard of a husband of yours. Maybe you should have cut them off when you had the chance.'

We sat tearing strips of newspaper under Matron Wright's watchful eye. I sensed she was waiting for any chance to send me back to the refractory ward. I had created an enemy when I used my talent to escape and spoiled her plan to trumpet the Christmas Play as a great success under her direction.

Edna waited until she was distracted by tea and biscuits. 'Look, the Great Wizard of the North is performing in London. His show sounds intriguing. Lily saw him years ago and wrote to me about it. I could almost believe in magic from what she described. Lily befriended his daughter, Alice, in recent years. She performs as Flora in his shows. She frustrates Lily to no end, as she will not reveal any secrets.'

I glanced at the article. 'Wouldn't it be wonderful if he could come here and use magic to make me disappear? Far better than Dr Butcher's way.'

I expected her to offer a grimace of sympathy. Instead, her eyes lit up.

She clapped. 'That's it! That can be the theme of the ball. The Magic of Healing. I know Matron will think this is a wonderful idea. I have heard her talking with Nurse Talbot about some shows she has seen at The Egyptian Hall. She knows people will flock to a ball with a magic show. They will be so distracted, you could disappear during it.'

I was desperate. 'That might work.'

Edna stuffed the article in her pocket. 'We can only ask and hope for the best.'

I followed Edna into the deserted music room as she requested. I had not been in the room since my last-ever conversation with Leonora, and I'll admit I gave the room a nervous sweep, as if I might see a glimmer of her ghost at the harp.

Edna waved a letter at me. 'You don't need to be worried about the dead. It's the living that are of more concern.'

I could not read her expression. Was it a mix of sympathy and rage?

'All is set for the performance' Edna seemed far from content that her plans were coming together.

I rubbed my chilled hands together. 'What's the matter? Why do I need to be concerned about the living?' I asked.

She pulled a letter from her apron. 'I asked Lily to keep an eye on your Dr Parker. She has discovered some disturbing news. He has secured funds from a widow to proceed with a divorce.'

My brain froze as if she was speaking in tongues. A divorce? I did not know of any person who was divorced. Slowly, my thoughts caught up. Prudence had not been lying when she mentioned Spencer's intentions to divorce.

'Why would he do that? Does that mean he might not bother with the operation? You'd think he wouldn't go to the trouble of getting a divorce if he thought I might die here.' As her eyes darkened, I could see Edna did not share my flicker of hope.

She folded the letter. 'No, I think this just means he is ensuring he is free to pursue someone else if you survive. That way, no matter what damage is done, he is not responsible for your upkeep here. So, if you are damaged beyond repair rather than conveniently dead, you would end up at the mercy of the public asylums. Lily heard whispers in the wind that he is escorting Lady Elizabeth Telford to the ball, supposedly as a potential patron of the asylum and its good works.'

My legs folded and Edna guided me onto a sofa in the corner. It smelt slightly mouldy with disuse.

'He will tell me of the divorce at the ball and flaunt his new conquest in my face, while ensuring I know of the impending operation.' I closed my arms around my stomach. 'Even if we find the ward of broken women and display them, he has won.'

With a creak of her bones, Edna knelt on the rug in front of me and took my hands. 'No. If he is divorcing you, you will be free of him. Once you escape, Mr Ashton will be waiting. He will not desert you in your hour of need.'

'It is kind of him, but I do not wish to be a burden to anyone.' I swallowed hard. Even if I managed to escape and hide for two weeks, my future looked as bleak as the clouds scudding across the sky outside.

She released my hands, and with a groan settled next to me on the pale pink sofa. 'If you will not let the man who truly loves you help you, then there is no hope.'

Heat radiated through my chest.

'I know you love him too, so let's forget the "burden" nonsense and focus on our plan. Nurse Talbot has been searching and believes that the women are in a basement ward that Mr Bugwell long ago told her was abandoned because of its poor ventilation and only used for storage. Yet only this morning she observed nurses going to and from the area. When she questioned them, their explanations for being there were rather suspicious.'

My thoughts of Morgan were quickly dashed by the horror of knowing that Olivia and other poor women who had endured goodness only knows what were being abandoned or further experimented upon beneath our very feet.

'Even if my head were not on the chopping block, I could not leave these women to suffer. We must get Olivia out.' I rubbed my cheeks to release the tension from my clenched jaw. 'Can Nurse Talbot gain access to the basement ward?'

Edna nodded. 'She knows where Mr Bugwell has a copy of every asylum key. We will take Olivia out and hide her, then reveal the others at the ball and speak of what horrors have been inflicted upon them. How will we move them all to the ball?'

I smiled. 'Tell Lily to ask Mr Walsh for more wheelchairs. Nurse Talbot will persuade Mr Bugwell that we will gather the most able to demonstrate how useful the self-propelled chairs are, and how they enable nurses more time to assist those unable to manage. They can be wheeled in, covered in cloaks as if they are part of the magic show. Agnes can be taken in, cage and all. I hate to think of her trapped like an animal. What we reveal will be the reality behind the illusion. Not the magic of healing at all.'

'What a grand idea.' Edna bustled from the room, muttering to herself. I rubbed my stomach, hoping to soothe the jitters below. Whether I was ready, the wheels were in motion. If this plan failed, my brain would be pierced with a metal rod. Perhaps I would die; perhaps I would be left a drooling imbecile.

My thoughts turned to Spencer. How could he ... there were too many evil acts to list. My fingers trembled. If I had known he was going to divorce me, flaunt his new conquest in public and leave me to my surgical fate, would I have been so willing to put aside the scalpel? The stone of regret weighed heavy. I dumped it into the well to land on the many others already there. No, I would not draw from the poisoned well of hate.

CHAPTER

FIFTY-FOUR

I held my breath as Nurse Talbot turned the key and we entered the basement ward. My eyes watered at the stench that assailed us. I coughed and gagged while Nurse Talbot put a handkerchief doused in peppermint oil to her nose. I took another that she offered with gratitude. Now I could stand to look around.

It was as gloomy as my cell in seclusion, but much colder. There were ten occupied beds. I scanned the room for Olivia. Some women lay as still as a corpse, with matted hair and frozen features. I peered closer to see if their chests were moving. The slightest rise told me they were. When one of the women's eyes popped open and she groaned, I crashed back into the wall. A scream caught in my throat.

A woman with dirty blonde hair cackled, reminding me of Agnes. She was strapped to her bedstead; dried blood caked her cheek.

Nurse Talbot ignored her grunts of protest as she removed the woman's bonnet. 'Oh.'

I crept forward. 'Is that ...?'

Nurse Talbot removed a hand from her mouth. 'Yes, it's her brain.'

With a grimace, I scratched my head. How could this woman be alive with part of her skull missing, her doughy wet brain exposed like that?

'I read their casebooks ... I did not believe Dr Butcher would do such a thing.' She pointed to the huddled woman next to her.

'He has removed some of their ovaries to cure them of hysteria, as Dr Baker Brown suggested. I am not sure any will recover.'

Nurse Talbot's face seemed to age before me. 'This is far worse than I had anticipated. Some of these women were taken from paupers' asylums under the promise of receiving the latest cures. It is obvious Dr Butcher is using them to trial his treatments before he enacts them on the wealthier patients. I have no doubt those hidden casebooks will be destroyed upon their deaths.'

My shock at the state of these women mutated into a wordless mass of larvae.

I pointed to an obese woman strapped to a strange-looking chair suspended from a frame. 'What is that?'

Nurse Talbot frowned. 'I think that's a swinging chair. I cannot fathom why it would be here at all. Swinging chairs were used last century to rotate unruly patients. It is hardly progressive. How terrible to leave her strapped to it.'

My stomach grew leaden as we explored further. In the far corner, an odour grew stronger than even the stench of unwashed bodies, urine, and faeces. I saw a box with slatted sides, much like a child's crib. I peered through the slatted lid. Milky eyes stared back at me.

'Oh Lord, it's Olivia.' I grabbed Nurse Talbot's arm. 'Do you have the key?'

With fumbling fingers, she tried all the keys on her ring. The last one released the spring lock. The lid was not much above Olivia's head; the crib was like a coffin, with no room for her to turn over – and a coffin it had become.

'She's dead,' Nurse Talbot said.

My vision clouded.

'Adeline?' I could hear my name coming from somewhere so far away.

CHAPTER

FIFTY-FIVE

D espite my frail state, I tried my utmost to clean the kitchen pots. Matron Wright had allocated me here after a night in the infirmary to allow me to prove I was in a state of robust health, fit enough to attend the ball. I was determined to be there. Wisps of images haunted me as I scrubbed. Olivia's waxy blue face, Papa's sunken eyes, my marble babe, and Dr Griffiths. No pleasant smile upon his lips … more of a leer.

The kitchen was a hive of activity, dominated by the solid, black presence of the double oven and the equally solid woman who ran the kitchen, who told me to address her only as 'Cook.' She wiped sweat from her brow and complained yet again about how long the new closed range took to heat and get to cooking point. No one bothered to comment, so she came to examine my work.

'How are the pots coming?' she asked as she re-rolled her sleeves.

I continued to scrub at the cast-iron pot as if I could scrub myself clean along with it. 'You are right, the brick dust works better than sand, but it is harder on the fingers.'

My arms ached and my chapped fingers were cracked and bleeding, but on I scrubbed. While I had worked hard as a midwife, the asylum had given me a new appreciation for the few servants we had employed and the washing women we had given our linen to.

'Yes, it is grittier. Oh, Dr Griffiths, how can I help you?' Cook rolled down her sleeves and smoothed her apron.

I did not look up.

'Oh, I was told Mrs Parker was here, and I wanted a quick word.'

I clenched my teeth as Cook moved away from the table where I was working. My nerves were tingling in an alarming way. Something was wrong.

'Mrs Parker, how did you sleep last night? I hope the powder I gave you assisted?' Dr Griffith's usually mellow voice was husky in my ear. 'You seem to heal well.'

I gripped the long pot handle so tight my knuckles looked like bones.

With a gust in my brain, the clouds blew away and clarity was mine. Now, I understood the ache in my tender privates and the staccato of my heart. He had drugged me and assaulted me. I sucked in a breath. He must not know that I was aware of his heinous act. I was sure my eyes held more ice than the Thames in the coldest of winters, but I forced what I hope passed for a smile.

'I slept very well. I am quite recovered now and am sure I will have no need of any more powder. Thank you, Dr Griffiths.'

I saw a flicker of uncertainty in his eyes. I turned back to my scrubbing and tried not to shudder, and he left the kitchen.

A slender woman came into the kitchen and dumped her basket of peas from the garden onto the table. She tilted her head at the departing back of Dr Griffiths and whispered, 'He's as slimy as a toad, that one.'

I looked over as she began shelling the peas. This seemed to be all the opening she needed.

She threw peas into a bowl with a shrug. 'He likes the pretty ones, but I think he knows I'd clock him on the head with that pot if he tried it on me. The cheek of 'im.'

I gave a wry smile. Lizzie was an attractive woman with a languorous, feline way of moving, and I knew she knew much of what lay beneath a man's civilised mask. That she saw with such clarity was a relief to me.

'I thought of doing that.' I held up a knife. 'Perhaps sticking this somewhere might have been quite satisfying too.'

She arched an eyebrow and threw back her head, laughing with snorts that had me joining her, before she finally stopped and gazed at me.

My skin prickled under her scrutiny. 'I can usually peg a person down. Can't say I believe you've got a mean streak in you at all.' Her eyes narrowed. They were a pretty colour, almost violet. 'Not that I'm saying you're weak. I think you know how to take care of yourself if you need to.'

That was the problem. I was still expecting someone else to do the caring. Papa, Spencer then Morgan. The only time I'd really believed I could take care of myself was when I was working as a midwife. I'd think nothing of following the link-boy who lit the way on a foggy night to a woman in need of me wherever she lodged. Any drunkard blocking my way was met with a kick to his shin or the sharp end of a stick I kept on my person just for that purpose.

'Thank you. I have done nothing except escape from an asylum where my husband had me unfairly committed.' I rinsed my hands and sat to help her shell the peas.

'That's rough. Mine took off, leaving me with too many to feed. It was a mighty fall that ended in walking the streets. When some mongrel tried to strangle me, I took a razor to him.' She kept her hands busy, not looking at me or removing the ebony curl that fell in her face. 'That's what I got for marrying a man for love ... far beneath my station, as my mother often complained.

If it hadn't been for her still caring, I don't know where I would have ended up.'

'That's terrible. Why did you not go to her much earlier?' I asked.

She shrugged. 'I was too proud. This isn't so bad here. Apart from what happens to some. I keep me head down, don't want to end up in the basement.'

I gasped. 'You know about that?'

She flicked the curl back. 'You do?'

'I've been down there,' I whispered.

Her eyes widened. 'You need to stay away. Do nothing stupid, or you'll end up buried in the field.'

'Stop yappin' and get those peas done,' Cook ordered.

I gulped. I had already done some stupid things. Was everything Edna and I had planned stupid? Leading me to a shallow grave in a field behind an asylum? I released some crushed pea shells onto the table. It had to work.

FIFTY-SIX

I wiped my sweaty palms on the folds of my donated ball gown. If it had been any other dance, I would have been pleased to be dressed in such a divine cream silk taffeta dress. It's off-the-shoulder neckline with layers of thin black and pale blue ribbons, fitted waistline and bell-shaped skirt, overlaid with petal-like drapes and dangling tassels, was most becoming. Even though I was still trapped in an asylum, I looked forward to swirling on the dance floor in the arms of the man I loved.

Once again, the hall had been transformed for the Lunatics' Ball. Candles and flickering torches illuminated the silvery stars hanging by threads from the cavernous ceiling, as if the night sky had dropped in upon us. Blue velvet was draped over chairs and tables on the outskirts of the dance floor. Vases dotted around the hall displayed the waxy yellow blooms of winter sweets, the scent of spicy perfume heavy in the room. If all went well, I would forever associate this aroma with revelation and freedom. If not, then it would mean failure and imminent death.

'While I may not stop you dancing with Mr Ashton, I will watch you, Mrs Parker.'

I jumped at Matron Wright's stern words.

'I will behave,' I promised. She gave a sniff and moved off to scold Prudence, who had clearly removed some of the material of her blue satin and velvet striped ballgown to reveal far too much cleavage.

'All set,' Edna said with a wink as the band warmed up and the first guests arrived.

I gulped and scanned those entering. It had been so long since I had laid eyes on Morgan that I feared his affections might have cooled. The burn within assured me that mine had not.

My heart thudded as Morgan strolled in and searched the room. He grinned widely as his eyes locked with mine and he made his way towards me. It then sank as Spencer cut him off, stepping right in front of me, with an elegantly dressed Lady Elizabeth Telford on his arm. Morgan submitted to the introductions and ignored Spencer's sneer. Spencer took my arm for a moment, leaving a startled Lady Telford to entertain Morgan. Prudence stood nearby, seeming to sway with shock at the sight of Spencer and Lady Telford. I nearly felt a twinge of sympathy.

'I do not understand how they can permit you to be present at this event – or for Mr Ashton to be so obliging as to forgive your terrible deception,' Spencer hissed at me.

I unclenched my jaw. 'You are a fine one to bring up deception. How could you leave me in the clutches of these mad scientists, then flaunt a mistress in public?'

His eyes glinted. 'It won't matter *if* you survive your next operation, for soon you will no longer be my problem. Within weeks, you will no longer be my wife. Who knows what asylum you could end up in next?'

Before we could snarl at each other like street dogs, Morgan took my arm and swept me onto the dance floor.

'He is quite insufferable, isn't he?' was all he had to say on the matter. 'Let's not let him ruin what could be a wonderful evening.

I cannot tell you how long I have wished to have you in my arms again.' He pulled me closer than was appropriate, and I did not care. I moulded into him for a moment and soaked in his citrusy scent. Tears formed in my eyes. It would be perfect if Spencer was not present. If I was not still trapped in an asylum and ...

'Not long now. I hope my plans meet with your approval. We will make flight to France tonight,' he whispered into my ear.

I nodded, not able to speak. I was oblivious of the other dancers, the attendants and nurses that watched on, the sturdy asylum walls. My world was Morgan. I almost snapped at the man who bowed at my side and requested a dance as the music moved on to another tune.

'Oh, forgive me Isaac ... Mr Walsh,' I said with heat in my cheeks.

'Believe me, I did not want to interrupt a beautiful reunion, but daggers are being thrown around the room by so many women,' he said, nodding to Prudence, as we waltzed. It was only then that I saw Charity waving to me as she took Morgan's hand. She looked beautiful in a swathe of rose silk and lace dotted with beads.

I waved back, eager to talk once this dance was done.

Isaac gave me a cheeky dip to get my attention. 'I could choose to be offended by your preference for the company of others.'

I gave him a bright smile. 'Please accept my humble apology. I find you to be delightful company.'

He returned my smile. 'You are forgiven. Now, as you are the closest thing to family and therefore a father to Charity, uh, I was hoping ...'

His steps faltered, and I trod on his foot. 'What has got you so flustered?' Then I let his words sink in as he exaggerated a limp. 'Oh! Charity?'

He became serious. 'I would like to ask her to marry me. Do you think she would agree?'

I looked over at my dearest friend, chatting and laughing with Morgan. 'I have no idea. She is rather independent and enjoys being a midwife.'

He frowned. 'I would not expect her to stop. I like her free-spirited approach to life. Do you believe she would think of marriage as a tether she would rather be without?'

I did not want to meddle and be the reason Charity was not given a chance to voice what was in her own heart. 'Do not be a coward, Isaac. Ask her. She may not want to marry anyone at all, or she may think that you are a good man and trust you to do right by her. I can't speak for her, though I will say I approve.'

His shoulders dropped in relief. 'At least you think we are a good match. I will brave rejection and ask her soon.'

I watched with interest as he thanked me for the dance and swooped on to Charity before Mr Bugwell could claim her. I saw the light in Charity's eyes, the twitch of humour in her cheeks, and the gentle care with which Isaac held her. I hoped she would give love a chance.

A ripple moved through the dancers, and I turned to the entrance door to see what the fuss was.

'We are looking for a Dr Parker.' A group of men dressed in deep blue, high-collared tunics moved into the room. A solid man with a hook nose hanging over a droopy moustache stepped forward, and the custodial helmet plate glinted in the candlelight. I knew from his stance there would be little use in denial or running for Spencer.

Dr Griffiths grabbed Spencer's arm and took him to the man. 'This is Dr Parker. What is the meaning of this?'

Spencer twisted his arm from Dr Griffiths's grip, only to be seized by two of the policemen.

'I am Police Sergeant Brydon. You are to accompany my men to the police station, where your charge will be read to you.'

Morgan's warm hand dropped from my back. 'What is going on?'

'I believe his evil acts have caught up to him.' Edna caught my eye and nodded. Lily had obviously been hard at work, ensuring Spencer was followed and his medicines were checked for poison. I sent her a prayer of thanks.

'No, tell me now. What do you think I have done? If it's my gambling debts, I repaid them only last night.'

Sergeant Brydon shrugged. 'I know nothing about that. If you insist on me telling you in front of these people here, so be it. You are wanted for the murder and attempted murder of some of London's finest and wealthiest women.'

Lady Telford gasped and stepped back, while Spencer howled in protest. I was glad I had not succumbed to my darkest desires. Now he would pay for his sins, and I would be free of him. Surely, they would know of Spencer's treachery and release me now.

Spencer's eyes rolled about, much like a terrified horse's, until they came to rest on mine. 'This is *her* doing! I do not know what falsehoods she has told, but don't listen to the words of a lunatic!' he yelled, pointing at me.

'How could I possibly do anything from in here?' I asked sweetly.

Mr Bugwell and Matron Wright moved in to calm the situation, but Sergeant Brydon could not be persuaded.

'You are making quite the scene,' Matron Wright admonished the policeman. 'Could you not have done this deed more discreetly elsewhere?'

The crowd continued to stare. 'What a debacle,' I heard a woman mutter behind me. 'It might be best to leave. It's obviously not safe here.'

Matron's cheeks flamed. 'Go, then. Get him out of here.'

Mr Bugwell nodded in agreement, and Spencer was frog-marched away.

'I apologise for such a terrible interruption to our night,' Mr Bugwell announced. 'Please, take some supper to soothe your nerves. We will continue the entertainment once all is well.' At first people remained frozen to the spot, blinking as if unsure they had indeed witnessed a man being arrested. The clink of cutlery and aroma of plum pudding soon had them moving towards the supper table.

Prudence glared at me.

CHAPTER

FIFTY-SEVEN

Morgan joined me in a sigh of relief. 'That should be the last of him, then.'

'Let's not risk getting caught tonight. After this, I am sure I will be released, and we can make plans then.'

Morgan gave a slight pout. 'I was looking forward to us sailing off to Paris together.'

'We can still do that, only it will be much nicer to do it without the asylum hunting me down.'

Charity and I embraced. 'That was quite a show,' she said. 'The only thing I would enjoy more would be watching him hang in front of Newgate.'

'I had some other ideas for punishing him, but a hanging would be justice served.' Even though I may not have sliced his testicles off, I was still angry with him. I gave a sigh and tried to relax and enjoy the dance.

The ball had attracted a mix of curious local villagers (as we did not have a male section to the asylum, male dancers were needed), wealthy patrons, and asylum staff. Matron Wright swooped on the latest arrival, who I recognised from sketches in the latest *Illustrated London News,* which I had torn into strips only yesterday. Mrs Seacole. She was a well-known (though lesser known than Florence Nightingale), female hero of the Crimean War.

Apparently, Morgan was acquainted with her. I raised an eyebrow as he greeted then guided her towards me for an introduction. Her russet eyes regarded me with a mix of curiosity and warmth.

All eyes were on her. Whether it was for her vibrant dress, her fame, or her Jamaican origin, I did not know. I smiled.

'Please call me Mother Seacole, like everybody else, Miss Ward.' She rubbed her arms. 'I had forgotten how bitterly cold England can be.'

How did she know my maiden name? As if seeing the question on my face, she laughed.

'Cha, forgive my manners. In previous discussion with Mr Ashton, I realised I knew your papa. I met him during the war at my little British Hotel. You have his look in your eye – curious and open.'

I sensed the heat in my cheeks under her scrutiny. 'Do I?'

'Yes, you do, child. Ah, we had many talks. He, a rare doctor, gave his ear to someone like me. Your pa agreed mustard rubs and poultices were most helpful in treating cholera and gave the boys boiled water with cinnamon as I told him to. He said his wife was a wise woman too. I was sorry to hear the cholera claimed him.'

Her soft, lilting voice penetrated to my heart, and I ached with loss. I nodded as she sighed.

'I knew his father too, a very different type of man. 'Tis good your papa turned from him and his money, made off the back of slaves.'

My eyes widened. This is why Papa had not touched the money. Should *I*?

She snorted. 'I am too blunt for you.'

'Ah. I guess I have not heard of such things being discussed. I knew Papa and his father had a bitter argument and spoke no further. I have not heard slavery come up in much discussion, so I admit my deplorable ignorance.' My stomach roiled.

She waved a gloved hand. ''Tis a bone of contention in your family. Many men thought little of how the sweetness of sugar came to their table or the coins in their purse. Your grandfather lived on his plantation in Jamaica for a time, so he knew better than most.'

My throat tightened. 'I did not know.'

'I did not know,' she echoed. 'No, why would you? The West Indies no longer interest an English person. What happened there, something to be tipped out of a chamber pot, maybe washed down the street into the Thames, eh?'

Morgan cleared his throat in my silence.

'Ah, I am not here for this. I have come back to London to raise funds for my army boys. I anticipate another war drawing near. I hear you find yourself a captive of this fine establishment.'

I accepted her change of topic with grace and was touched by her concern. I explained that all should be well now that Spencer had been arrested, although the stigma of being a lunatic and married to a criminal might follow on my release back into society. I did not know why I felt the need for such candour with a stranger.

'I know what it is to sit on the fringes of London society. If you are your papa's daughter, you will survive. Do what your heart tells you. Don't wait for some man to say what you can and can't do.' She scanned the room and whispered, 'Just see that the darkness does not drown out your light.'

I wondered at her parting words. Was she talking about the darkness of society, or could she peer into my soul?

Charity was bursting with curiosity about our conversation and grabbed my arm as soon as Mother Seacole accepted Morgan's offer to dance. Isaac gave up on getting another dance for a while, and we laughed as he twirled Matron Wright around. My thoughts were bittersweet. We should not be at a lunatics' ball together. How wonderful it would be to bring in a new year somewhere else ... anywhere else.

The magic show began. The Great Wizard of the North had accepted our invitation, and all gasped at his Great Gun Trick, in which he appeared to catch a bullet fired from a gun, and we marvelled at his Animated Oranges. Matron Wright had decided it was best he did not perform his Inexhaustible Bottle, which was said to produce whatever drink members of the audience requested.

I clapped as hard as anyone else in the audience, my heart puttering. Soon, Edna and some other cloaked women would wheel in the women from the secret ward as if it was the finale of the magic show. The cloaks would come off, and I would disappear with Morgan as the pandemonium broke out.

I looked to the closest side door and frowned. Edna beckoned me over. I squeezed Morgan's hand and sidled over, checking that the corridor was empty. 'What is it?'

'Something is terribly wrong. They are all gone.'

My head thudded as my mouth went dry. 'Gone?'

She bit her chapped lips. 'Gone. The ward is empty and cleared of everything.'

'Someone has betrayed us and removed all evidence,' I mused. 'Maybe one of the nurses that Nurse Talbot asked to help us wheel in the women. No matter who it was, we are in serious danger.'

Her eyes widened, and I turned around. I motioned for Edna to run.

Dr Butcher stood behind me, a wry smile curling his lips, as Edna brushed past. 'Do not think for a moment that Dr Parker's absence will prevent me from continuing your treatment. He made a sizeable donation before the start of the ball tonight to ensure it goes ahead. For the good of humanity, I will do it.'

My bladder tingled. I would not give him the satisfaction. 'I do not think Mr Bugwell would consider that a good idea, as surely he will see that I have an evil husband who cannot be trusted. Mr Bugwell will release me from this madhouse.'

He gave a soft laugh. 'His priority lies in funding this madhouse rather than in dealing with your unfortunate circumstances. Regardless, it will be over before he knows it. Don't expect any help from your Nurse Talbot. Even if she is related to Mr Bugwell, I will have her dismissed for the role she played in your devious plot. The arrest of Dr Parker at his charitable ball created sufficient scandal ... and your intentions to damage the esteemed name of this institution are unforgiveable.'

Strong arms gripped me and tugged me down the corridor, my screams drowned by the band. Even with the cacophony, I swear I heard Prudence laugh.

FIFTY-EIGHT

The soft hum of a familiar lullaby filled me with a sense of calm ... until I opened my eyes and realised where I was.

'Adeline, are you awake?' Agnes whispered.

I groaned and sat up, my head bumping against metal bars. With a hand to my head, I realised I had been placed in a cage next to Agnes's. I tried to ignore the burn of my bladder.

'What have you done now?' Her voice was croaky, but gentle.

Images of the ball flashed through my mind, and I groaned again. 'I have ensured I will never escape this place.'

Agnes wiped her mouth and edged closer. There was the slightest scent of lavender in the air. 'Thank you for trying.'

My eyebrows shot up. I did not know her hair was as blonde as mine, nor that she had dimples in her now-clean cheeks. With the dirt removed, she had an elfin face; her green eyes were all that seemed familiar.

'Nurse Talbot snuck in. She got me a sponge bath and all. Some fresh clothes.'

One look at her forlorn face melted any resolve I had to be stoic in my fate. I had sealed hers, too. Tears coursed down my cheeks.

'No, don't cry. I don't remember anyone caring about me like that before. I will die a smiling woman.' Agnes tried to reach through to touch me, so I stretched my hand out and grabbed hers, and we cried together.

'He's coming to get us tonight. I heard him trumpeting his plans to that meater, Granville.' She dropped my hand and wiped her nose on her shawl. I agreed we could not depend on the younger doctor to be any more than a coward. I picked at my stockings, glad for their warmth, then horrified that I had obviously had my ballgown layers peeled from me and been placed by unknown hands back into my asylum clothes.

'Edna will tell Morgan and the others. They will stop him.' Why hadn't we already been found and released from this morbid room?

She sniffed. 'The scratches I made on the floor aren't there. Smells different. Earthy.'

I swallowed my rising panic. 'How will they find us if he moved us?'

I tried to calm myself. Even if we had been moved, Edna would know to point them in Dr Butcher's direction.

A finger to my lips, I observed the nearly noiseless movement of the iron inspection plate as it turned away from the circular opening. I could hear breathing through the wire.

It closed, and with a tinkle of keys the door opened. I squeezed my eyes shut. I could hear the heavy thud of Dr Butcher's boots coming closer.

'I know you are both awake. Not for long, though.' I heard the rattle of the cage doors being opened, and I readied myself to run.

No such luck.

I was dragged out by two burly attendants, with another on standby, while Dr Butcher backed up to the door.

With little ceremony, they bound Agnes in some kind of jacket, and left her thrashing, trying to land her teeth into soft flesh.

'Stop this nonsense now. Chain her legs,' Butcher instructed.

They put manacles on Agnes, as if she was a dangerous criminal. I followed meekly behind, not wanting to be chained too. Agnes's face was a mask of terror.

At the end of the corridor, we entered a surgery. Agnes was slapped onto a table in the centre, while I was told to sit in a chair. Butcher dismissed the attendants.

'You may watch with interest what will befall you for creating such havoc at the asylum.' I held my wrists stiffly as he strapped me into the chair with restraints, hoping he wouldn't notice they were looser than they should be because of the angle at which I'd held my hands. My eyes rolled wildly around the room. My breath stopped when I saw what loomed above me. It was the metal helmet of my nightmares. Metal spikes jutted down from it.

Dr Butcher laughed. 'Oh, yes. That is merely used to pinpoint various parts of the brain, not to pierce it. Although it could, I suppose,' he mused with a rub of his jowls. He picked up a sharp spike. 'No, I will use this today. It is time to begin.'

He waved in a man. 'As a woman with a knowledge of medicine, Mrs Parker, please note, that we are using Samson's chloroform inhaler today. It is much smaller and simpler than Snow's. His tubing often gets in the way, and I'm told the water jacket makes it too heavy. See how this is a tiny, metallic cylinder, and the tubing perforated?'

I'd never experienced such terror at the sight of a tiny metal tube.

My body trembled and my breath rasped as the chloroformist prepared his equipment. He set his contraption up and sat on a stool next to the table as Agnes thrashed about. When the chloroformist bent forward to attach the mask to Agnes, she stretched up and smashed her skull into his jaw, knocking him unconscious to the ground, where he lay immobile. Dr Butcher waddled over to his aid, and I used the moment to release my hands. I grabbed the stool and smacked the back of Dr Butcher's head hard enough to make him collapse on top of the chloroformist.

With a grunt of effort, I rolled him off. I took the dangling mask and held it on Butcher's face, hoping it was ready. His eyes fluttered open, but I held the Sibson's face mask firmly to his face. Try as he might not to, he had to breathe in. Once both men were slumped on the floor, I held the mask to each of them alternately until I was certain they would not be conscious for a while.

I released Agnes from her bindings and manacles and embraced her as she collapsed into my arms. 'That was a whisker too close.'

I waited until she stopped trembling. 'We must go.'

My foot sent something clanging into the torture chair. It was the metal spike. Fear evaporated and shadows formed.

I had not uttered a word, yet Agnes beckoned me over to help lift the corpulent form of Dr Butcher into the chair. With great strain we managed, although he spilled over the sides, so Agnes used a strap from the jacket to bind him in. 'See how he enjoys being strapped to a chair? It might take a while for anyone to find him. Hope his bowels are nice and full.'

I managed a dry laugh. She kicked his shin.

'Give me a moment to adjust my drawers,' I said, hoping my voice was even and she couldn't hear the crackle of my icy heart.

With a nod, she left me. The only sweetness in the room was the scent of chloroform. Any feminine reluctance to harm another had fled in the face of this monster. I had thought Spencer had no redeeming features. He too preyed on the vulnerable, taking advantage of a woman's good nature. He had been responsible for my predicament. However, he did not mutilate those in his care with the righteousness of an honourable man serving humanity.

With a big breath, I shoved that metal helmet down on his bent head as hard as I could. I watched the blood drip from his chin, staining his waistcoat. He would never harm another woman again.

CHAPTER

FIFTY-NINE

I did not think it was possible to have my soul droop any further, but when faced with the granite gloom of Newgate Prison, every part of me sank. A whimper formed on my lips as I was led through the solid gate by a wardsman with a fox-like face.

I flinched at each door that clanged shut and was locked behind me. Ascending the gallery stairs, I pondered how many predecessors had contemplated a plunge over the railing onto the stones below. I glimpsed the dankest of cells to the side and peered in.

A small half-moon window with a double row of heavy crossed bars greeted me, and I shivered in the still chill of spring air. Near the window, a water tank and basin sat in the corner. In the opposite corner was a plank bed and a small rolled-up blanket. A shelf held a Bible, plate, and mug. The only other furniture was a wooden stool and table.

The wardsman beckoned me to continue. 'There's no mattress, as the new policy is hard beds for hard crimes. There's no light once the sun's gone.'

Before I had the opportunity to utter a word, the door was slammed shut to the empty cell, and we moved on.

We walked by the yard, and I blocked my ears to the curses and foul language mingling with cackles and taunts. The yard was a miserable affair, with high stone walls tipped with sharp iron spikes that I could easily imagine might once have held the heads of those who had been hanged here. Gazing at the spiked wall, then the other wall dotted with barred cell windows, I felt as if I had been plunged into a deep pit. Even the grey, smutty sky was oppressive.

The wardsman pointed to a black flag drooping from a pole above. 'When you hear the clang of the bell, there'll be another one for the yard. I miss the crowds yelling at the devils. It's all done in the execution shed now.' She pointed to the debtor's door. 'Used to walk straight out onto a scaffold. Everyone made a hullabaloo, then bam! No matter whether the crowds were screaming for mercy or death, the prisoner was hanged. They end up in the old yard.'

I shivered as I noted the old exercise yard, roofed with iron bars. On the rough stone walls and path were some names and brief epitaphs.

'That leads to the Central Criminal Court. When you come back accused of murder, you're walking over what will be your own grave.' Her cackle froze like amber in my blood. She smoothed down her uniform and nodded to two wards men.

'She's for the glasshouse, even though there's no attorney.' She gave a nod. 'Hope you enjoyed the tour.'

I discreetly handed her a small purse of coins.

I was led into a glass room, where the warder on watch squinted at me from outside the transparent walls.

A chaplain came in, tugging at his collar. 'Mrs Parker. May I introduce myself? I am the Ordinary of Newgate. I take care of those condemned to death.' He glanced through the glass at the wardsman watching us. 'I provide spiritual care and listen to confessions and so on.'

I cleared my throat. 'I am no longer Mrs Parker.'

'Yes, that's right. I apologise.'

I wiped my hands on my dress. 'I have little to say, I'm afraid. I have not been one of the flock since my mother died.'

He pursed his generous lips. 'It is very generous of you to visit a condemned man. He asked for a chance to beg your forgiveness before he meets his Maker.'

Black spots danced before me. Could I ever forgive Spencer? How easily it could have been me in his shoes. When they discovered Dr Butcher's body, they also discovered other hidden rooms in which he had placed women from the pauper's asylum, and it was assumed one of them had done the deed and escaped. The doors on these rooms had been unlocked, and no one could identify who the violent escapee might have been.

'Would you agree to such a thing?'

I jolted in my seat. 'Oh, uh. Yes. I am sorry, I am quite shocked to hear he wants this.'

Beads of sweat formed on his upper lip and at his temple, dribbling into his beard. It was warm in the glasshouse, but I embraced its heat.

He leaned forward. 'Many wish for forgiveness before they meet their Creator.'

I blinked fast. As much as Spencer had wounded me, to be hanged was a terrible punishment. I rubbed my neck, well aware this too could have been my fate. I still had nightmares in which I was taunted by Dr Butcher.

He tapped his steepled fingers together.

'Of course, I will do my best.' While I had some shred of sympathy for Spencer, I did not know if I could forgive him.

He smiled and nodded to the men standing outside. He ambled off, and I waited.

Spencer looked gaunt, with deep shadows under his eyes, and he'd grown a beard.

'I won't waste time with niceties. Is there anything you can do to stop this?' Spencer reached out to grab my hand. I pulled it back and gripped the arm of my chair. He was not interested in my forgiveness at all. 'Surely you would have your hands on your true inheritance money by now.'

I shook my head. 'My father was wise to hide it. I would not waste a farthing on you. I have put it to much better use.'

His face grew even more pinched as he debated, no doubt, whether to hurl abuse at me or appeal for mercy. 'I have been trapped here for so long ... in the common wards and now the cells for the condemned. My pleas have fallen on deaf ears. Do you know of anyone who could have more influence and get clemency for me?'

I did not have any mercy left. 'I know what it is to be trapped. But if I knew, I would not tell you. You murdered innocent women for their money.' I rubbed my pounding temples. I had to focus on that word *innocent*. I was also guilty of the sin of murder; I was no better than Spencer. I consoled myself with the knowledge that at least the man I'd killed was guilty of horrendous acts against many innocents. 'I am not surprised that Queen Victoria failed to pardon you. One woman you poisoned was well known to her. I don't know why you think I would offer you any hope. No one would dare go against the wishes of the Queen.'

His eyes darkened and his lips thinned. 'I wanted nothing but the best for you after you flew at me. Attacking me for trying to give you what you wanted, another baby.'

I dropped my hands. 'No, you wanted me to do my "duty", and I was not ready. How could you have left me to rot in an asylum? How could you organise that horrendous operation?'

'I was told it would restore you to your sweet self.'

'You mean make me docile and compliant.'

He took my wrist. 'Yes, a good wife. But you escaped and lived with a man and dressed in gentlemen's clothing. My reputation was in tatters.'

I shook his hand away. 'You ruined your reputation yourself with your gambling, cavorting, and thieving. It is good to know that the full extent of your treachery is now known, Dr Leycroft. You should be punished twice over for what you did to little Molly.'

He had the grace to at least hang his head.

'The only favour you did me was to declare our marriage null and void due to me being supposedly already insane at the time. Better than trying to prove me guilty of adultery, I suppose. Not that it matters now.'

He stood, wiping his hands as if I was tainted. 'Fine, I see asking you to come here was a mistake, as was marrying you.'

I shook my head. 'That we can agree on. Our marriage was just another of your frauds. You and Prudence might have been a better match.'

His eye twitched at her name. He gave a snort. 'She's pathetic.'

'Oh, I should let you know. I heard that her predilection for poisoning has finally caught up with her and she is now a prisoner in here, too. It appears she will follow you anywhere. Even to the grave.'

He swallowed hard. Opened his mouth and then closed it.

I stood up, trying hard not to reveal the weakness of my legs. 'Goodbye, Spencer.'

He did not look up as I hurried from the glasshouse.

I had nothing left, not even a morsel of pity for Spencer. I knew many people believed death by hanging to be instantaneous. My father had explained to me once that this was not always the case. It could take two or three minutes or even up to an hour. Some unfortunate men had even had their head snapped off. Perhaps I would have had a slight pang if Spencer had endured the old penalty for treason; to be hanged, cut down while still alive, and then disembowelled, castrated, beheaded, and quartered would be a most horrific way to die. Being hanged would suffice.

Nurse Talbot ... Sarah – I didn't know if I could ever get used to using her first name – sat in the carriage, letting me mull over my visit with Spencer in silence until we arrived at our next destination. 'Are you sure about this?'

I nodded. 'I want to know he is in there.'

CHAPTER

SIXTY

I t was with some relief that I stepped down from the coach and
sucked in the crisp, clean air after a long journey. Set among
tall, dense pines, Broadmoor Criminal Lunatic Asylum awaited.
I was met outside the gates by a handsome attendant with vivid
green eyes. 'It is a pleasure to finally meet you, Mr Hall.'

His smile was so like Olivia's. My breath caught.

'Please, it's Sam to you.'

We walked under the central archway leading to a cloistered
courtyard. As we continued, I have to admit I was disappointed to
see that the new red Romanesque-style buildings were so handsome
and the gas-lit corridors so bright. As we passed a billiards room
and library, I saw much that reminded me of the cheerful façade
of Bloomfield House. From a window, I glanced at men playing
cricket on the lawn outside, with a lovely view of fields beyond. I
had anticipated it would be more like Newgate than Bloomfield.

'Dr Griffiths made a clever choice, didn't he?' Sam said as I
followed him into a darker, gloomy corridor.

'I guess it would not be difficult, with his expertise, to convince
an alienist that he was insane. Far better he be a "Queen's pleasure"
patient here than an inmate in prison. I would have thought that
a man in collusion with another man who was no better than a
body snatcher would be punished.' That Griffiths had helped and

supported Dr Butcher in his madness rankled. The thought that his abuse of the women in his care would never fully come to light, and that those women would never receive justice, had my nails digging deep into my palms.

Sam stopped in front of a sturdy door. 'He might think he has escaped the worst of it. I ensure he spends far more time in seclusion than his behaviour here warrants. Seems to put some chinks in that smug armour.'

He opened the viewing slot. In a scruffier state than I had ever seen, Dr Griffiths sat on a small bed, staring into space. His eyes locked onto mine and he hummed the lullaby I used to sing to Agnes. A shudder ran through me. He knew. He knew exactly what Dr Butcher had been doing. He had seen me caged and had sat outside that stench-filled room and listened to me sing.

I nodded to Sam, and he shut the door. I had wondered if I would have any sense of pity for Griffiths. I did not. 'I agree with you he is having far too easy a time of it,' I said. 'It is time he got "mistakenly" transferred to block one to spend some time with the more dangerous convicts.'

Sam scratched his well-groomed beard. 'I know of more than a couple of men in there who might enjoy their own measure of justice. Seems one had a sister and another a mother taken from the pauper asylum.'

My boots clipped along the wooden floors at a great pace, and I did not breathe until I was beyond the brick gateway and the twin three-storey towers.

Sarah was still waiting for me in the carriage. I told her that Dr Griffiths was committed there, but then once again found myself lost for words. My mind was plagued with images from the past of both Spencer and Griffiths.

Eventually, Sarah cleared her throat and began a conversation on a different topic. 'Are you apprehensive about giving your lecture?' she asked.

I turned my gaze from the carriage window to her kind face. 'Yes, now that that unpleasant business is attended to, I had better prepare my thoughts. No, I am quite keen to share my experiences with the Nightingales. I hope it will equip them with the necessary knowledge and skills to work in the asylums. Your contribution has been invaluable. It should really be you lecturing.'

I smiled as she blushed and stuttered. 'Oh, no. That's not for me. Mother Seacole has been rumoured not to see eye to eye with Miss Nightingale, so it is wonderful that she listened to her in this case. I am sure that your insight as a midwife and previous inmate will be very useful.'

Sarah Talbot's firm belief in me soothed my now-jittery nerves.

B y the time we arrived at the Nightingale Training School at
St Thomas' Hospital the next day, I was eager to share my
experience and views. It would be exciting to tell them of our
new venture, Ashton Retreat. Where women fleeing from a man's
fists or those who became melancholy after the birth of or loss of
a babe and needed a gentle hand could go for refuge. My body
tingled with a life and passion I had believed lost to me forever.

Seated at long tables, the young student nurses looked strangely
like a sea of nuns to me. Dressed in grey tweed and plain white
aprons, the twenty students were distinguished as such by wearing
a beret rather than cap. The uniforms and neatly pinned hair
produced an air of cleanliness, but made it difficult to distinguish
one girl from another. I gave a skeleton on a stand at the back of
the room a wink, which made a couple of them giggle. The gloom
of the wood panelling was balanced by the three French windows
through which sunshine poured in. I did not sit at a large desk
placed in front of them, preferring to walk back and forth, as I
began my lecture.

I could see by the curious eyes glued to my face as the women
perched on the edge of their chairs that they had found my thoughts
on nursing in an asylum interesting, so I continued. 'I know you
have been told to be a good nurse. One must strive for improvement,

for stagnant waters eventually grow corrupt and are unfit for use. Please continue to be open to learning, not only from your teachers and mentors at St Thomas but also from your patients. Listen to them, as often the doctors forget to.' That caused a stir.

I looked at Sarah Talbot. 'I was most fortunate to have a nurse listen to me. Many medical men reduce you to a pound of flesh and bone that must be cured by any means they deem possible. They dislike being questioned or thought to be mistaken. You are a mediator between a patient and a doctor. Remember that these patients are people, and remind the doctors of the same. Sometimes their cures do far more harm than the presenting problem. They may not consider what a person needs or whether this operation, with all of its hidden complications, is best suited in the long term for the life of that person. They may sweep a hand at the patient who asks questions rather than blindly trusts. Know what you are assisting a doctor to do,' I said with sombreness.

Tears glistened in a few eyes. They had already seen some of the damage of which I spoke.

I walked across the small lecture-room stage. 'I know you will be told to do as you are ordered by a doctor and not question him in any manner. Your livelihood may depend on obedience. If, however, your heart stirs you otherwise, there may be other doctors who do not agree with whatever methods or practices are disturbing you. It is right to question a system, or how else can we ever improve it?'

I thanked them and gave a bow at the smattering then thunder of clapping. Afterwards, we responded to the students' questions while we took tea with them. Sarah looked more than comfortable discussing her various experiences of nursing. We were both invited to speak at future classes.

'Do you think it was wise to have discussed Elizabeth Barnwell drowning her infant son in the canal?' I asked. 'I had meant to argue that she was suffering from puerperal insanity and needed compassionate treatment rather than a gaol cell. The horror on some of their faces tells me such a woman would still be condemned by them.' I knew it would be hard to nurse such a woman.

Sarah clicked her tongue as we settled onto the carriage cushions. 'Many who suffer from ills of the mind are perplexing to nurse. It is far simpler to understand the suffering caused by an ulcer or to recognise the need for a bone to be set than to address the unseen anguish.'

'That is true,' I agreed. 'As it is to ascribe blame to the person who is supposedly demented than search for reasons for how they came to be in such a state. It is hard to think that perhaps their affliction is no more their fault than a man's weak heart is *his*.'

Sarah sighed. 'It is good that we are beyond the time of believing insanity is caused by mischievous devils taking over a body or being cursed by God.'

As we clopped along the streets of London, no doubt past many with one illness or another, I too sighed. 'Yes, it is. There is still a long way to go.'

CHAPTER

SIXTY-TWO

I stepped down from the carriage and waved to Edna and Lily, who were tending to some plump, red roses in the garden. Edna beckoned me over.

'Welcome home. How was the visit with the spawn of the Devil?' Edna asked, fanning her face with her straw bonnet.

I sighed. 'He did not want my forgiveness to free his burden of guilt. He merely made a desperate plea for help to save him. A waste of time.'

'As expected. Now, onto a more worthy cause. We must meet and discuss which politician we will target. He must be sensitive to public opinion,' Edna began.

Lily touched her arm. 'Give the poor woman a chance. Now is not the time to be discussing our plans to combat wrongful confinement in lunatic asylums.' Lily's vivid blue eyes regarded me. 'You look wrung out. All of this is not good for the babe. Go and rest. We will catch up on how the visit and lecture went later.' She shot Edna a warning look, and I grinned.

'I must agree, I am not up to discussing amendments to the Lunacy Law at present. As for other news, Miss Busy Body will have to wait,' I said. 'Where are Morgan and Charity?'

'Mr Ashton is in the study wading through the accounts, and Mrs Walsh is at the women's cottages attending to Mrs Harper.

Being the fifth, I assume it will slide on out,' Lily said. She shared the same *joie de vivre* that Edna had. Both might have snow-white hair and wrinkles, but such spirit radiated from them they seemed years younger. Edna had blossomed even more with the presence of her love, as if the hard years of living in asylums were now melted away.

Lily was right about my being wrung out. I was exhausted.

A flutter in my belly prompted me to gently stroke it. Under my travelling clothes, my blooming shape had not been clearly visible. I had no desire for Spencer to know of my condition.

I entered Ashton Retreat and made my way to the study. Morgan had been very busy renovating and preparing his fine house to become a true retreat while I was locked away. His face lit up at the sight of me, and he rushed from his desk to hug me.

'Adeline, come, sit. You really should have let me go to London with you,' he said after a warm embrace and delicious kiss.

'Stop fussing. Nurse Talbot was a wonderful companion. We are well.' I sank into the armchair by the fireplace with a groan of relief. 'Ahhh.'

There was a clatter at the door, and I smiled at Charity. 'Come in.'

Charity beamed at me. 'Mrs Harper has a baby girl, and all is well. I hope the travel did you no harm?'

'No. Seeing Spencer may have stirred some feelings ... it is a sorry situation.' I ignored her snort. 'I know. He brought it upon himself.' My shoulders gave the slightest shudder as the clock on the mantel chimed. 'He will trouble no one further.'

Kitty came in and set down the tea service. 'I, for one, am glad to hear it. Will I run you a bath?'

'That sounds heavenly. After tea would be wonderful. How is Agnes?' I asked.

Bloomfield House had been closed down until new staff and administration could be arranged, and Morgan had ensured Agnes was transferred to our retreat, even though some authorities wanted her for Broadmoor. Upon further enquiry – which would not have taken the police much effort to have done in the first place – it was discovered that the mistress had been the one to kill Agnes's husband.

'She is still having nightmares. The music room is very therapeutic, though. She may never recover.' Charity's forlorn face resumed its cheer. 'She did laugh when Edna pulled a face at Lily yesterday.'

Though many things needed addressing, I grew drowsy. With a pointed nod to the door from Morgan, they both left us in peace.

Morgan laughed. 'When we set up this retreat, I did not expect it to be so difficult to get you to myself, Mrs Ashton. Do I need to whisk you away to Paris again?'

I grinned as flickers of memories filtered through my mind.

We strolled among The Exposition Universalle's many displays and national pavilions at the Champs de Mars. The French had definitely tried to outdo Londoners with their Exhibition of 1862. I sniffed the scent of rich chocolate from a one-legged cocoa vendor before it blended with smells of sweat from the crowd, then lime and bergamot from Mr Rimmel's perfumery exhibition.

While I thought it odd as an exhibition piece, I was transfixed by a full-size Gothic cathedral in the park. It had painted glass in the windows, beautiful chandeliers, ivory figurines, and even a grand organ.

'Imagine being married in a church so grand,' I whispered to Morgan.

He pointed to the Egyptian temple and then the cast-iron lighthouse on the other side of the windows. 'There's no need to whisper. It's not a proper church. What a strange assortment of structures. This is beautiful though, I agree.'

It was odd to move from a cathedral to a schoolhouse. As I sat at a tiny desk in a rustic American one-room schoolhouse, I was astounded by not only the building but the ideas that the Exposition was promoting. 'What a clever display for such a noble cause. Wouldn't it be wonderful to offer free education to every child?'

Morgan nodded. He picked up the slate pencil and began writing on the slate.

I cringed as the pencil shrieked on the quarry slate set in its wooden frame. Some refined French people frowned our way. I handed Morgan the sponge to wipe the slate clean, saying, 'I do not think we are meant to use the—'

He held the slate up, as a proud child in class would.

Would you do me the honour of becoming my wife, sweet Adeline?

The world beyond Morgan disappeared, and I melted into his embrace. I knew I could live well, with passion and purpose, on my own. But I chose to open my heart, rather than barrier it shut. 'Yes, Morgan. I will marry you.'

A towering structure illuminated the sky at night, as high as the mood I was in. There was so much at The Exposition to explore, yet I wanted to hurry back to London and begin married life. My joyful eagerness contrasted with the lethargy I had known alongside Spencer.

Morgan craned his neck to look up at the tower. 'Some think it awful; others want to construct an even taller tower for the next world fair. I think it is quite striking.'

We moved on and tested our courage, trying out the new invention of the elevator. When our energy finally flagged, we made our way past the artists at their salon shows. I had to stop and admire the works of one cheeky man, Manet, who had dared to set up across from the exposition grounds.

Once back at Le Grand Hotel, built especially for visitors such as us to the Paris Universal Exhibition, Morgan abandoned all propriety and came into my room. It was a luxurious suite, done in what we were told was a Second Empire style. Most decadently, unlike Morgan's room, it had a bathroom. A fire crackled, casting a warm glow upon the room.

Morgan stepped towards me and touched a tendril of hair, wrapping it around his finger as he had done so long ago when he had first caught me naked.

He leaned into me. A gentle meeting of soft lips, then a groan. As I peeled off his shirt and waistcoat, then pants, he tugged at my dress and corset. With delicate speed and much kissing, we were soon bare to the world,

I moved his fingers to my breast. His eyes widened, but his fingers stroked. I would not smoulder down what I wanted to ignite.

He nuzzled my neck and cupped my buttocks as I pulled him into a tight embrace. I moved him to the bed. Morgan ran his lips from my neck to my breast, and I tingled with pleasure. Heat flared from within, and I did not draw back. I kissed his neck and held him tight.

As his lips travelled, everything fell away. I stroked the smooth, firm muscle of his back. A flicker of doubt flared. Then, riding on pure instinct, I drew him into me. I moaned as his soft tongue licked my nipple, and he moaned with each lift and slide, until he arched up and shuddered in release.

We lay curled in silence.

In the morning, doubts niggled at me. I had not been behaving at all like a lady. Did he think I was ... was I different down there? Did he ...

'Adeline. I always knew you to be a passionate woman, but last night was beyond my expectations and only makes me want you more,' Morgan said as he nuzzled my neck.

It seemed that the whole body is an instrument of pleasure, and the most powerful part was my mind. Even with the operation, all was not lost.

'Ah, Paris. It is the most romantic city in the world,' Morgan said.

I blushed and stroked my belly. 'I will not forget our special months there. You are the perfect accomplice to have when I am on the run. It is wonderful to be surrounded by so much love and comradeship from all my friends.' As he pouted, I said, 'Put that lip away. You know I have more than enough love for everyone in this heart, and an extra dose for you.'

Thank God that Agnes and I had not been caught making our way to Ashton Court, and that he had been there waiting.

He swooned like a lady. 'Oh, to have the love of my Adeline.' He dropped his humour, and I blushed at the smoulder that replaced it. 'I have missed you.'

I had thought I would never trust another after Spencer's devastating chain of betrayals.

'I love you, Morgan.'

'I love you too, Adeline.'

It was that simple, and that complex.

AUTHOR'S NOTE

The Lunatic Asylum, Bloomfield House, is a product of my imagination based loosely on information about Moulsford Asylum presented in Mark Stevens' book *Life in the Victorian Asylum*.

Unfortunately, Dr Isaac Baker Brown is a true historical character, and the use of his 'harmless operation', the clitoridectomy, was based on fact. The other doctors mentioned are a blend of fact and fiction, though the debate and downfall of this operation and Dr Baker Brown is based on fact.

The 19th century saw psychiatry in its embryonic state. There was a shift from treating those with mental illness no better than vermin to building new palatial buildings for patients, where they were well-fed, warm, and comfortable, in the belief this would cure whatever ailed them. Unfortunately, for many reasons, such as overcrowding, issues with staffing and training, the management of 'lunacy' – mental illness – often remained problematic.

The Victorian period had very definite expectations of how a woman was supposed to behave, and in this emerging male-dominated field of psychiatry, many women were found to be 'abnormal'. Was this treatment medically motivated or a means of exerting control over women's lives and bodies under the guise of medicine? Tread in fear those women who broke societal norms.

ACKNOWLEDGEMENTS

This novel was written in COVID-19 lockdowns, so there was never more a time that I appreciated support, and encouragement in my writing journey.

Itu Taito continued to cheerlead and generously sent a box of treats with the card attached to 'Keep Writing' during lockdown. Arna Radovich also offered support from afar. It was wonderful to have writerly catch ups again with Beth Amos and Angela Long once restrictions were lifted. Other writers (many from Fiona McIntosh's masterclass group – Emma, Chrissie, Jo, Beck, Sharyn, Leonie, Nerida) added support for the long publishing journey.

Thank you to those who have enthusiastically embraced and shared the love of my first novels, many of them my old school friends. It means so much to hear kind words. Thanks Wendy, Emma, Maxine, Heidi, Warwick and Julie. I'll stop now as I know I will miss people out – I am grateful to you all.

Once again, this novel would not exist if it hadn't been for Fiona McIntosh's belief in me and the concept of the novel. I attended her masterclass a few years ago, and she has always offered so much enthusiasm and belief in my writing that I continue to battle on.

A huge thank you once again to my book editor extraordinaire, Jane Smith. She is a dream to work with and this novel is much improved with her attention to detail and enthusiastic support.

My daughter, Brooke, has read all of my awful first drafts. I know she must groan when I hand her another manuscript, but

I trust her to share her wisdom and am grateful for her support (besides we were in lock down together so she couldn't escape).

My son, Zac, wasn't too keen on the subject matter for this novel so while there was little discussion about it, he's still proud he has a mum who writes.

To my husband, Darren, who has finally read my first novel and now gets it a little bit. Thank you for giving me precious time, space and the nod to spend money on developing my craft.

Thanks to Mum and Dad for instilling a love of learning and reading in me.

Mum, you continue to support me in countless ways. One day I'll get to writing a novel inspired by your side of the family. Thanks to my sister Kathy for her support to my Author Fund and endless encouragement.

I appreciate the belief my family and friends have in me. Thank you to those who buy my books, share them, or tell other people about them. It's always wonderful to hear back that what you've written was enjoyed. Please tell others, write a review or share on your socials.

To you, the reader. Thank you for taking the time to read *The Cure*. Jen x

If you'd like to reach out, you can contact me via
www.jenkingsford.com.